ABOUT THE AUTHOR

Brought up in Lincolnshire, Judith Thomson studied Art in Leicester before moving to Sussex, where she still lives. She is passionate about the seventeenth century and has gained much of her inspiration from visits to Paris and Versailles. In her spare time she enjoys painting, scuba diving and boating. She is the author of four other Philip Devalle novels, 'Designs of a Gentleman: The Darker Years', 'High Heatherton', 'The Orange Autumn' and 'The Distant Hills'.

Follow her on:-

www.judiththomson.com

and on Twitter @JudithThomson14

DESIGNS OF A GENTLEMAN

The Early Years

Judith Thomson

Matador
9 Priory Business Park,
Wistow Road, Kibworth Beauchamp,
Leicestershire. LE8 0RX
Tel: (+44) 116 279 2299
Fax: (+44) 116 279 2277
Email: books@troubador.co.uk
Web: www.troubador.co.uk/matador

ISBN 978 1789016 468

British Library Cataloguing in Publication Data.
A catalogue record for this book is available from the British Library.

Printed and bound by CPI Group (UK) Ltd, Croydon, CR0 4YY
Typeset in 11pt Bembo by Troubador Publishing Ltd, Leicester, UK

Matador is an imprint of Troubador Publishing Ltd

1662

ONE

John Bone looked up at the sound of a horse's hooves. Although only twelve years old, John worked beside his father picking the scarlet apples that were hanging heavy upon the orchard branches. Sometimes he carried the heavy baskets to the carts, for he was well built for his age, but now he sat in the highest branches to throw down the fruit for those who waited with a net below.

"It's Lord Philip," he said to his father, Sam, as the horse and rider came into view between the chestnut trees. "Can I go with him, father?"

Sam Bone shrugged. "Aye, if he wants you. He is your master."

John slid down the trunk of the apple tree and waved as Philip, the Earl of Southwick's younger son, drew closer, bringing his mount to a magnificent halt a few yards away from him.

"Are you well, my Lord?" John asked him.

Philip was the same age as John, slim and graceful with fair hair curling about his shoulders. He had eyes of deepest blue, and these now solemnly surveyed his friend.

"I am well but I am very bored, John. Will your father spare you for the rest of the afternoon?"

"He says I am to do exactly as you say, Lord Philip."

"In that case you shall come swimming with me." Philip reached out a hand to help John climb behind him on the horse and then they galloped off between the trees. "How's your nerve, John Bone?" he called back over his shoulder.

"Good as yours, Lord Philip."

"Hold tight, then."

John gripped him firmly round the waist and a second later they cleared the high flint wall that divided the orchard from the lane and raced on toward the woodland, both exhilarated by the speed of the sturdy little animal and the prospect of an afternoon of glorious freedom.

"You're a fine horseman, Lord Philip," John said when they finally stopped beside a deep pond surrounded by trees.

"It is well I am. A gentleman should be possessed of one talent at least," Philip said as he leapt lightly to the ground. "It seems I am never even to learn to read and write properly, much less be taught the etiquette of a courtier. Did you hear that my tutor left last night?"

"I did hear so, Lord Philip." News travelled fast on the estate of High Heatherton. The abrupt departure of the tutor had not caused much surprise to those who knew the family, for it was a common occurrence. "How many have you had now?"

"Six, and every one driven away by the ranting of my brother. He threatened to strangle this one, if you please! Well I don't care. I wait only for the day when I am old enough to join the army, then my father, my brother and this house will see no more of me, for I shall never come back."

"Not even to see your father?" John sounded shocked.

"No. What do I owe him? If he loved me at all then he would have my brother put away in a place where he can do no harm."

"Would you do that if he were your son?" John asked, stripping off his clothes ready for a dip into the cold, dark water of the pond.

"If he were mad then yes, I would," Philip said emphatically, "particularly if he terrorised his younger brother."

As he spoke he removed his own coat and shirt, and Bone looked pityingly, as he had many times before, at the marks which Philip would bear all his life, marks which told of the years that he had suffered at the hands of his brother, Henry. His back was

4

a mess of scars for Henry, when the fever in his brain was at its worst, would beat him.

Both boys raced into the pond, yelling as the cold, muddy water enveloped them. The sun rarely penetrated through the trees to warm its depths, but they were young and careless of discomfort. For a brief time, too, they were equals as they ducked each other, wrestled in the water and dived for stones.

Despite the daintiness of Philip's build he was strong, and he owed much of his strength to his companionship with the brawny lad with whom he had swum and fought since they were little children.

His father had allowed Philip to mix with few people outside of the estate for fear that the truth about Henry should be discovered but even so, as time went on, it had become increasingly difficult to hide it. Philip himself appeared to be untouched by what the locals called the 'Devalle sickness', which had cursed the family for several generations. Certainly as he played that afternoon with Bone, matching him challenge for challenge, he was no different from any boy of his age enjoying the delight of splashing naked in a woodland pond.

"The Race?" John said, when they were panting from exhaustion.

Philip nodded and ran out with him to the foot of the great oak tree whose branches overhung the water. They counted together out loud.

"One…two…three…four…" At the count of 'five' they both sprang at the tree and began to scale it, their wet feet slipping on the rough bark.

Grabbing branches, they hauled themselves up, forcing their already tired bodies to accept a further challenge. Higher and higher they climbed, their muscles throbbing from the exertion as they both fought to reach the branch from which they must dive to complete the test of strength and nerve they called 'The Race'.

John reached it a second ahead of his young master, but in this contest there was no quarter given, nor any expected. Even as Bone sat upon the branch to edge his way along, Philip was beneath him, gripping like a monkey with his arms and legs and travelling nearly as fast, for all that he was upside down!

When they reached the end of the branch John stood up and dived down into the water, but Philip, letting go first his hands and then his legs, hurtled after him and they hit the surface of the pond at the same second.

"That was a cheat," John said as they came up spluttering and laughing, "but a bold one!"

They staggered out, both thoroughly exhausted, and collapsed on the soft earth of the bank. They lay for several moments getting their breath back and enjoying the feel of the cool autumn breeze upon their bodies, happy to be still and let their muscles rest.

"I shall be sorry when you go," John said at length.

"I can't stay here; Henry will kill me one day." Philip sat up and began to pull on his clothes, which stuck to his damp skin. "My father says he might send me to school. I don't much relish that, if I am honest, but at least it is a step into the world."

"The world?" John looked at him blankly. "Do you mean London?"

"London, certainly, perhaps France too, in time. There is a great deal more than this, you know." Philip made a gesture that embraced the woods and fields around them.

"I suppose so, but it is all of the world that I shall ever see, and it will be an empty world without you here, Lord Philip."

"Shall you miss me, John?" Philip rather liked that notion. "You will hear about me, I've no doubt, for I shall be a very famous soldier."

"First you have to go to school," John reminded him.

"It hasn't been decided yet. I would rather go to Court but my father will not hear of that, for he says it is a den of idleness and corruption! It's my intention to speak to our agent, Mr.

Wilson, on the subject when he arrives tonight. His office is in London and I want to learn everything about it that I can."

The mention of the visitors who would shortly be arriving reminded Philip that he must go back to the house in good time to bathe and change for supper. Although young, he was already very conscious of the courtesies expected from those of his rank and, besides, visitors were such an unusual occurrence that he welcomed the prospect, even if the arrivals were only Wilson, who dealt with the sale of High Heatherton's timber, and a new clerk from Wilson's office.

Philip's French maid, Nanon, gave a shrill cry when she saw the state of him and raised her hands in horror.

"Why, Lord Philip, what have you been about? You look just like a labourer's child."

"At times I wish I were," he muttered as she tugged off his muddy clothes. "I'll bet they don't get scolded all the time as I do."

Nanon always spoke to him in her own tongue and he always answered her in the same. Philip's mother had been French and, although she had died when he was only three years old, Nanon had made sure that her mistress' favourite son was fluent in that language.

She exclaimed afresh when she saw the muddy streaks upon his skin and she was still carping on about young gentlemen behaving like young gentleman long after he had climbed into a tub of hot water and scrubbed himself clean.

"Oh don't go on so, Nan," he interrupted her when she paused for breath. "You know you love me."

She smiled suddenly. Philip thought Nanon was very pretty when she smiled.

"Of course I do. I loved your mother and you are every bit your mother's child. I'd better wash your hair, it's full of leaves."

She bent over the bath, pulling him toward her. Philip relaxed, enjoying her nearness. In his idle moments, which were many, he had lately begun to conjure up delicious fantasies of Nanon.

She finished his hair and helped him from the bath and towelled him down. Philip often wondered whether Nanon ever had thoughts similar to his own but he had never quite known how to broach the subject! She combed his hair and whilst she worked he watched her in the mirror. The heat of the steam had made her sweat and her damp clothes clung to her in a way he found exciting. He stored the memory.

"The visitors from London have arrived," she told him. "Mr. Wilson and a very handsome young man."

"Is he as handsome as I am?" Philip said, studying his own pleasing reflection.

"Such conceit, my Lord," Nanon reproved him.

"Aren't I handsome then?" he persisted as she helped him into his clothes.

"You know you are. I fear the ladies of the Court will eat you up alive!"

"I hope they do, but first I have to get to Court. Oh, Nanon, would I not make a splendid courtier?"

"Splendid," she agreed, fastening his cravat and buttoning up the coat of rich blue velvet that exactly matched his eyes. When she was satisfied she swept him a deep Court curtsey, such as she had often seen her mistress perform. "My Lord, I am most honoured to make your acquaintance."

"Are you making fun of me?" he said, hurt.

"Why, no." She took his hands in hers. "I forget how sensitive you are. You will be, I'm sure, the finest looking man at Whitehall. How proud your mother would have been of you."

They both looked toward a painting which hung above the fireplace. Philip's mother, Madeleine Pasquier, had been a famous beauty at the Court of Louis X111, and Philip had inherited her good looks. There had been many occasions in his young life when he had wished most fervently that his mother could have been with him still. He sometimes used to go into her rooms, which had been left exactly as they had been when she was alive, and sit there all alone, as though within those walls her love enveloped and protected him.

After a final glance in his mirror Philip hastened down the stairs to the gallery, where he was to meet the others, pausing to compose himself before he entered the room.

His father, the Earl of Southwick, was already there, showing the visitors the billiard table which he had just purchased. Henry sat alone, staring ahead of him at nothing in particular. He glanced round as his brother entered then quickly looked away.

Five years older than Philip, Henry was larger of build and his features were coarser. He lacked, too, his younger brother's grace and charm but Henry's tormented mind believed that these gifts had been bestowed upon him by the devil and were, therefore, visible proof of Philip's wickedness.

Wilson, a round and pleasant little man, greeted Philip respectfully and introduced his assistant, Daniel Bennett.

Bennett was young, about twenty years of age Philip guessed, and handsome, just as Nanon had said.

Philip noted approvingly that he was very well dressed. Best of all he had a black beauty patch fixed just below his right eye. Philip thought that particularly splendid and resolved that he would always wear one when he lived in London!

"Lord Philip. I am enchanted."

Philip was somewhat surprised as their guest bowed so low before him that the handkerchief he held actually swept the ground.

"Do you ever go to Whitehall, Mr. Bennett?" he said.

"I have been there several times on Mr. Wilson's business, I am very glad to say, for it has afforded me the opportunity to study the manners of the courtiers, Lord Philip."

Philip was thrilled. It was the first time he had ever spoken to anyone who had actually been there! "And have you met King Charles?"

"Oh no, but I have seen him very close and once he nodded in my direction."

"I intend to be presented to him one day," Philip said.

"But you have the advantage of a noble birth, my Lord, whilst I am but a scrivener's son."

"Even so, you're very elegant."

Philip was noticing that, whilst Bennett talked, he gestured constantly with the dainty handkerchief which he held between the third and fourth fingers of his right hand. He decided there was much this guest could teach him of the ways of fashionable folk and he resolved to learn from him all that he could.

They walked the length of the long gallery so that Bennett could study some of the family portraits that were hung on the panelled walls. Philip stopped before one of his mother that he especially liked because it showed himself standing by her knee. It was the only one that had ever been painted of them together.

"A handsome woman," Bennett said.

"She was considered one of the finest at the Court of France," Philip told him proudly.

Philip's father came to join them. "It is Philip's most avid wish to go to Court himself but I am loath to part with him just yet."

"And I can well see why, my Lord. He is a boy that any father would be proud to have beside him."

There was a sudden movement from the other side of the room. Henry still sat in the same place but Philip, who tended to observe his brother very closely, noticed that his hands had begun to twitch.

The visitors stayed a week, during which time Philip sought out Daniel Bennett's company whenever possible. The young clerk contrasted soundly with anyone Philip had ever met before. His father's friends were country people, still dwelling upon the dismal days of the Commonwealth. Those few who had been to London since King Charles' restoration had gone only to obtain loans to restore their ruined estates.

He studied Bennett constantly, imitating many of his affected little mannerisms. Others, he decided wisely, would be too ridiculous for a person of his age but the low bow, which he practised before his mirror, was Philip's special accomplishment and he was very proud of it.

So absorbed was Philip in his new friend that he neglected to notice he himself was being observed. Henry watched them, sometimes hiding in the bushes as they walked in the formal gardens, or lurking behind the little banqueting house if they sat talking in the lengthening shadows of the autumn evenings. Sometimes he even crouched with his ear to the keyhole if he discovered them in a room together. To one with a more rational mind it would have been obvious why Philip, starved of company, delighted in the chance to speak to someone from the outside world. Henry saw only further evidence of the devil at work inside the brother he detested. He decided to tell his father that Philip had bewitched their guest.

His father listened to him in amazement. He generally humoured Henry a good deal, not because he was himself afraid of him but because he feared for Philip's safety, since it was upon him that Henry vented all his spite. Even so, he found it difficult to endure the accusations Henry was making now, and he said so.

"But I have seen them," Henry insisted, clenching both his fists. "I tell you they say wicked things together."

"What kind of things?" his father said, perplexed.

"They talk too quietly for me to hear," Henry had to admit, "but they are vile, disgusting things."

"How can you know that?"

"Because I have heard Philip laugh. You know as well as I that he never laughs."

"That's true. The poor boy has very little cause for joy, but I still think it is innocent pleasure that he finds in Bennett's company."

"Do you doubt me? Have you ever known me to lie?" Henry's face turned red and the veins stood out upon his neck, as they always did when he was enraged.

"No, not lie," his father said carefully, "but I think you might, in this case, be mistaken. After all, Philip is scarcely more than a child."

"He is evil," Henry insisted, "and he makes others evil."

Southwick sighed resignedly, recognising only too well the beginning of yet another tirade of hate against his younger son. "What would you have me do?"

"Just hide with me and try to hear the things they say."

"Sneak around my own house and spy upon my son? I shall not do that," he said firmly.

"I am your son too, your elder son, though not the one that visitors fawn upon."

His father held up his hand. "Very well. Mr. Wilson's business here is almost concluded. I will suggest he leaves tomorrow and that he does not bring Daniel Bennett here again. That should make you happy."

Philip was far from happy at their guests' sudden departure the following day. He watched from his window as the coach containing Bennett and Wilson travelled the circular drive and disappeared from view. He was still staring disconsolately through the diamond-shaped panes when the door opened quietly.

Philip swung round as he heard the sound of the key being turned on the inside.

"Henry!"

"I had to come and see you. Father is displeased with you, Philip." As he spoke Henry drew a piece of rope from his coat pocket and then a cane, the ends of which he had split. This he laid it on the table between them.

Philip shuddered as his brother came toward him but he stood his ground, for he was no coward. "You are wrong, Henry. He is not displeased with me, you ask him."

"No, I can't do that. You see in order to protect you he would lie to me. My father shall not be made to sin on your account, like Daniel Bennett."

"What did you tell him about Bennett?" Philip demanded.

"That you had bewitched him, as you bewitch all who come near you."

"Well he has gone now." Philip viewed his brother with loathing. "You have driven him away as you drive everyone away from me."

"But there will be others. You have the power to put evil thoughts into the heads of all who come into my house. It shall be my house one day, not yours," Henry reminded him.

"You may have this house. I hate it, just as I hate you."

Henry made a grab for him and Philip dodged, but not quickly enough. Henry was bigger and stronger than him and pushed him easily to the ground. He grabbed both of Philip's wrists and wrapped the rope around them tightly, then used the rope to drag him to his feet

"The devil is in you," Henry rasped in Philip's ear as he tied him firmly to the handle of the door. He picked up the cane. "I must purge the wickedness out."

Philip flinched as Henry ripped the shirt from his back. Resigned to the beating that he knew would follow, he did not struggle, or even cry out, for he had discovered the futility of the first of these measures long ago and had more pride than to adopt the second.

As the 'purging' began he closed his eyes in mute acceptance of the pain but he could not close his ears to Henry's insults, which stung nearly as much as the whip that lashed the raw skin of his back. When Henry had revelled in his brother's helplessness long enough he stopped and looked at him contentedly. "That is a lesson learned, I think."

He untied the rope that had bound his captive's hands and left the room as abruptly as he had come.

Philip stayed where he was for a moment then rushed over to the china bowl that stood upon his washstand and, leaning over it, was violently sick.

Nanon must have seen Henry leaving his room and guessed the worst. She ran in and tried to put her arms around him but he pushed her away.

"Let me alone, Nan. The sooner I am away from this accursed house the better."

He ran from the room and down the corridor to the suite which had been occupied by the gentle mother whose comforting arms he could not remember. Drawing the velvet bed curtains around him, he threw himself face down upon the counterpane.

Now, safely hidden from the world, he cried bitter tears that he would not have let any witness.

When he returned later to his own room he found his father waiting for him.

Philip knew that his father had never been truly at ease with him, and he suspected it was because he knew that he owed it to Philip to do what he had never found the courage to do, which was to commit Henry into a place where he could do no more harm. It was because of his irresolution that Philip's back was scarred and because of it, too, that his education had been so severely neglected.

"Henry had convinced himself that there was something unnatural in your friendship with young Bennett," he began, somewhat awkwardly, since Philip did not speak. "Not that I believe it," he added hastily, "although, of course, because of your brother I cannot allow him to come here again."

Philip viewed him with disgust. He could feel neither affection nor respect for this man who had never once defended him or even taken his part.

"Try to appreciate how difficult it has been for me to bring you up without a wife to help me," his father begged. "Your mother would have understood you better, Philip. You are very like her."

"Yet that does not endear me to you, it would seem, my Lord."

"It does, more than you know, but still I cannot condemn your brother to a life of hell chained to his bed, as was your grandfather, and tormented by physicians."

"Then, if you will not abandon him, I beg you to let me go, or I will end my days as mad as he," Philip said passionately.

"If you truly wish to leave this house then you shall," the Earl said with a sigh. "Perhaps it is time you learned a little of the world, but you are still too young for Court. I shall enrol you at St. Paul's School in the city. We can travel in the morning."

It was not quite what Philip had wanted but it was better than nothing and at least he would be in London. "Thank you, my Lord."

"My Lord? My Lord? Will you not call me 'father' even now, when you are leaving me?" Southwick said sadly.

"No…my Lord."

Philip went back to his mother's bedchamber and he stayed there for a long while, for this was one farewell he did not want to make. This room had been his sanctuary, his refuge from the misery of his young life. As he looked around him for what he was certain would be the last time he was tempted to take some small article, a comb, a handkerchief or a glove, as a memento of the lovely lady who had comforted him so many times with her invisible presence, but he could not bring himself to do so. It seemed to be sacrilege to disturb this precious shrine.

"I know you loved me," he said out loud, "and because of that I need no object to remind me of you, for I can see your portrait any time I close my eyes. Instead I shall leave something of mine for you, lest you forget me when I no longer come to visit you."

So saying, he took off the black ribbon that tied back his hair and folded it, then went over to an ivory-veneered cabinet and opened a drawer which held the ribbons that Madeleine Pasquier had worn in her own hair. He tucked his in amongst them and closed the drawer.

The thought of what he had done pleased him for, although he rarely showed his feelings, Philip was a sentimental boy.

A little later he saddled his pony for the final time and rode over to the orchard where John Bone was working with his father. On this occasion Philip did not call to him but, instead, dismounted and approached the pair.

"I leave for London tomorrow," he said quietly. "I have come to bid farewell to both of you and to thank you, Sam, for all that you have taught me." Under Sam Bone's tuition Philip had learned to defend himself expertly without a weapon. It was an art he was to find invaluable in the eventful years ahead for, although he was not yet strong enough to be a match for Henry, there were to be few others he could not better.

"I wish to thank you too, John, for your companionship." Philip's voice faltered here but he quickly collected himself. "You two are my friends, the best that I have ever had."

"We shan't forget you, Lord Philip," Sam assured him.

"You had better, for you'll not see me again, though you may hear of me one day if I become a soldier, as I hope."

"You'll be a good one, that you will, Lord Philip," John said, "for you have great courage."

"Thank you." Philip reached into his pocket and brought out a gold coin which he held out to John. "This guinea is for you and it is my desire that when the Michaelmas fair is here you should spend it on some object that delights you."

John's eyes opened wide. "A whole guinea? I can't take that, Lord Philip."

"Yes you can, for it is mine and I would like to give it as a gift to you." Philip tossed his curls, a habit of his. "Friends though we are, I have always insisted that you obey me, have I not? So obey me now when it is most important."

John nodded, too overcome to speak and Philip, affected too by their parting, impulsively embraced him. It was gesture so unexpected and so out of character that it brought a tear to the eyes of Sam Bone.

"Think of me sometimes when you go to the pond where

we have enjoyed ourselves so often," Philip whispered in John's ear, "and when you climb our oak tree wish me good fortune wherever I might be."

"I'll do that gladly many, many times," John said, "though it will be a lonely place for me from now on."

Philip smiled. "At least you'll always win The Race!" He released him and without a backward glance ran to his horse and mounted it. As he did so John and his father could see the streaks of blood that had stained the back of his white shirt.

"Poor little devil," Sam said as Philip galloped out of sight. "You're right, he has great courage."

TWO

༄

"Lord Devalle, you have a visitor."

It was the first time Philip had heard these welcome words
and he wondered who it could possibly be, but he refrained
from asking. All the other boys had frequent visitors and he was
determined to behave in as casual a manner as they did on such
occasions.

He had been seven months at St. Paul's School and already
detested, in equal measures, its staff, its pupils and its disciplines.
The private tutors who had been employed for him in the past
had always treated him with respect whilst here, regardless of
his rank, he was criticised harshly by the learned doctors and
frequently rebuked in front of the other boys.

It was all very well for him to be told that the conquest
of the classics was a necessary trial that would train young
minds for leadership. For Philip, who struggled to read even
his own language, the difficulties of mastering Latin were quite
insurmountable, whilst the mysteries of mathematics were to
remain forever impenetrable to him!

What made matters worse was that the other boys of his age
were far ahead of him. Also, since the classes at St. Paul's School
were composed of pupils from varied backgrounds, Philip was
more often than not finding himself bettered by the son of a
lawyer or a clerk.

Dr. Harmon, his tutor, was a good enough man but he had
too little understanding of Philip's past. When he was unable to
comprehend Harmon judged him obdurate and when he refused,

for fear of looking foolish, to ask for help he was reckoned to be arrogant.

The lessons might have been less onerous and the curtailing of his freedom more bearable if only Philip had been allowed some privacy, but instead he was forced to share a comfortless dormitory with four other boys, none of whom he liked, or who liked him.

All things considered it was little wonder that he was unhappy.

Philip's nonchalance disappeared when he discovered that it was Nanon who waited for him in the Visitor's Room.

She made to curtsey to him but he would have none of it and, instead, kissed her upon both cheeks, in the French fashion.

"My dear Nanon, what brings you to the city?"

"I wanted to come and say goodbye to you, Lord Philip."

"Goodbye? Are you leaving Heatherton?"

"I'm leaving England altogether. I have booked a seat upon the coach to Dover. I shall be upon my way within the hour."

"You are going back to France?" he said, surprised. "But why, Nanon?"

"I've nothing left to stay for now that you have gone. You are the only one who needed me. Besides," she lowered her eyes, "I'm homesick."

"After all these years? I don't believe you." Philip sat upon a sofa and indicated that she was to place herself beside him. "Now," he said sternly, "tell the truth, or shall we part upon a lie?"

Nanon bit her lip but did not answer.

Philip tilted her chin so that she was forced to look at him. "I am still your master, am I not?"

"You are, my Lord, and always shall be."

"Then do as I bid you."

"I cannot. I made a promise to your father that I would speak to no-one of what happened. He did not even know that I would come to see you."

"And he will never learn of it from me, I promise. Please tell me."

"It's about your brother." Nanon said quietly.

Philip paled. "What has he done to you?"

"Two weeks ago he called me to his room," she began hesitantly. "I went, of course, as I would have gone if you had summoned me, but when I got there he was nowhere to be seen. Too late I realised he was hiding behind the door."

"Nanon! He didn't beat you?"

"No, not that. He locked me in and then he…, then he…," she looked away from him, tears in her eyes. "Please, my Lord, I have already said too much."

Philip jumped to his feet. "You mean he ravished you?"

"He tried to. Oh, I fought him off as best I could but you know well enough how strong he is. He ripped my clothes and tried to tie me to his bed with my own petticoat. I kicked out at him very hard and I must have hit a lucky place for suddenly he cursed and let me go."

"Continue," Philip said, sensing there was more to tell.

"I ran to unlock the door and had nearly got free when he grabbed me by my hair and threw me to the floor. I fell upon a glass that had been knocked down in the struggle. It cut me rather badly, I'm afraid, but it was fortunate for me all the same for the sight of the blood seemed to bring him to his senses and he ordered me to leave."

Philip went over to the window and stood for several minutes looking out upon the cathedral that towered high above them.

"Where was God at a moment like that?" he said bitterly. "Where, for that matter, was I?" He brought his fist down hard upon the window sill. "Confined here in this blasted house of learning whilst you suffered that ordeal. I should have been there to protect you."

"Do you blame yourself? Please don't," she begged.

"He only turned on you because he could no longer torment me. Oh, Nanon, I would not have had this happen to you for all the world."

"It could have been much worse. The scar has almost healed."

"Show me."

Nanon stood up straightaway and removed her cloak for, although she had often grumbled at Philip, she had never disobeyed him when he gave her an order. Beneath the cloak she wore a high-necked dress, trimmed with a little lace around the collar. He recognised it as her best dress, the one she had worn on special occasions, such as Easter or Christmas when the servants ate with the family.

Philip had not thought to ask where the scar might be and he was startled when she commenced to undo the buttons down the front and unlace her bodice.

Were it not for the circumstances, this would have been the fulfilment of his secret desires. As it was he stared in horror at the form around which he had woven his adolescent fantasies. A livid mark ran from the top of her right breast down to her navel.

"The bastard! I would like to kill him."

"You must not speak so, my Lord," Nanon reproved him. "He is your brother whilst I am but a servant."

Philip felt rather ashamed as he realised that the anger he was feeling was on his own behalf, as well as Nanon's. Henry had even managed to sully his dreams. "My brother is a monster, whilst you are very dear to me," he told her, though he wondered if he was not one as well. "What are you going to do in France, Nan?"

"I shall go back to Languedoc," she told him, getting dressed again. "I am sure your mother's family will take me in. I've no-one else."

Philip had never had any contact with his mother's family, the Pasquiers, for they had disapproved most strongly of Madeleine's marriage. They feared that the so-called 'Devalle Sickness' would taint their line and had taken no interest in their grandchildren, other than to grant Philip, being the second son, the title of Vicomte de Montpelier, but it was no more than a nominal honour, carrying neither lands nor income.

"I hope they are kind to you. If not come back and I'll employ you when I get to Court." In that Philip was sincere. Nanon, though over thirty, was still a fine-looking woman and her presence in his household would certainly bring no shame upon him.

Nanon nodded, obviously overcome by her emotions now that the moment had finally come to part from him. "May fortune follow you for all your days, my Lord, and may you always be as good a master to your servants as you have been to me."

She threw her arms around him and sobbed unashamedly upon his shoulder. Philip suddenly felt much older than his thirteen years; it was the first time that anyone had clung to him for strength.

"Don't be upset, dear Nan," he begged, when she had quietened down. "Rather be glad that you are free from the horrors of that house."

"And so, thank God, are you, my Lord."

"I? Oh no, Nan, I shall not be free as long as I live, for you see I can never be quite sure that the demons which inhabit my brother's body do not dwell in me also."

He spoke lightly, not wishing to cloud their last moments together, but it was a matter, nonetheless, which bothered him.

After she had gone he made his way slowly and reluctantly back to the dormitory. The boys had been permitted to spend the afternoon there, for it was May Day and a holiday from lessons.

The four other inhabitants of the room looked up curiously as he entered.

"Who was it?" one of them asked. "Your mother?"

"My mother is dead," Philip said coldly, "for all the business that it is of yours."

He lay upon his bed and looked up at the ceiling, wishing that he, too, was going to France instead of having to remain a captive, and he thought of himself as little else, in that austere establishment.

"I think it was his mistress," a boy called Richards jeered. Philip particularly disliked him. "See, there she goes across the courtyard."

The other three flew to the window and looked out. "That's his bedding piece for sure," another cried coarsely. "I wouldn't mind having her legs apart for half an hour myself!"

"Hold your tongues, all of you." Philip knew they only sought to goad him yet he could not bear to hear his Nanon spoken of so lewdly.

"So, his Lordship commands us to hold our tongues, does he?" Richards made a ridiculous bow. "You are not in your great house now, my Lord, with your servants to do your every bidding. Here you are no better than us; in fact, we should treat you like a servant for you are more ignorant than any of us. You cannot even write properly."

"An earl's son does not need to write," Philip flashed back. He was well aware that Richards, who was the son of a merchant, resented him chiefly on account of his noble birth. "Literacy is essential only to those who will need to earn their living."

It was a remark calculated to inflame all of them against him, since they each fell into that category, but Philip was in no mood to care. He had endured their taunts with surprising patience during the time he had been there, not because he was a coward but because he had long ago resigned himself to the injustices of life and he found their insolence to be but a mild inconvenience compared with the brutality of his brother. Today, however, after seeing Nanon, he wanted more than anything to be left alone.

He looked up at the four hated faces that surrounded him, as usual, and decided that, for a precious few hours at least, he would be free of them, whatever the cost.

There were some books on the table by his bed. Philip reached out and grasped one. It was a Latin grammar, whose cover bore the hopeful inscription 'A Delicious Syrup newly clarified for Young Scholars that thirst for the Sweet Liquor of Latin Speech'. Philip, for the first time, had found a practical use for it. He hurled the 'Delicious Syrup' with his full force at Richards!

His victim was a big boy but the heavy volume caught him squarely upon the side of his head and he dropped like a stone.

The other three stood stupefied for a second then with one accord, attacked the person who had felled their champion.

Philip was unperturbed. Even if he would not learn from Dr. Harmon he had proved himself a willing pupil of Sam Bone. He brought his knees up close to his chest then kicked his legs straight out, so that his nearest assailant careered backwards to fall across a chair and land, dazed, on the floor. Next he seized the arm of the closer of the remaining two and jerked him off balance, and then he lowered his head and butted the last one hard in the stomach.

Now none stood in his way. He crossed the room quickly and, opening a window, stood upon the sill and looked down.

The dormitory was on the first floor, a drop of no more than twelve feet onto the soft earth of a flowerbed beneath. Philip paused for barely a second then leapt down. Ahead of him was the boundary wall. He raced across the courtyard, the cries of his adversaries ringing in his ears before he reached it, but he was over swiftly and did not stop running until he was at the steps of St. Paul's Cathedral.

Now he stood in wonderment, taking in the sights and sounds of the city. The pupils of St. Paul's School were not permitted to wander about alone and, of course, no-one ever came to take him out so it was the first time Philip had left the school grounds since he had arrived in a coach with his father all those months before.

"So this is London," he murmured to himself.

Ahead of him was Ludgate Hill, a noisy, bustling thoroughfare where carts rumbled past and people jostled one another beneath the overhanging gables of the tall buildings on either side.

"Sweet lavender, sir?"

Philip glanced down. A young woman sat upon the steps by his feet, holding up a bunch of the purple flowers.

Philip stared at her. "Me?"

"Yes, young sir. Makes a pretty posy for your sweetheart. Only a penny, sir."

"No thank you." Philip hastily moved away from her, almost colliding, as he did so, with two men dressed in a manner he had never seen before. They both wore wigs and had huge hats with enormous coloured plumes. Both, too, wore powder on their faces, carmine on their lips and a dab of bright pink rouge upon their cheeks, as well as a profusion of the little beauty patches of which Daniel Bennett had been so fond.

Although Philip had no desire to paint his face or cover his blonde curls with a ridiculous, frazzled wig, he gazed upon their clothes in frankest admiration. They had silver buttons as large as sovereigns on their coats and so much lace upon their cuffs that it was difficult to see their hands at all. Shiny silver buckles adorned their satin shoes and white silk stockings showed their calves to best advantage beneath the frilled bottoms of their embroidered breeches.

As he watched they both purchased posies from the flower girl and held them up to their noses in a delicate manner as they strutted, arm in arm, into the cathedral.

Intrigued, Philip looked in after them and discovered, to his astonishment, that there were many similarly dressed, strolling up and down the aisles in twos and threes, chatting amongst themselves.

"Who are they?" he asked the lavender woman.

"Gentlemen of Fashion, sir. They meet here every day to show themselves off in their fine clothes."

"Fancy! Here, I've changed my mind." Philip gave her a penny. "I *will* buy a posy, since it is the fashionable thing to do."

He soon discovered that the fragrant ornament had other uses than for decoration. As he walked the length of Ludgate Hill he realised that the very air was different from that in the country. Down the centre of the street was a gutter filled with stinking slime and rotting refuse and there were piles of horse droppings everywhere.

Philip, who had always been a fastidious soul, pressed the lavender to his nose as he gazed with a child's delight upon the sights he had never seen before. It was as if he had entered a different world. From the ragged, dirty urchins who squatted on their haunches in the gutter playing with knuckle-bones to the egg-shaped cobbles beneath his feet, all was new to him and he was enthralled by it.

He did not even mind that he was being pushed and shoved and was made to stand aside to let through two wagons and a sedan chair. He caught up with the sedan again, for it was forced to wait whilst the driver of one of the wagons struggled to free a wheel from a deep rut in the road. The curtains were drawn back and inside sat a creature of incredible loveliness. Philip wondered if she might be Lady Castelmaine, King Charles' mistress. Her beauty, he had heard, outshone that of all others at the Court.

The lady, glancing round, caught his eye and smiled at him, fluttering the fan she carried in her small, white hand. Philip wished he had a hat that he could doff but, since he had not, he thought quickly of some other form of salutation. He still carried the little lavender bouquet and, on a sudden impulse, he held it out to her.

The fair inmate of the sedan reached out and took it from him, laughing gaily.

"Thank you. You are a gallant young man, and handsome too," she said. "Tell me, is it your custom to give flowers to every lady that you meet?"

"No, only to the fairest I see each day and it is for certain I shall not see any fairer than yourself this afternoon, my Lady," he replied, with an ease which surprised himself.

The way being cleared, the carriers picked up the sedan and she leaned from the window and blew a kiss to Philip as they moved on. Then she was gone but it seemed that, just for a second, a waft of her sweet perfume lingered in the air.

He was reminded suddenly of Nanon and he wondered whether she had yet left on the Dover coach and if he would ever see her again. It did not seem too likely that he would. That thought made him feel sad so he cheered himself up by inspecting the wares of a street vendor and purchasing a tiny mirror attached to a chain. He had noticed that some of the smartest people wore them hanging from their waists and he determined he would do the same.

There were no mirrors provided to encourage the vanity of the pupils at St. Paul's School, so Philip had not glimpsed the sight of his own face since he had watched Nanon brush his hair on the morning he had left High Heatherton. If he had altered at all, he decided now, it was for the better, for he had not the least idea of modesty. The gracious lady in the sedan had called him handsome and he knew he was. He knew also that his good looks would prove far more valuable to him than any amount of skill in Latin!

He felt happy again as he crossed the bridge over the River Fleet and walked the length of Fleet Street to the Strand. A small crowd was gathered there and he went to see what was the attraction. As he drew nearer he could see that the people stood around a tall pole, as high as the roofs of the surrounding houses.

On top of the pole was a crown and vane, with a gilded royal coat of arms, and below, to the strains of fiddlers, six milkmaids danced, their pails hung with garlands of flowers.

The scene was charming, and so unexpected in the midst of all the dirt and bustle that Philip stood upon Strand Bridge and watched it, quite oblivious to all around him.

"Pretty ain't it?"

Philip spun round and found himself looking into the smiling face of a girl of about his own age. She was pretty herself in a pert way, but he noticed that her face was streaked with dirt. He walked a little further across the bridge, hoping she would go away, but, instead, she skipped along beside him.

"Cromwell had that Maypole taken down. I remember well the day they put it up again after the Restoration. There were twelve great seamen pulling on it and everybody cried 'the golden days are here again. Long live King Charles'!"

"Really?" Philip said, turning away from her.

"Yes. I've lived all my life in Drury Lane. Not around here, of course, for this is where the rich folk live, but at the Covent Garden end." She tapped her small foot in time to the music. "Don't it make you want to dance?"

"No, not one bit," Philip said icily, for he was growing weary of her chatter.

She was evidently not a person easily discouraged. "It does me. Would you like to see me dance?"

"Not particularly."

"But I do it very well. Sometimes people throw me pennies when I dance."

"I don't have any money," Philip lied.

"Oh, I'll dance for you for nothing. Won't you watch me?"

Philip sighed. He figured that the best way to get rid of such a pest was to let her have her way. "Get on with it, then."

She commenced straightaway, following the movements of what might have been some old, traditional dance, for all he knew. She was a graceful dancer and so completely unselfconscious that Philip found himself watching her almost in spite of himself. He even noticed, when she lifted her skirts, that she had rather nice legs.

"Well?" she said when she had done. "What do you think? Am I good enough to go upon the stage?"

"Now how should I know that?" he said, exasperated. "In any case they don't have women on the stage; of that much I am aware."

"They soon will. Why should men take all the female parts? I want to be an actress, but I'll have to catch the eye of Mr. Killegrew."

"Then I hope you do." Philip had no intention of admitting that he did not know who Killegrew was.

"I don't suppose you are acquainted with him, are you? He's a gentleman like you, though not so good looking."

"No, I'm sorry," Philip said, feeling a trifle better disposed toward her for her compliment.

"But surely you go to Court. As well as being the manager of the King's Company of Players he is also Groom of the Bedchamber to King Charles."

"Be that as it may, I'm not acquainted with the gentleman."

"No matter, I am sure to find someone to introduce me to him. The new theatre will be opening next week." She sighed wistfully. "I've heard it is very grand inside, with huge wax candles standing on brass cressets to light the stage. There is no roof, though, else it would still be too dark, so it's better that it does not rain during the play or all the people in the pit will get half-drowned, so they say!" She leaned over the rail of the bridge and looked down at the muddy water. "What wouldn't I give to be there on the opening night? I wouldn't care how wet I got."

"Why don't you go, then, if it means so much to you?"

She glanced at him. "You wouldn't understand. From the looks of you I'll bet you've always had everything you've ever wanted."

"What nonsense! That is not the case at all," he corrected her, rather crossly. "If it were then I should be at Court now, instead of wasting my time in listening to impudent chits venturing their opinions without so much as a by your leave. I asked a civil question, kindly answer it."

"I can't afford to go," she said in a subdued voice.

"Is that all?" Philip reached into his pocket and pulled out a crown. "What does it cost? Is this enough?"

Her eyes widened. "Enough and more. You can go in the upper gallery for a shilling. Why even the pit only costs two and sixpence."

"Good. Take it then and sit where you like." He tossed her the coin. "And now I really should be going."

He started back the way he had come but she caught up with him and barred his path. "I can't take money from you." She clutched it to her all the same. "Even though I would dearly love to see the play."

"Then see it." He dodged around her. "Don't be tiresome, please."

"But it's charity," she said, catching up with him again, "and I am not a beggar."

"No, you're a dancer and you danced for me. Call it a token of my appreciation, if you will."

She smiled. "That's alright then. Wait, you told me earlier that you had no money," she recalled.

"I thought that way I might be rid of you," Philip said honestly, "but I really do have to go now and that's the truth."

"If ever you are passing by this way again call at the Coal Yard and ask for me," she begged. "They all know me there. My name is Nell."

"I will," he promised, little thinking that he ever would. "Goodbye, Nell."

"Am I not to know your name?" Nell called out after him.

Philip shook his head. "Enjoy the play."

There seemed little point in attempting to re-enter the school in secret, for Philip knew his enemies would have lost no time in informing Dr. Harmon of what he had done, so he presented himself boldly at the main entrance.

Harmon himself appeared directly he heard of his return and Philip was ordered to his study.

"My Lord," he began sternly, "I have received today most grave reports of your misconduct and have called you here in the hopes that you can explain your wayward actions. What do you have to say?"

Philip viewed him without the least concern. "I decided to go for a walk."

"You decided to go for a walk?" Harmon repeated. "Is that why you absented yourself without my leave, and by leaping from an upstairs window and scaling a wall?"

"Yes." There seemed little else that Philip could say to that.

"Having first brutally assaulted some of your fellow students?"

"There were four of them against me," Philip reminded him. "If you term that an assault then yes, I did assault them."

"Why?"

"They were annoying me," Philip said simply.

"There is a rule forbidding fighting within the walls of this establishment," Harmon said angrily, "a rule which you have blatantly disobeyed and, in addition, you have left the school without permission. Your father, shall hear of this."

Philip turned to go, imagining that the interview was at an end. He had no fear of his father and was, therefore, not in the least bothered by Harmon's threat.

"One moment, my Lord, I have not dismissed you. We have a remedy for disobedient boys here, no matter what their rank." As he spoke Dr. Harmon opened the drawer of his desk and drew from it a long cane.

Philip stared disbelievingly at this ghost from his unhappy past.

"Approach, my Lord."

"No."

"What?" Harmon brought the cane down hard upon the surface of his desk.

Philip did not move a muscle.

"Approach," Harmon said again.

"I shall not, and if you attempt to use that odious object upon me you will regret it," Philip said warningly.

"My Lord, you have deliberately flaunted the rules of this fine school and for that you should be punished."

"I care nothing for your school, Harmon, and I care even less for you."

"Now you go too far." Harmon took a step toward him.

It was not a wise move. Grasping a table behind him, Philip kicked out, striking the master soundly in the chest. Harmon staggered back, all but winded, but before he could regain his balance Philip leapt at him and brought him crashing to the ground. Whilst he was still dazed Philip seized the cane and struck him with all his force.

Harmon cried out in pain but Philip did not care. He brought the cane down again and again. When Harmon held that cane he had become Henry and Philip was wreaking a lifetime's revenge upon the unfortunate man.

Philip's father arrived from Sussex, summoned in haste by the governors of the school.

"You must surely appreciate the seriousness of what you did," he said to Philip, in a vain attempt to remonstrate with him. "Were he so inclined then Dr. Harmon could take legal action against you for this attack."

Philip was unrepentant. "It was his own fault. I warned him not to touch me."

"But what am I to do?" his father demanded. "They have decided to expel you and I shall never find another school to take you now."

"Good! I dislike being at school even more than I disliked being at home," Philip said. "As for what you ought to do, is the answer not obvious?"

"You are still determined to go to Court? That is why you have done this, I'll warrant. You think now to get your way."

"What else is to be done with me?" Philip said reasonably. "I can't stay at St. Paul's, nor will I be accepted, as you say, in any other place of learning. I'll not come back with you to Heatherton and I am too young for the army."

His father sighed. "I suppose the Court is the only choice, although I wish there was some other solution."

Philip did not trouble to reply. He had got his heart's desire at last and words were now superfluous.

The next morning they went to Whitehall and made their way to the Stone Gallery. His father told him that it was hung with some of the paintings which had been collected by the old King, and which had now been returned to their original hanging places. Philip reckoned that the gallery must be the very hub of the palace, for it was crowded with people talking and laughing amongst themselves as though at a social gathering.

"Are all these people courtiers?" he asked his father.

"Some are. Most, like those in the outer chamber, are petitioners. The war left many without land and some without even the means of earning their livelihood. King Charles has opened the gallery to all so that it may be for the pleasure of any who wish to see it and if, whilst doing so, they should also see him and gain a favour then it is their good fortune. Some come every day for as long as they can afford to remain in town."

Philip looked at the velvet curtain that hid the doors to the royal apartments. "Does King Charles pass by this way every day?"

"Yes, several times on his way to the Privy Gardens or the offices of his ministers, but we shall not have to waylay him here. I have requested a private audience so that I may introduce you to his Majesty properly."

Philip was glad of his father's title as the guards admitted them to the Withdrawing Room, for only those entitled to appear at Court were permitted to enter Charles' private apartments.

There was no fire lit, as it was May, but there was a magnificent mirror hanging above the fireplace and Philip studied himself in it, which saved him from having to make conversation with his father. This had always been difficult for him, for they had so little in common, and they remained in silence until they were summoned to enter the Royal Bedchamber, where they were to be received by the King.

Charles stood with his back to them, looking out upon the river, which flowed beneath his window, but he turned as he heard them enter. He was exactly as Philip had pictured him; extremely tall, six feet it was said, with black hair and moustache. Philip noted with approval that he carried himself very straight and with a natural dignity that would have easily set him apart from other men, even had he not been a king.

"Your Majesty." The Earl went down upon one knee. "I am most honoured by the favour that you have shown me in the granting of this audience."

"My Lord Southwick, I do not forget my friends," Charles said, indicating that he was to rise. "You and your brothers helped me in my days of peril and I was saddened to learn they had paid for it with their lives. If you have come to request any favour of me you shall find my gratitude of far more substance than a few fine words."

"Your Majesty is gracious, but I am happy to say that High Heatherton flourishes and that I come here to ask nothing of you but that you receive my son."

"Is this he?" Charles looked at Philip. "Come forward."

Philip approached him and went down upon one knee, as his father had done.

"Rise, my Lord, and let us look upon one another."

Philip studied him closely. Charles was handsome, he decided, despite the somewhat prominent Stuart nose, and his dark eyes seemed alive with humour.

Charles smiled. "I see you take me at my word! That is good.

You are very like your mother. Such a pretty lady, I recall. Is Philip your eldest son, Lord Southwick?"

"No, your Majesty. Philip is my younger son. I have one other, Henry, but he enjoys poor health, I fear."

Charles nodded and Philip guessed that he probably knew only too well the usual nature of the Devalle's ill-health. "And do you seek a place here at Court for this handsome son, my Lord?"

"It is his wish, your Majesty. I must return to Sussex before the week is out and I hope, before I go, to find a suitable patron to watch over him."

"I am sure you will. How old are you, Philip?"

"Thirteen, your Majesty."

"Then you would make a fine companion for my son, the Duke of Monmouth. All the ladies make a fuss of him, too much perhaps, but he has not many friends of his own age."

Charles spoke of his illegitimate son with obvious fondness and Philip resolved that, come what may, he would make a friend of Monmouth.

The audience being over, Philip's father began the task of seeking a protector for him. He first sought out the office of John Maitland, the Earl of Lauderdale, who had fought alongside the Devalle brothers at the battle of Worcester. Lauderdale had been captured by the Parliamentarians and held until the Restoration, when he had been rewarded for his loyalty to the Crown by the appointment of Secretary of State for Scotland.

Philip regarded this coarse, red-faced man with horror. His voice was loud, his manners ugly and, even worse, he had a habit of spitting when he talked! It was a great relief to him when Lauderdale said that he was now but rarely at Whitehall and therefore would be unable to offer Philip any patronage unless he accompanied him to Scotland.

Philip's father declined that offer and they called next upon another of his old acquaintances, Lord Arlington, the Secretary of State for England. Arlington was a severe-looking man who sported a black patch across his nose, which Philip's father had told him concealed a wound he had received in fighting for the Royalist cause. Notwithstanding this, Philip found it a rather comical sight and, although not much given to laughter, found it quite difficult to keep a straight face.

His father glared at him, but kept the visit short. "Quite apart from the obvious merriment that you derived from his appearance," he said heavily, when they were outside, "how could I ask Lord Arlington to take care of such a difficult child as you when it appears he is already so heavily burdened with affairs of state? As for Lauderdale, from the look of him he has become a heavy drinker. I really don't know what I'm going to do with you."

Arlington's office was beside the Privy Gardens and Philip looked longingly toward them as his father stood considering his next course of action. The lawns were peopled with the most exquisite creatures, ladies in rustling silks, their arms and shoulders bare in the warm Spring sunshine, and elegant young men, grand in their lace and embroidered coats.

"Can't I stay here for a while, my Lord?" he asked. "You can come back for me."

"May I remind you that it is your future we are trying to settle," his father reminded him. "I thought you were eager to find a patron."

"Not if he is going to be like those two," Philip said, somewhat ungraciously. "Do you know no-one save politicians?"

"Those with whom I am acquainted have either been rewarded for their services by a position of responsibility or else they prefer to spend their time usefully upon their estates, rather than frittering it away in idle pleasure. The people you seem to so admire have either only recently arrived at Court or else are those who accompanied his Majesty into exile and they were, in the main, a worthless bunch who thought of nothing save roistering and wenching."

"Are there none of those that I could meet?" Philip said, for roistering and wenching sounded a great deal more fun to him than affairs of state!

"Not through me, but if you think that you can find a patron for yourself then go ahead, for I am tiring of the whole business. I will meet you back here in one hour."

Left to his own devices, Philip walked contentedly around the gardens, happy to merely watch and mingle with the colourful people who laughed and chatted there.

He was standing by the sun dial, where, he had heard, Charles went every day to set his watch, when someone touched him lightly on the arm. He swung round to behold the lovely lady he had last seen seated in a sedan chair on Ludgate Hill.

"If it is not my young gallant! Am I now to learn your name?"

Philip bowed to her delightedly. "Lord Philip Devalle at your service, but I trust you will forgive my ignorance if I confess I do not know yours."

"I am Elizabeth Hamilton." Elizabeth looked even prettier to Philip now than she had upon their previous meeting a few days ago. She was very fair with a sweet mouth and a delicate, turned up nose. "Are you to stay here at Court, my Lord?"

"I would like that very much but my father is afraid to leave me here alone."

"And I don't blame him one bit, for you are far too handsome for your own good!" Elizabeth tapped him playfully with her fan. "Does he not know someone who can watch over you?"

"No-one who is likely to advance me much in society."

Philip went on to relate his experiences so far but, whilst they talked, he became aware that he was being watched. A handsome man, in his early thirties and magnificently dressed, kept glancing in their direction.

"Who is that?" he asked Elizabeth.

"Why, the Duke of Buckingham, and he appears to be taking quite an interest in you."

Philip had heard of Buckingham and knew he was a hero of the Civil War. "What kind of man is he?"

"A good man to count amongst your friends, for he is well-liked."

"So his name would open doors to me?"

"There is no door in Whitehall that would not be open. He's invited everywhere, for he is a great wit, though not so great as he thinks he is," Elizabeth giggled. "Also, he's prepared to lose vast sums at the gaming table. That always makes for popularity now that there are so many who have birth and breeding but no substance!"

Philip had heard enough to know what course of action he should take. Buckingham, brought up in the royal nursery alongside King Charles, was exactly the right choice to be his patron.

"Would you introduce me to him, please?"

"Willingly," she said, leading him over to where Buckingham was conversing with some friends. "Your Grace, allow me to present to you Lord Philip Devalle."

Philip stepped forward and made the elaborate bow he had practised so often before his mirror at High Heatherton. "I trust your Grace will forgive my boldness in requesting that Miss Hamilton introduce us, but it is not often that I have the opportunity to meet so famous a person."

Buckingham beamed at him. "And it is not often I have the opportunity to welcome such a charming newcomer to Whitehall."

Elizabeth's lively eyes conveyed to Philip that she thought he would cope very well without her help now and she withdrew, winking at him as she went.

"A charming girl," Buckingham said. "They all pursue her; de Grammont, Richmond, Jermyn and the rest, but she will have none of them, and even less of me."

"She likes you well enough, your Grace. She said you were a great wit." Philip did not tell him the remainder of Elizabeth's remark!

"Did she now? She certainly seems to have taken to you. Do you suppose that if I were to invite her to a little supper party she would come, if you were going to be there as well?"

Philip realised now the purpose behind Buckingham's interest in him and he smiled to himself. He knew the way that he must play this game.

"She might," he said, "but unfortunately I may not be staying in London for very long. My father is anxious to return home and I fear he would not allow me to remain here without him."

"Can't you persuade him to let you stay even a week?"

Philip looked sorrowful. "I doubt it."

"Not even if you were my guest at Wallingford House?"

Philip could have shrieked for joy, but he managed to appear calm. "I am sure I can persuade him to agree to that, if it will help you."

"You help me and I'll help you," Buckingham promised him. "Stay with me for a week and we will see how we agree with one another."

They were to agree extremely well. When the end of the week came no mention was made of his leaving and Philip had achieved the first of his ambitions.

He was a courtier.

THREE

Philip found it easy to win the friendship of the young Duke of Monmouth, who took to him right away. Philip liked him well enough and enjoyed his company, although Monmouth could be a trifle wearing at times, for he was not possessed of great intelligence.

They had much in common, however, including the desire to be soldiers one day, and they both worked hard at their fencing lessons with Signor D'Alessandro, the Italian fencing master.

"Don't forget that my father is planning to go to Bath at the end of August," Monmouth said as they left D'Alessandro's studio one afternoon. "You are coming, aren't you?"

Queen Catherine was still barren and it was hoped that the waters of Bath would enable her to produce the heir for which all England waited but, of course, the trip was also an excuse for a splendid holiday and most of the Court were to accompany her.

"I would not miss it for the world," Philip said. "What of Lady Castelmaine, is she still determined not to go?"

"She'll go," Monmouth predicted. "She can't really do much else, not with Miss Stewart so much in favour."

Charles had lately taken a fancy to a newcomer at Court, Frances Stewart. She was beautiful and stylish but so devoid of intellect or conversation that Philip could not understand how he could prefer her to the dazzling Castelmaine, who Philip thought must be the loveliest creature in the world.

They said goodbye and as Philip walked off in the direction of St. James' Park he saw the diminutive figure of Lord Ashley appear at Monmouth's side.

Philip frowned. Of all the people he had met at Whitehall, Ashley was the one of whom he felt most wary, yet without quite understanding why. The guileless Monmouth seem to find him the most agreeable of men, yet Philip could not help but feel there was some motive in Ashley's friendly overtures towards him. When he arrived back at Wallingford House Philip decided to mention Lord Ashley to Buckingham, who knew him well as they were both Privy Councillors.

"Ashley?" Buckingham looked surprised. "Why do you want to know about him?"

"He intrigues me, that is all, for he makes a most extraordinary fuss of Monmouth. I have heard my father talk about him and he called him a traitor to the Royalist cause, yet Ashley has been made a Privy Councillor in reward for his service to the Crown. How can this be?"

"It can be if you are as clever and devious as Ashley, and not ashamed to be a trimmer," Buckingham said.

"A trimmer?" Philip was not familiar with the term.

"When war broke out he raised a regiment of foot and a troop of horse for the Royalists, all at his own expense, but when Parliament began to gain the upper hand he changed sides," Buckingham explained. "He was one of those who cried out loudest for the old King's death and yet, just before the Restoration, he was one of the commissioners sent to Breda to invite the new King home."

"I see." For once Philip felt inclined to agree with his father.

"You haven't heard it all, for his next move was to sit upon the commission which tried his old regicide friends! You see now why he is not a man who should be underestimated, and if he takes an interest in Monmouth it is sure to be for a purpose."

"Whatever his purpose, Monmouth is flattered by it, for Lord Ashley praises his intelligence, so he says, and his political awareness, yet I know him to be quite empty-headed and interested in little but his own pleasures. It makes no sense at all."

41

Buckingham agreed. "Has Ashley spoken to you?"

"No. I think he dislikes me, though I don't know why. If I'm with Monmouth he doesn't speak much to him either, but Monmouth always tells me everything so it makes no difference."

Philip strummed thoughtfully upon the guitar which Buckingham had recently bought him. In addition to fencing lessons, the Duke was also paying for Philip to take lessons with the music master, Francisco Corbeta, but he did not find these nearly so enjoyable, for he had no real love of music. He was trying to learn, however, to please Buckingham, who had been very good to him and was making sure that he was schooled in dancing and all the other social graces so necessary to a courtier. He was also very generous. Philip's father sent him an allowance but it was to Buckingham he turned for such essential items as cravats of finest Genoa lace or silver buckles for his shoes! In return he had more than fulfilled his side of their bargain. The Duke's house was now often graced by pretty girls come to call upon Philip, for they loved to take him promenading in Hyde Park or riding around the Coach Ring in their carriages. He enjoyed the fuss they made of him and the compliments they paid him, and was very happy to oblige them with his company, since it seemed to give them so much pleasure!

"I thought we might go to see a play this afternoon," Buckingham said. "They have a woman on the stage at the King's House now, Mrs. Hughes. I hear Prince Rupert goes to see her every day and will soon make her his mistress."

Prince Rupert was at the theatre, as usual, but there was someone of far more interest to Philip as he looked down from the box where they were seated. He could see into the pit where a line of orange women stood with their backs to the stage, holding their baskets of fruit, covered over with vine leaves and, to his surprise, he saw one that he recognised. It was none other than the dirty-faced creature he had met a few months ago on

Strand Bridge, although she was looking considerably smarter than when he had last seen her. "Well I'm damned!"

Buckingham followed his gaze. "What are you looking at? Not one of those pox-ridden whores, I trust."

Philip ignored that. "Do you see the pretty one? That's Nell." He pointed her out. "I met her once."

Buckingham sniffed. "I don't believe I wish to hear the vulgar details of your encounter with an orange girl! Don't touch 'em, that is my advice, unless you want a bad dose of the clap."

Philip would have liked to have spoken to her, nonetheless, and he resolved that he would seek her out when he returned from Bath.

He had a fine time there and he was too busy to think much about either Nell or Lord Ashley. The courtiers were accommodated at various pleasant lodgings all around the wells and met in the morning to drink the waters and walk in the shade of the trees. There were also shops which sold the finest gloves, stockings and lace, as well as a market where everyone purchased their own provisions to be cooked for them at their lodgings.

In the afternoons there was no shortage of play for those who wished to risk their luck at cards or dice. Philip was already beginning to have the urges of a gambler, which was hardly to be wondered at since money was being wagered upon something every hour of the day, and Buckingham was always prepared to cover his losses.

Queen Catherine had asked for the King's Theatre players to be brought along to entertain the party. Mrs. Hughes was amongst them and there could no longer be any doubt as to Prince Rupert's feelings for her.

The holiday atmosphere caused a good many other romances to flourish too, amongst them that of Elizabeth Hamilton with the sophisticated French Comte de Grammont. It was a union of which Philip very much approved, for he liked de Grammont.

He spoke to him in French as often as he could, for the Comte was able to instruct him in some of the niceties of the language that would have been beyond his dear Nanon.

Philip was attracting a good many admirers of his own, but for him there was no-one there to compare with the beautiful Lady Castelmaine. The feelings that she stirred in him were, at times, acutely painful, yet he could not take his eyes off her if she was near. Once she actually turned and smiled at him, and that was the worst torture of all. He was unable to even breathe, let alone respond!

The Court returned to Whitehall in the Autumn. In October the Queen was taken very ill.

Philip was genuinely concerned, for he had come to feel very sorry for her. Queen Catherine had been considered a great beauty in her own country of Portugal but in England her slightly protruding teeth were frequently ridiculed by the more unkind and her olive skin was not at all fashionable at a Court where the ladies prided themselves on their milk-white complexions! Mostly, though, he pitied her for having as her rival the incomparable Lady Castelmaine, and Philip had noticed how often Catherine's lovely, dark eyes were turned sadly upon her husband's mistress.

For a week the Queen lay delirious with fever and it was full month before she was counted to be even out of danger.

Buckingham was among the few permitted to visit her. The next day Philip was astonished to receive a message from none other than Lady Castelmaine, requesting that he attend upon her.

He stared at the servant who had delivered it to him at Wallingford House. "Are you sure this is meant for me and not the Duke of Buckingham?"

"It is for you, my Lord," the servant said. "Shall I tell her you will come?"

Would he go? There was no power on earth that could have stopped him, although he guessed that if Buckingham had been at home he would have made a good attempt! Fortunately, he was not, so Philip did not even have to endure any tiresome warnings.

He dressed quickly but quite carefully, choosing his best brocade coat, which was adorned with some silver lace. When he was satisfied with his appearance he took two beauty patches from his patch box. He had discovered that these black spots, which had so fascinated him when he had seen them worn by Daniel Bennett, were essential for any wishing to be truly fashionable. He had learned, too, that they could speak a language all their own and that messages could be conveyed according to where a patch was placed. Near the eye it indicated passion, nearly on the lip was flirtatious, upon the nose was saucy and worn boldly on the cheek meant that the wearer was in love! After a little consideration he affixed one upon his right cheek and one near his left eye.

Philip had never felt so apprehensive as he did when he presented himself at the apartments of Barbara Palmer, the Countess of Castelmaine. Whilst he was dressing he had practised what he would say to greet her but the words which had come so easily to him then would not come now that he actually stood before his idol.

Barbara advanced to meet him, offering her hand. This was easier. Even if he was at a loss for words Philip did know how to behave and he made her a graceful bow.

She smiled at him delightedly. "You are even more handsome than I thought you were. Come and sit beside me so that I can talk to you properly."

Philip sat down with her upon a small sofa, carefully arranging the folds of lace around his wrists. It was one of the many little affectations that were becoming a part of him, and which were going to grow considerably more pronounced as he grew older.

"There's no need to fuss with yourself, you look divine." Barbara put her hand on top of his. "I've always thought you very elegant."

"Have you, my Lady?" Her touch seemed to send warmth through his whole body. "I didn't think you had ever even noticed me."

"How could anyone not notice such an accomplished young gentleman?" She pouted prettily. "Every woman at Court has set her sights on you, including me."

That was too much to believe, even for one with Philip's vanity, and he felt certain she was mocking him. He had never taken that from anyone, and he never would. "You are making sport of me, I think, my Lady," he said, a little hurt. "Please don't."

"I assure you I was not, but I see that I must tread more carefully if I am to gain your friendship, Philip." She still had her hand on his and she squeezed it gently. "May I call you Philip?"

"If you wish." Philip's heart was pounding. To hear her merely speak his name was making it difficult for him to breathe.

If Barbara was aware of the effect she was having on him she gave no indication of it. "Do you know why I've asked you here, Philip?"

"I have no idea," Philip said truthfully, "unless it concerns the Duke of Buckingham."

"What if it does?"

"Then you ought to know that I would never speak or act against him."

"Loyal too. I like you more and more," she said, "although why you waste your loyalty on such as he I don't know."

Philip smiled, for he knew how little regard the pair had for one another. "Should I not, then, be loyal to someone who enables me to be at Court?"

"You don't need him. You're well bred, talented and pretty. You'd do very well alone."

"But my father would not have left me here alone."

"And do you think your father would be pleased at the way Buckingham looks after you?" Barbara said, touching one of his curls.

"He is very generous," Philip said guardedly, for he was unsure of where this particular topic of conversation was leading. Even the feel of her toying with his hair could not make him completely forget that Barbara was an ambitious schemer.

"Oh, he indulges you, no doubt, and buys you every mortal thing you want, but at the same time he allows you to associate with whoremongers and even orange girls. Am I not right?"

Philip thought a moment before replying. The description of whoremonger could have fitted a legion of his new friends but the only orange girl he knew was Nell. He guessed that Barbara had spotted him one day when he was talking to her outside the theatre.

"I am flattered that your Ladyship has been paying so much attention to me."

"You are rather difficult to ignore, you know. Also, being a confidante of Buckingham's, you are in a somewhat unique position, are you not?"

"Am I, my Lady?" Philip was beginning now to suspect the real reason that he was there, and to fear that it had nothing whatever to do with his charms!

"You certainly are. Charles has no secrets from his old friend, Buckingham. I hear he even took him to see the Queen yesterday."

"What of it?"

"So you must know if it is true."

Philip stared her, nonplussed. "If what is true?"

"Why, that she is pregnant, of course."

"I don't know," Philip said coldly. "We did not discuss it." He was mortified that she had invited him to her apartments because he might know whether there was any truth in the rumour that was circulating the palace and not, as he had dared to hope, because she really wanted his company.

He stood up and made her a stiff bow. "If that is all, my Lady, I think perhaps I should go now."

Barbara looked surprised. "But I have barely had the chance to get acquainted with you."

"If your purpose in making my acquaintance is to try to discover things I do not know then I fear you waste your time." Philip was not so easily won over, especially when his pride had been wounded.

"That was not my only purpose, "she said softly, "and I certainly never meant to make you cross. It's just that Charles and I have argued lately. You must have heard that he now favours Frances Stewart over me."

"That little simpleton?" Philip said dismissively.

Barbara laughed at his frankness. "Yes, that simpleton, but it is I who have been the greater fool, for I befriended her, little thinking she was only using me to get to Charles."

"I doubt she'll keep him long. She has too little wit."

"Who needs wit when they have a face so fine that Philip Rotier is copying it for the face of Britannia on the new coins?" Barbara said pettishly. "It is not my image that Charles has ordered him to use but that of a simpering little virgin who swears she will never renounce her chastity before she's wed. And now I hear his damned wife is with child."

Philip decided to put her out of her misery, for he did know the truth and Barbara would learn it soon enough in any case. Buckingham had told him that Catherine, whilst she was delirious, had thought she was pregnant but it had turned out that she was still barren, despite the waters of the Wells.

"She's not with child."

"Truly?" Barbara leapt to her feet and danced around the room. "That is the best news you could possibly have given me."

Philip did not answer, for he was absorbed in watching her. Barbara put to shade every woman he had ever met and he could not hide his admiration.

She smiled at him. "Are you still in a hurry to leave me, Philip?"

Philip shook his head. He felt as though he never wanted to leave her, although he had not quite forgiven her yet.

"Then why not stay and sup with me?" She took his hands in hers. "Do, please. I made a bad beginning with you and I'm sorry, but I want us to become friends."

Philip's resistance melted away. "In that case I should be honoured to be your guest, my Lady, but won't the King mind?"

"Charles will never know unless you tell him, for he's on his way to Newmarket by now. Besides, he's treated me abominably lately, flirting with Stewart and sitting for days at his pathetic wife's bedside, and then disappearing to the races without me. I don't believe he could begrudge me a little diversion."

Philip was not so sure, but he allowed her to pull him closer.

"You are very tall." She ran her hands over his shoulders then down his arms. "Strong too, I'll wager. You have firm, hard muscles. Where did you develop those? Fencing in Signor D'Alessandro's studio?"

Philip knew she was not really asking him questions, or rather not any that required answers, but was merely giving herself the excuse to touch him.

"Wait here whilst I change," she instructed him, going into her bedroom. "I will summon you when I am ready."

Left alone, Philip took a deep breath to calm his nerves. He studied himself in the silver-framed mirror on the wall. "I just hope you know what you are doing," he said to his reflection. "Well at least you look the part of a gallant, even if you don't truly know how to act it."

He had rarely encountered any situation that he could not handle and he little doubted this would be any different, that is until he entered Barbara's bedroom. She was reclining upon her bed clad in nothing but the flimsiest robe, and that had fallen open to reveal one shapely leg up to her thigh.

Philip was stunned for a second but he soon recovered his equanimity. He had heard that she was partial to younger men but not even Barbara, he guessed, would throw herself so wantonly at someone she scarcely knew, so he suspected that this little display was intended as a test for him.

A table had been set up in the room and laid for two so he seated himself. Giving her no more than a cursory glance, he poured the wine and pushed one crystal goblet towards her.

"Bring it here to me," she said.

Philip did not move. "I am not your servant, my Lady."

"But you are my guest."

Philip regarded her coolly. "Then you should serve me."

She laughed. "I should dismiss you right now for your audacity." Instead she came to join him at the table. "I won't, though, and do you know why?"

"Because I'm pretty?" Philip guessed.

"That's part of it." Barbara took one of the glasses and raised it to his lips. "Here, drink, sir, since you would have me serve you! You fascinate me, Philip, that's the truth of it."

Philip stayed her hand, fearing she would pour the whole glass into him. "I do?"

"Yes, indeed. You are very self-assured for one so young, but tell me, have you ever had a woman?"

This threw Philip for a second, but he soon recovered. "Is that a question you usually put to your guests, my Lady?"

"No. Answer it."

"Very well. I have never had a woman."

"Would you like to have one?"

"That depends," Philip said carefully. His pulse was racing but he was determined to remain calm. If she were teasing him, as he reckoned she was, he vowed she would not have the satisfaction of seeing him make a fool of himself by playing into her hands. "Since I have been at Whitehall there has been only one woman I have really desired."

"And who is that? Elizabeth Hamilton, I suppose," Barbara said, archly. "You're always talking together."

Philip smiled. Barbara certainly had been watching him. "No, you, of course."

"That's nice!" Barbara blew him a kiss across the table. "Did you tell anyone about your feelings for me?"

"Only Buckingham."

"Good. You are discreet."

"Afraid," he corrected her. "I saw what happened to Henry Jermyn."

Jermyn had recently been banished from Court for bragging that he and Barbara were lovers.

Barbara commenced to pick daintily at a piece of cold pheasant, which she now held out to him. Philip found something unbelievingly erotic about sharing food with this sensuous woman.

He was in no doubt now that she truly did intend to seduce him and, if he'd had doubts, the rubbing of her thigh against his would have dispelled them! What was strange was that he no longer doubted his own capabilities. The early stirrings of manhood had now become the fiercer urges of an animal, and it was these most bestial instincts which were guiding him, and would have done so even if she had not been making it so plain that she desired him.

Barbara took him by the hand and led him over to the hearth where a fine fire burned. She put out all the candles in the sconces so that the only light in the room came from the flames. As she stood beside him he could see, in the flickering red glow, the outline of her body showing through the filmy robe.

She undressed him slowly then ran soft hands all over his naked body. Philip gave himself over completely to the pleasure of her touch. He did not even care that she could see the ugly scars upon his back.

Barbara's breath came faster and faster until, quivering with excitement, she slipped off her robe and knelt down to devour him.

Philip offered no resistance; indeed, he would have been incapable of doing so as Barbara took total possession of his body and his will, becoming, in turn, his expert teacher, his tender mistress and his willing slave.

FOUR

❧

Philip was walking in the Privy Gardens when he came across young Harry Killegrew, staring morosely at the ground.

"What troubles you, Harry?"

"I'll tell you what troubles me, my Lord," Killegrew said. "It troubles me to discover that a man I considered to be my friend is nothing but a treacherous dog. "

"Who are you talking about?" Philip said, although he feared he knew.

"Who else but Buckingham. You know he's stolen Lady Shrewsbury from me, when he knew that we were happy together? Have I not extolled her virtues ever since she became my mistress?"

"You have indeed, and I believe that was the very reason he pursued her," Philip said frankly. "Buckingham is a man who judges only by outward appearances and he told me that, in his opinion, Lady Shrewsbury did not seem half as tempting as you claimed. I guess his curiosity got the better of him and he decided to see for himself whether it was true or false."

"Well it was false," Harry flashed back. "She has no wit, her breasts are padded and it takes an hour to rouse her to a passion, and when you do it is hardly worth the effort. What do you think of that?"

"I think you should guard your tongue," Philip advised him. "Buckingham will not take kindly to your slighting her."

He was right about that. Buckingham was furious the next day when he heard the tales that were being spread by Lady

Shrewsbury's ex-lover. Philip had never seen him in such a rage and he could do nothing to calm him.

"I shall challenge him to a duel," Buckingham decided.

"How can you do that? She is married to someone else and so are you," Philip reminded him.

"Very well then, I shall let Lady Shrewsbury have her way. She wants to have him set upon in the park when he returns from the Duke of York's tonight, and serve him right for his insolence."

Philip was horrified. "How can you possibly condone that? Besides you risk being involved yourself. What of his father?"

Harry's father was Thomas Killegrew, the manager of the King's Theatre and a favourite of Charles.

Buckingham shrugged. "If any blame comes my way I am certain Charles would forgive me. He always does. Don't you interfere in this, Philip," he warned. "Harry may be a friend of yours but he is due for a lesson."

Philip could not help but agree that Harry had behaved imprudently but he thought a scare would be sufficient. Buckingham's relationships had always been short-lived in any case and, since Lady Shrewsbury had the reputation of being a fickle jade, he hardly thought the matter warranted such drastic measures.

Of course, being Philip, he had not lost sight of how the matter would affect him personally! Buckingham would be in disgrace if his involvement was discovered and that was certain to reflect on Philip. It might even jeopardise his position at Whitehall.

He decided he could not afford to leave such important considerations to chance. Loyalty to Buckingham was one thing but, for reasons which he hoped were noble, he knew he must thwart the plan, and without the Duke ever knowing it.

It was midnight before Harry left York's. Philip was waiting in the park, wearing a long black cloak and with his hat pulled low over his eyes. As Harry's sedan chair approached, three figures appeared from the shadow of the trees, their swords raised. Philip fastened on the black velvet mask which he wore at masked balls and crept towards them.

When the sinister figures reached the sedan, Harry's servants dropped the poles and ran. Harry cried out in pain and fear as the three swords pierced his chair, but Philip was upon the men before they could retrieve their weapons. Drawing his own sword he lashed out at them and, defenceless, they ran for their lives, leaving their swords embedded in the chair.

Harry staggered out, clutching his arm, which was bleeding. "Thank you, whoever you are."

But Philip, seeing that Harry was not seriously wounded, had already turned to make his own escape. He might have managed it too had not a gust of wind lifted his hat, so that his fair hair showed plainly in the moonlight.

"Philip!"

"Blast! Breathe a word of this to anyone, Harry, and I swear I'll finish you myself," Philip threatened, replacing his hat quickly before anyone else came by and recognised him.

"Was it Buckingham who set those ruffians on me?"

"Lady Shrewsbury actually, and it's your own fault. If you have a grain of sense you'll leave her to Buckingham and find yourself another mistress."

Harry looked so dejected that Philip could not but feel sorry for him, despite all the trouble he had caused. "Are you in much pain, Harry?"

"No more than I deserve to be, I suppose. I don't know why you did this but I am truly grateful. How can I ever repay you?"

"With your silence," Philip said simply.

The following day he was a little concerned to receive a message to attend upon Harry's father, Thomas Killegrew.

Killegrew soon put him at his ease. "Lord Devalle, the world believes that Harry was set upon last night by common vagabonds intent on stealing the contents of his purse and that he defended himself so valiantly that he sent them packing with only one wound to himself. Only *we* know differently. What can a father say to the man who saved the life of his son?"

"I did not act entirely for Harry's benefit," Philip had to admit. "For all his faults, I am fond of Buckingham and I am reluctant to see him risk disgrace on account of a whore like Lady Shrewsbury."

Killegrew laughed at that. "You are a remarkable young man. Not one, it is plain, who should be underestimated. Is it true that you were expelled from St. Paul's School as ungovernable?"

Philip flicked an imaginary piece of fluff from the cuff of his velvet coat, another affectation of his. "There were some who felt me to be a disruptive element in the school."

"I can well believe that! I do not see a way I can reward you for what you have done, for anything I did for you would soon be noticed by Lord Buckingham and cause you to be placed in an invidious position. Can you think of any favour I could do you that would not arouse his suspicions?"

Philip smiled as an idea struck him. "Yes, I can. I would have you meet a girl of my acquaintance who very much desires to be an actress at the King's House."

"Has she any talent?"

"She can dance and she's pretty."

"Then bring her to me before tomorrow afternoon's performance," Killegrew said. "Is that all you want?"

"That's all."

"You're easily contented! What's her name?"

"Nell. Nell Gwynne. She's one of the orange girls."

Killegrew smiled knowingly. "And is this the reward you offered her for her favours, an introduction to the manager of the theatre?"

"Hardly! I met her quite by chance a couple of years ago. I have not troubled you with this before because I thought she might come to her senses."

"If you say that then you can have no understanding of the passion some have for the stage," Killegrew said. "When I was a child with no admittance money I would wait nearly every day outside the theatre doors until one of the actors came out to enquire who would act the 'Devil', then I would volunteer so that I could witness the performance for nothing."

Philip looked at him, bemused. "I have absolutely no idea what you are talking about, but if you would be kind enough to give Nell this chance then you would ensure me a little peace and discharge any debt you feel you owe me."

Killegrew was as good as his word. When Philip brought Nell to him the following afternoon he put her through her paces, watching her dance and hearing her sing and read a part.

Philip thought she did rather well. He waited for her afterwards in the auditorium, which was beginning to fill for that day's performance. The Company were playing 'Mustapha', a popular play written by the Earl of Orrery, with Mrs. Betterton taking the lead part of Roxolana.

As Philip looked about him, noting who was there and with whom, he felt someone touch him on the shoulder. He turned to see that it was the Comte de Grammont.

"I thought you still in Paris, Comte."

"Alas, it seems King Louis has not yet forgiven me, as I had hoped, so I stayed only long enough to play a few games of cards to raise the money for my passage back to England."

Rumour had it that the reason de Grammont was in England in the first place was because he had been exiled for attempting to steal a mistress from the King of France and Philip reckoned it unlikely that he would be welcomed back there for quite a long while!

"So your trip was for nothing?"

"Not quite, for I do believe my absence has served to quicken Miss Hamilton's feelings for me."

"You are a lucky man," Philip said. "Were I a few years older I would woo Elizabeth myself!"

"The damnedest thing is that she would probably accept you! Here's a pretty little piece," de Grammont remarked, "and I do believe she comes to join us."

The pretty little piece was Nell.

"It's all agreed, I join the Company right away." She threw her arms around Philip's neck. "I am so grateful to you, dearest Philip."

Philip hastily disengaged himself, aware that de Grammont was watching him with merriment.

"It seems you are keeping secrets from us 'dearest' Philip! Aren't you going to introduce me?"

Philip did so and de Grammont bowed. "I hope to see more of you, Mistress Gwynn."

"You will, sir, on the stage of this very theatre," Nell said pertly, "thanks to Philip. I owe everything to him."

"I'll bet you do!" De Grammont winked at Philip as he left then to take his seat, for the play was about to begin.

"Would you like to see 'Mustapha'? Philip asked Nell.

"What, with you? I certainly would! You can't take me into the boxes, though, where all the lords and ladies sit."

"Then I must be contented with the pit, if I'm to have the pleasure of your company," he said, laughing at her excitement.

He always enjoyed being with Nell. Perhaps it was because of the strange way they had met or simply because she was such an unpretentious creature herself, but he felt completely at ease with her, as he had with few people in his life. It was as if, whenever they were together, they were still those same two children who had stood upon Strand Bridge delighting in the dancers around the Maypole.

They had just found themselves a place to sit when King Charles and Barbara entered and took their places in the royal box.

Nell sighed enviously. "Look at her, the lucky bitch. That dress, those jewels!"

"The rewards of being a king's whore," Philip whispered.

"I could bed him for no reward at all," Nell said. "He is the handsomest man that I have ever seen. Apart from you, of course," she added cheekily.

Philip ignored that. "We will have to see what we can do to bring you to his attention."

"Don't tease."

"I'm not. I see no reason why you shouldn't catch his eye now you're going to be upon the stage."

"But I'll not get the big parts right away," Nell said, "even though Mr. Killegrew does like me."

"Wait and see. I have some other influential friends now apart from Thomas Killegrew."

Just at that moment, almost on cue, Barbara looked down from her balcony at the crowd below. Catching sight of Philip she blew a kiss to him, shielding herself from Charles' sight with her fan.

"Was that meant for you?" Nell said.

"Yes, I believe it was."

"But why? What is the Countess of Castlemaine to you?"

"Hush! The play begins."

"Have you bedded Castlemaine?" Nell persisted as the tall wax candles were lit to illuminate the exotically decorated stage.

Philip said nothing.

"You'll get no peace until you answer," Nell warned. "Well, have you?"

"Yes. Now be quiet and watch the play."

"Did you say 'yes'?"

"I shall abandon you right here and now if you cannot behave," he warned.

"Oh, don't do that. I will do absolutely anything you ask if you bring me to the notice of the King."

"So you believe now in my capabilities? That's gratifying!"

"A man who can take a mistress from a king is capable of anything."

"I haven't taken her from him. I merely borrow her from time to time, and you had better keep it to yourself or you will be the ruination of me," Philip said, remembering the Comte de Grammont's fate.

"I will, of course." Nell was silent for a little while, then she tugged at his sleeve. "If, on account of you, I did become Charles' mistress, what would you want for your reward?"

"Reward, you saucy jade?" Philip turned once more from the play, whose plot he was, understandably, finding difficult to follow. "What reward could you possibly offer me?"

"I thought, perhaps, that you could borrow me from time to time, as you do her," Nell said hopefully. "I wouldn't mind a bit."

He smiled at her affectionately, for he was fond of her, but no more than that. "Don't you reckon it is a little early to be offering favours in return for a service I have not yet performed?"

Nell linked her arm through his with a familiarity he did not mind, although he knew he should. "Philip, even if I never become his mistress, for what you have done for me this day you shall have my friendship and my gratitude for all my life. Let's watch the play now."

"What an excellent idea!"

Philip was not entirely surprised to find a summons from Barbara awaiting him when he arrived home. Knowing that she must have seen him with Nell he guessed she would not be in too good a mood, and he was right!

"Who was she?" Barbara demanded.

"She?" Philip said innocently.

"Don't play games with me. I saw you at the theatre with some common little strumpet."

"What makes you think I was with her? She must have just been someone in the audience."

"Not so, for she had her arm through yours. I saw that very clear."

Philip was also seeing something very clear - a side to Barbara's character that he had not seen before, and it was not one he much liked. Whilst he felt extremely flattered by the attention she showed him, he had not expected such possessiveness from a married woman who had several other lovers, including King Charles!

Nevertheless, he knew he must be careful, and not only for his own sake. If Barbara was determined it would not take her too long to find out for herself who his companion was, then Nell's career upon the stage would be blighted before it had even begun, along with her hopes of catching the eye of the King.

"Can I help it if women find me irresistible?" he said, feigning pettishness.

"You can if you encourage them."

"Do you imagine I would enjoy to be pawed by some filthy serving slut when I am privileged to enjoy the touch of the most beautiful woman in the world?"

Compliments always worked with Barbara and her expression softened a little. "Why did you allow it then?"

"Because the stupid creature misunderstood my civilities. I could not rid myself of her so I thought to take her to the play, hoping to slip away afterwards and avoid a scene in public." This sounded a bit unlikely, even to Philip's ears, but he thought it worth a try.

Barbara seemed to accept it, however. "And did you escape, or did you take her back to her lodgings? No, don't trouble to answer that for I can easily tell if you have been with another woman. Come here."

Philip went to her, deeming it wiser to do as he was told. "What are you going to do?"

"Undress you."

That was not unusual; Barbara dearly loved undressing him and it had become a ritual part of their lovemaking. She always did it slowly, tantalising herself, but on this occasion she fairly tore the garments from him. Philip found it strangely exciting.

Barbara must have seen that he was aroused, without quite realising how she was doing it. "What are you thinking about?" she wanted to know.

"Actually of Nanon," he said wickedly. "You remind me of her."

"And who the hell is Nanon? Some French whore?"

Philip laughed, despite her fury. "Nanon was my maid."

"Your maid? You saucy bastard! How can I remind you of a damned maid?"

"She used to take my clothes off in the same way as you are doing now, for she was usually annoyed with me on some count or another." Philip lay back on the bed and smiled as he recalled his early fantasies about Nanon.

"What did she do then?" Barbara said.

"She used to bath me. I enjoyed that most of all, and while she did I would imagine such divine things that, at times, I quite shocked myself!"

"And do you still think of her?"

"I haven't thought of Nanon since I was at school." Philip recalled the last occasion of their meeting and put it from his mind. His memories of Nanon were forever soured. "But why are you talking to me, sweetheart?" he said, to change the subject. "Am I not still that same fornicating wretch I was a few minutes ago?"

"That is what I intend to discover. Stay there, wretch, while I examine you."

"There's surely not much more to see than what is already in plain view," Philip said, obligingly keeping still whilst Barbara scrutinised every inch of him.

"Very well," she said at length. "I cannot see another woman's marks upon you. I reckon you were probably telling me the truth."

"You sound disappointed!"

Barbara ran her fingers lightly over his firm stomach. "In a way I am. I rather fancied teaching you a lesson. Well perhaps I'll teach you anyway." Without warning the hand that fondled him turned into a claw and the five sharp points of her nails dug into his flesh.

Philip sucked his breath in sharply, but he did not move a muscle.

Barbara laughed. "I see I must do worse than that to punish you. Who is the most desirable woman you have ever seen?" The talons scraped him this time from his navel to his groin, drawing blood.

"You are," he panted.

"Very good! Let's try another question." This time she fastened the nails of both hands into the soft flesh just below his neck and brought them down across his chest, leaving clear, red welts. "Who is the woman you want more than any other in the world?"

"You, you bitch, although I don't know why I should." He tried to sit up but she pushed him back and sank her teeth deep into his shoulder.

"And have you been unfaithful to me?"

"You were supposed to be finding that out for yourself!" Philip said, dabbing the blood from his shoulder with the bed sheets. "May I get dressed now, please?"

"No, you may not." Barbara kissed him savagely upon the lips. "I've not finished with you yet."

"Why, what are you planning to do to me now?" he asked warily.

In answer Barbara pointed to the gilded bath which stood in the corner of the room.

"Guess!"

FIVE

⌘

"Philip, I want you to be the first to hear my plans. I am going to war and I have applied for the command of a ship."

Philip looked at Buckingham in amazement. He had known that the fleet was being made ready to fight the Dutch, but he had never expected his pleasure-loving patron to volunteer. It was good news, however, for several of Philip's friends were already talking of going, including Monmouth, and he was longing for the chance to see some action for himself.

"But you are not a sailor," he said, laughing at Buckingham's enthusiasm. "Surely York will never give you a ship when you have no experience of fighting at sea."

Charles' brother, James, the Duke of York, was Lord High Admiral, and not one of Buckingham's greatest admirers.

Buckingham dismissed York with an airy wave of his hand "Of course he will. How can he refuse me? This something I must do, Philip, for I feel I have lived the life of an idle wastrel for too long."

"More likely you are doing it to impress a lady," Philip said, for he had come to know him very well.

"Lady Shrewsbury," Buckingham admitted. "I'm in love with her."

Philip groaned. "Why must you always fall in love with them?"

"You used to say you were in love with Barbara once," Buckingham reminded him.

"I could love her still when I am close to her but afterwards I have no feeling for her whatsoever," Philip said truthfully. "When are we leaving?"

"We?"

"Why yes. I assume I will be sailing with you, if the navy does entrust a ship to you."

Buckingham looked uneasy. "I'm sorry, Philip, I'm not taking you."

"What?" The excitement Philip was feeling at the prospect of the coming adventure left him abruptly.

"This will be my first command of a ship. I shall have sufficient worries and responsibilities without adding you to their number."

"Is that all I am to you, then, a worry and a responsibility?"

"No, of course not. You're a dear friend and a good companion," Buckingham said. "That is why I would never forgive myself if anything happened to you on account of me."

Philip knew he should be flattered by Buckingham's concern but he was desperately disappointed. He could not believe he was being deprived of his first opportunity to go to war.

York, as Philip had expected, was far from grateful for Buckingham's offer to command a ship. It presented him with a delicate problem. Buckingham was wholly ignorant of naval tactics, so he could not be trusted with a large ship. On the other hand, with his rank and station, he could hardly be given charge of a gun-brig or a sloop. After some deliberation it was decided that he could serve upon the flag ship without doing too much harm. He would not be in a position of extreme command but, as the captain was a friend of his, Buckingham was quite agreeable and sent word to Philip of his success.

The letter arrived at a most inopportune moment, just as Philip was receiving a parting visit from Monmouth, off to join York upon the 'Royal Charles'.

"He bids me not to follow him, lest he should have my death upon his conscience," Philip told him despondently. "It seems that everyone is going to fight except me."

Monmouth read the letter himself. "He does not tell you not to go to war exactly," he said, with a flash of astuteness which was unusual for him. "He merely says that he will not have you serve on his ship."

"He means for me to stay here."

"He may mean that, but it is not what he has said. Why don't you come with me aboard the 'Royal Charles'?"

"Don't you think I would if I could? Buckingham would not hear of it."

"But he won't be able to stop you now, will he? He's already on his own ship, so he won't even know until it's too late. Besides, he surely can't refuse to let you go if you have already been accepted on board by the Lord High Admiral himself!"

Philip's face lit at the thought. "Would your uncle agree to it without Buckingham's permission?"

"Leave him to me. Have you sufficient money to equip yourself?"

"I think so. My father's name is good for credit anyway."

They both laughed to think how easily the problem had been solved. "Join me at the gun fleet as soon as you can," Monmouth said as they parted. "Can you believe it? We're actually going off to fight a war, just as we always used to say we would!"

York left London by river on the last day of March. His wife and King Charles accompanied him as far as The Hope then, as Commander of the Royal Squadron, he sailed on to join the fleet. It was an impressive sight, ninety-eight ships in all, with forty guns apiece, together with the fire-ships and various other craft. York boarded the 'Royal Charles' to meet Prince Rupert, who was Vice-Admiral of the White, and the Earl of Sandwich, the Rear-Admiral of the Blue.

He did not look particularly pleased to find the Duke of Buckingham waiting with them. He looked even less pleased when Buckingham demanded to be present during all councils of war.

"That is unthinkable," York said. "You are quite unqualified. You were a soldier, not a sailor."

"But Prince Rupert was a soldier, too, before he became a sailor, and he will be there."

"Prince Rupert is Vice-Admiral of England," York pointed out as patiently as he could.

"Well I am a Privy Councillor, the same as he, so I am entitled to sit upon the council here, just as I do in London."

"Indeed you are not!"

"You are refusing me?"

"I fear I must. There is no place for you in my council."

"Then there is no place for me in your fleet," Buckingham said hotly. "I withdraw my service and that of those of my household who accompanied me."

"Does that include your charge, Lord Devalle? By arrangement with my nephew he is due to join me aboard this ship in a few days' time."

"Is he indeed? The devious little bastard! I can assure you that Philip will not be sailing with the fleet, and nor will I."

Philip viewed Buckingham a little apprehensively. "I little thought to see you back so soon, my Lord."

"Evidently, from your expression, it is not a pleasant surprise," Buckingham said tartly, "and I can well understand why."

"Of course I'm pleased to see you," Philip lied. It was past midnight and Buckingham had awoken him from a deep sleep, but he had his wits about him sufficiently to know that he must tread carefully. "Do you not have preparations to make before the fleet sails?"

"I am not sailing with the fleet." Buckingham said.

Philip's heart sank. This was not what he wanted to hear. "Why ever not?"

"I have decided I cannot serve under the Duke of York, since he has refused to allow me to be present during councils of war. As a Privy Councillor it is my right, and I told him so."

"But you were not there in your capacity as Privy Councillor, but as a volunteer serving beneath a captain," Philip said.

"What has that to do with it? He refused me for no better reason than that he dislikes me."

At any other time, Philip would have been sympathetic, but his only thought now was whether this would ruin his own plans. Buckingham's next words confirmed it.

"I told him you would not be sailing with the fleet either, no matter what arrangements you and Monmouth have made behind my back."

"You had no right to do that," Philip said furiously. "York had already agreed to have me on board the 'Royal Charles'."

"He is not responsible for you. I am, and I say you are too young to go to war."

"I am practically the same age as Monmouth!"

"He is also too young, in my opinion, but he has the permission of his father. Yours, I think, would not approve of your going, any more than I do."

"But you were hardly any older than I am now when you left your studies and went to fight for the Royalists."

"I was lucky to escape unharmed, but there were others less fortunate, who should not have died so young," Buckingham said quietly. "My mind is quite made up, and you'll not change it, not this time."

"Because you yourself have been deprived of a chance of glory?" That was unkind and Philip knew it, but he didn't particularly care. Buckingham had never refused him anything before and yet it seemed now, when it was most important to him, that he was not going to get his way.

"You must have a low opinion of me if you truly believe that," Buckingham said in an injured tone, "and a low opinion also of the regard I have for you."

"What regard can you have for me if you wish to deprive me of the one thing I truly want?" Philip said passionately.

"So this is what you truly want? Forgive me but I was under the impression that it was a courtier's life you wanted," Buckingham flashed back. "Fine clothes and other fripperies, dancing lessons, a fencing master and a thousand other expensive privileges it has been my pleasure to provide for you. That was what I thought you wanted - mainly because that is what you always told me that you wanted."

They faced each other angrily. Philip was well aware of how much Buckingham had done for him, and he was really very grateful, but he was too disappointed to be reasonable at that moment. "You can keep your money," he said huffily. "I want no more to do with it, or with you. Barbara has already asked me to move into a room near her in the palace and I think, now, that perhaps I shall."

Buckingham looked hurt. "If that is what you would prefer."

It wasn't really, but Philip could hardly admit that. "I have nothing more to say."

"Not even any words of thanks for all I've done for you?"

"You had your reasons, I've no doubt."

"That was true at the start," Buckingham admitted, "but I have enjoyed your being here. I'd even go so far as to say that I would miss you now. Let's put this behind us, Philip, and continue to be friends, as we have always been."

Philip was tempted, for he was genuinely fond of Buckingham, but he had gone too far now to relent. "I think it better that we part company, my Lord."

Buckingham sighed. "Very well. If you choose to disdain my patronage that is your affair. You may live independently from me on the allowance your father sends you, but you remain my responsibility. That means I am still able to prevent you from going to sea."

Philip knew then that he was beaten, and he was not a good loser.

⌇

The fleet sailed two months later, on the second day of June. Barbara brought word to Philip only a few minutes after she had heard it herself, for Charles had been dining in her apartments when Samuel Pepys, the Clerk of the Acts, arrived from the Navy Office to report the news.

"Charles is more worried over Monmouth than he lets show," she said to Philip. "Just as I would have worried over you if you had gone."

Philip made no reply. He had still not forgiven Buckingham.

"I have another piece of news as well," Barbara added, as an afterthought. "Apparently some illness has started in the city and is spreading fast. There have been several deaths, but never mind. We're safe here, and that is all that matters."

"Is it?" Philip looked at her, thinking how shallow she really was. "Is that all that matters."

"Yes, of course."

"Then it is of no consequence that the citizens of London are dying or that our friends may be soon engaged in a battle for our country? None of that is in the least important, just so long as you and I and a hundred other useless creatures that spend their lives decorating Whitehall Palace are kept safe?"

"My, but you are disagreeable today," Barbara snapped, her colour rising.

"Sorry, sweetheart." Philip held out his hand for her to strike him with her fan, which she did, quite hard. "It is of no use to rail at you, for none of this is your fault."

"Buckingham has asked me to tell you that he wishes to be friends again."

Philip knew what it must have cost Buckingham's pride to send this message through Barbara, who disliked him, but he did not care. "Buckingham can go to hell."

"And what about me and the hundred other useless creatures here?"

"The others may do as they please. You, I hope, will spend the night with me, since Charles, no doubt, will now be engaged elsewhere."

Barbara laughed. "You are impertinent! You don't deserve my favours." Nonetheless she seated herself beside him, laying down her gloves and fan and raising her petticoat to show her neat, slim ankles, bare in the warm weather. "If this disease does spread I reckon Charles will move the Court out of London, don't you?"

"How should I know?" Philip lifted her skirt a little higher to look at her legs. Barbara had wonderful legs. "Anyway, it may be nothing but a rumour, for you know how these tales grow."

"Yes, I'm sure you're right," Barbara said, "indeed the more I consider it the more I'm certain that we have no cause to worry. It is very likely nothing but a silly rumour."

The battle of Southwold Bay was a glorious victory for the English, though not without cost. Monmouth and the Duke of York returned home safely but amongst the dead was the young Earl of Falmouth, who had married one of Elizabeth Hamilton's friends only months earlier.

"The shot that killed him burst on the quarter-deck a few feet away from my uncle," Monmouth told Philip. "He was spattered with Falmouth's blood. It was dreadful."

Dreadful or not, Philip still wished he had been there. The English had sunk or captured over twenty Dutch ships and had killed five thousand of their men, whilst losing only one small vessel. As Monmouth told the tale, with the enthusiasm of a boy returning fresh from his first campaign, Philip's hatred of Buckingham deepened.

"What are you going to do now?" he asked Monmouth, when he thought he could no longer bear to hear his friend speak of his adventures.

"My father and my uncle wish me to join them on the royal barge to sail from Hampton Court to Greenwich and inspect the buildings that are being added to the palace, and then we go to Salisbury with the rest of the Court."

The sickness in the city, far from being an empty rumour, had reached such terrifying proportions that it was already being dubbed the Black Death.

The play houses were closed, along with every other place of public entertainment. Even the shops were boarded up, for the citizens had more to fear than catching the fever; crime was rife upon the streets and looters ransacked any empty houses.

Now that the fleet had returned, Charles had reluctantly agreed to move the Court and Parliament to Salisbury, just as Barbara had predicted.

"Lord Ashley has invited my father and me to stay with him in Dorset for a week before we go to Salisbury," Monmouth said. "Why don't you come too?"

"Lord Ashley has not invited me."

"But I'm sure he would if I requested it."

Philip shook his head. "No thank you. I think he dislikes me and, besides, I don't really want to go."

"Oh." Monmouth looked disappointed. "Philip, is there something I have done that has displeased you?"

"Of course not."

"You have been so odd with me since I returned. Believe me I do understand the way you must be feeling but you know it wasn't my fault that you could not come with me on the 'Royal Charles'."

Philip smiled. Despite his bitterness it was impossible to remain cool with such an earnest creature as Monmouth.

"There is nothing wrong between us," he assured him, "but I would prefer it if you went to Dorset without me. I'm not certain if I'm even going to Salisbury."

"But you must," Monmouth said. "This plague will soon be everywhere in London. It will not be safe here for you. Everyone else is going."

That was not quite true. The Duke of Albemarle, though only recently returned from the fighting, had elected to stay. He rode out daily, in the midst of death and danger, keeping the peace, comforting the sick and protecting the property of those too weak to defend themselves.

Philip admired him very much for it, though many others thought he must be mad.

"If you stay I'll stay too," Monmouth said impulsively. "We'll keep each other company."

"Don't be a fool, James. You must do what your father says. I'll see you just as soon as this is over and the world grows sane again," Philip promised. "And one more thing. Please do be careful of Lord Ashley."

Monmouth laughed. "Ashley? I am not afraid of him."

"Then perhaps you should be. Call it, if you will, a premonition but I feel he's dangerous. He seeks to gain your friendship and your trust. I think you ought to wonder why."

Monmouth left the following week, along with most of the Court. Philip remained in London and so, perversely it seemed to him, did the Duke of Buckingham.

"I suppose you do know he is staying on account of you?" Barbara said when she came to say goodbye.

"Nonsense! If he stays then it is because it suits him to stay. Most likely he has some mistress that he will not leave."

Barbara shrugged. "I've done my best to reconcile you pair. We've had our differences, Buckingham and I, but he is still a cousin of mine, after all, and I pray that you come to your senses soon."

"It's good to know that I am in your prayers! Safe journey, sweetheart."

"Oh, Philip, I can't bear to leave you here. Come with me," Barbara begged. "I can invent some story for Charles."

"And do yourself no good at all. I shall be perfectly all right." Philip was touched by her concern, for he had not expected it. Indeed, as Barbara hugged him, he saw she was very close to tears.

"You are so stubborn. I ought to hate you," she sniffed. "It may be that I will learn to hate you when we are apart."

"Then perhaps it would be best if I caught this plague so that I might die remembering the tenderness that I see in your face right now," he teased her.

She gripped him still harder. "No. You will not dare to catch it. You must promise me that you will not go into the city."

"Now why should I do that?" Philip tried to kiss her to distract her but, for once, she resisted him.

"Because I've heard you speak of Albemarle and I'm afraid that you might offer to help him in order to prove that you can be a hero even if you could not go to war."

"Are you implying that my motives would be those of glory rather than philanthropy?" he said dryly.

"Yes, because I know you very well and you are selfish, like me."

"Why do you suppose Albemarle concerns himself in the city?" Philip asked her. "What has he to prove, since he is already a hero many times over?"

"There are those who think that Albemarle might be so unhappy with that mean-bred, plain and shrewish wife of his that he no longer cares if he should live or die! Anyway, I'm not concerned for him but for you. Shall you promise me or not?"

"No." This time Philip did succeed in kissing her. "I positively shall not promise anything. You will just have to trust to my good sense and selfishness!"

SIX

༄

Barbara had guessed exactly what Philip planned to do. Just as soon as the Queen's coach, with Barbara inside, had departed from the palace he went to see the Duke of Albemarle where he still lodged, near the tennis court.

There had been considerable pressure put on him to leave, since many of the courtiers were convinced that he carried on his person the very sickness which they were trying to escape. This being the case, he had few visitors and he greeted Philip cordially, even though the lines of exhaustion were plain enough upon his face.

Philip had never actually spoken with this courageous fighting man who, when he was General Monk, had led Cromwell's forces but who had later paved the way for King Charles' restoration. He suddenly felt a little overawed to be in the presence of the famous soldier.

"Philip Devalle, is it not?" Albemarle said, without standing on ceremony. "You must excuse my rough appearance, but I've spent the greater part of this day in a pest house."

"It is on account of that I am here. I've come to offer you my services," Philip said.

Albemarle looked surprised. "And what do you think you could do?"

"I could help you to keep order on the streets."

Albemarle laughed. "You would be better keeping step upon a dance floor, my young sir. They'd make piecemeal of you out there."

Philip flushed angrily. "I am handy with a sword and not afraid to fight."

"Then why did you not fight for your country?"

"That is my affair."

"It is," Albemarle agreed, in a kinder tone, "and I do know that you were to have sailed with York."

"Then you must also know the reason why I did not go."

"I do, and I can understand that you must have found the Duke of Buckingham's decision unjust, but you should not be too hard on him," Albemarle said. "You may have misjudged his motives."

"I am not here to discuss the Duke of Buckingham," Philip said sulkily.

"Nonetheless you are in his charge, and he did make himself responsible for you. If he refused to let you fight the Dutch it is for certain he'll not countenance your risking a fouler end in the streets of London. Come to think of it I'm not sure I would either."

Philip was disappointed. It seemed he had been thwarted yet again by Buckingham. "So you have no use for me?"

"God knows I have use for any man with the courage to stand beside me, yet I shall not take you, Lord Devalle. Follow the Court to Salisbury. You are too young and handsome to be smitten with this Black Death."

Philip sighed. "Doubtless you, too, think I am doing this to prove that I can be a hero even if I could not go to war," he said, recalling Barbara's words. "It's not the truth."

"What is the truth, young sir?" Albemarle said softly.

"The truth is that I do not think it right to run away and hide if I can stay and help those who do not have the chance to run."

Albemarle nodded. "Yes, I think that too, but I am nearly sixty, you are nearly sixteen."

"At what age can I be held responsible for my own life?" Philip said in exasperation.

"Soon enough, my Lord," Albemarle said, "and then you may find that there is not one sod on earth who truly cares if you're alive or dead! Go make your peace with Buckingham, if you value good advice."

But Philip was not in a mood to take advice, good or otherwise, as he returned to his own lodgings. He lay upon his bed, lost in his dark brooding, and thought suddenly of Nell. He had last seen her some months before when she had appeared in her first play, 'The Indian Emperor'. Her performance had been very well received but he had not visited her or heard from her since.

He wondered now how she was managing, or whether she was even still alive. That thought he could not bear, for he had grown extremely fond of her, even though he had been too much wrapped up in his own problems to think much about her of late.

At least, he vowed, he would help her, even if he was permitted to do nothing else.

Philip rose early the next morning and took out most of the money that he had in his strongbox. Even though couriers came less frequently to the city now, he was certain that his next allowance from Sussex would reach him before too long. Next, he paid a call on Anthony Hamilton, one of Elizabeth's brothers, who owned a house in Hampstead and rented rooms in it to friends so that they could house their mistresses. Philip ascertained that the house had space for another lodger. Then he walked across the park to Wallingford House.

He avoided the house, having no wish to run into Buckingham, and went straight to the stables. Loving horses as he did, Philip had spent many happy hours with Buckingham's magnificent animals and he had grown well acquainted with the grooms and coachmen whilst he had lived there. One driver in particular he knew to be sufficiently greedy to take a chance in exchange for the generous reward Philip was prepared to offer him.

A little while later Philip drove boldly out of the gates in Buckingham's second-best carriage. As they turned the corner into Charing Cross he sucked his breath in sharply. It was the first time he had set foot outside the palace grounds since the plague had been reported, and he was quite unprepared for the sights he was to see.

It was the start of another sunny Summer day, but the usually busy thoroughfare of the Strand was practically deserted. There were no shops open, no hawkers upon the streets and the silence that replaced their raucous calls was eerie. Even as Philip contemplated the strange peace all around him, the stillness of the morning air was broken by the tolling of a great bell.

"The death bell of St. Dunstan's," the driver called down to him. "You can hear it nearly all day, every day."

Philip had heard it, of course, many times during the last few months but the sound had seemed less poignant when heard from within the Privy Gardens or whilst contemplating the pleasant vista of St. James' Park. Now, but a mile away from the very church of St. Dunstan's, he associated it more fully with suffering and death.

He swallowed hard as he heard a scream, not of pain but of despair, for it was followed by loud sobs.

There was no-one else to be seen so he guessed the sound emanated from one of the shuttered houses and as he turned his attention to them he saw that upon the doors of some were daubed a bright red cross, a foot high. There were words written above one of these crosses, words he could not quite read as they went along, and he leaned out of the window to talk to the driver.

"What does it say?"

"It says 'Lord have mercy upon us' Those houses with the crosses have the plague."

"So many of them?" Philip dreaded now what he would find at Nell's lodgings.

He had to leave the coach at Strand Bridge and continue on foot. Drury Lane was strewn with debris and even furniture from the looted houses, so that they would not have got the vehicle through.

Philip said a quick prayer to himself when he reached the Coal Yard but, to his relief, there was no cross painted on Nell's door.

He rapped upon it loudly. There was silence so he knocked again, this time more urgently.

"Go away," he heard a woman's voice shout. It was Nell without a doubt.

"Nell, it's Philip."

Nell gave a little shriek and ran to unlock the door. "I never dreamed it would be you." She clung to him like a frightened child. "The Court's left London, so I heard, and I guessed you would have gone with them and that I'd not a friend left in the city. I never thought you'd come to see me."

"Not just to see you but to save you if I can." Philip stroked her tousled hair. "I know a place for you to go where you'll be safe."

"You mean I can escape?" She raised her pretty, tear-stained face to him. "This is like waking from a nightmare. I have been so frightened."

"I shouldn't wonder at it." Philip laid her head back on his shoulder, for it was pleasant to feel her leaning on him, though he had never entertained the least desire for her. "I should have come sooner. Are you well?"

"Yes, perfectly, I've not a mark, but it has not been just catching the plague that I've feared. There has been looting everywhere and women raped in daylight on the city streets. There's nowhere safe except your own home. I've not been out this last week except to get food, and there's not too much of that about. There are no shops open save for those that sell coffins. Two days ago, I stole a cabbage from the garden of Essex House," she confessed.

"And is that all you've had to eat since then?" Philip said, appalled.

"Oh no. I've had some candied fruits as well," she told him brightly.

"Wherever did you get those?"

"They were a present a while ago from a gentleman admirer who saw me on the stage. To be truthful I was not too fond of them at first but I'm glad I kept them now!"

Philip smiled, pleased that she had not lost her spirit. "Poor Nell! Never mind, you'll soon be back upon the stage accepting gifts of candied fruit from gentlemen."

"Oh, Philip, do you really think so? I sometimes wonder if things will ever return to normal. We have to be within doors by 9 o'clock so that the sick may go outside to take the air and it is pitiful to see them, for they know that they are dying. Then, in the night, the carts come and that's the worst of all. You hear the cry 'bring out your dead' and as they throw them on the cart you can hear the sobs of those who loved them. Always there is someone weeping and the sound of those damned bells hour after hour."

"You'll not hear them anymore," Philip reassured her, tilting her face toward him and kissing her very gently on the lips. "I'm sending you to Hampstead. There is no plague there."

He had not intended to kiss her; indeed, he honestly did not know why he had, but it had seemed the natural thing to do.

"Are you coming with me?" she said hopefully.

"Only until I've seen you from the city. I am safe enough at Whitehall. Those of us who have elected to remain are supposed to stay within the environs of the palace."

"Then what are you doing here?"

He winked at her. "Disobeying orders. Get your things together quickly. Buckingham's coach waits by Strand Bridge. I could not bring it any nearer."

Nell did as he bade her and was ready speedily enough.

Despite her recent success upon the stage of the King's House, she had pathetically few possessions of any consequence, and these were soon rolled up into a bundle, which Philip carried for her out into the street.

Nell took his arm and they walked briskly in the direction of the Strand. He recalled the day they had met there, by the Maypole. There was no music now and no gaily-dressed milkmaids. The death bell, tolling its relentless rhythm, was the only music to be heard and the only human sounds were the cries that came from inside the paint-daubed houses.

"It's like another world," Nell said. "Built just like ours, but peopled by invisible beings."

"Not quite invisible," Philip said, seeing a movement in the shadows by the side of them. Two men were edging out of one of the narrow passageways between the houses in Drury Lane. "When I give the word let go of my arm and run for all you're worth to the bridge. Don't stop until you reach the coach."

Nell's eyes opened wide with fear, but she nodded. "What about you?"

"I'll follow as soon as I can. Get going! Now!"

She obeyed immediately, running as fast as she could, whilst Philip drew his sword and turned toward the two men.

They had black hoods over their heads. Their eyes, which showed through the slits cut in their masks, were those of desperate men. Both carried knives, but Philip stood his ground as they approached.

He waited until they were a few yards from him then, feinting quickly, he hurled Nell's bundle onto the blade of one, lunging at the other with his sword. Caught off guard, by the sudden movement, the man raised his knife to strike, but doubled over in agony as the tip of Philip's sword went between his ribs and into his lung. He collapsed onto the cobbles, blood pouring from his mouth.

Philip turned his attention to the other, who had extricated his knife from the bundle. "Your friend will die," he told the man, "you need not. Get back to your home. I've nothing you can steal, at least nothing that's any good to you right now."

"What's in there?" the man said in a hoarse voice, pointing to the bundle. "Food?"

"No. Clothes and a few trinkets, that's all."

"But you're a gentleman. I'll warrant you've got gold upon your person."

"What if I have? What would you do with it? There's nothing in this stinking city you can buy. Besides, if you attempt to take it from me I shall kill you, as I did your friend."

"He was as good as dead already, but I am not, young gentleman, and you shall not escape me."

"With a horrible cry the masked man came toward him with the knife held low. Philip quickly shifted his position as he guessed the blade's intended target. Bringing up his foot he kicked his assailant's arm with such force that the weapon clattered to the ground. The man went down, knocked over by the impact of Philip's boot, and then screamed, the last sound he was ever to make as the sword pierced his heart.

Philip looked with no satisfaction at the two he had been forced to kill. He wondered what the man had meant when he had said that his companion was as good as dead already. He shuddered as a dreadful thought occurred to him. With the tip of his sword he gingerly lifted the mask of the first wretch he had killed.

"My God!" Philip paled as he looked upon him. The face he had exposed was a mess of oozing sores. Fighting back the revulsion that he felt at the ugly sight, Philip grabbed Nell's possessions and hastened toward the waiting coach.

He was glad to reach it, for the noise of his encounter had brought more ragged creatures onto the street and the sight of their covered faces filled him with horror.

"Thank heaven you're safe." Nell hugged him. "If you had been killed because of me I'd never have forgiven myself."

Philip smiled. "If I am not allowed to fight for my king at least allow me to fight for his future mistress!"

"Can you honestly see me as the mistress of King Charles?" Nell said and, indeed, Philip thought that he had rarely seen a more disreputable-looking female. Her face was dirty, her hair was all awry and she had ripped her skirt whilst running.

"Not like that." he admitted. "Here, you'll need this whilst you are away." He pulled out a leather purse and put it into her hands. "Here's fifty guineas. Don't refuse it," he advised, seeing that she was about to protest. "It will pay your lodgings in the house I've found for you and I would have you spend the rest upon some luxuries, such as a ball of soap maybe!"

"Oh, Philip, why are you so good to me?" She seemed quite overcome at his generosity.

He shrugged. "I feel responsible for you, don't ask me why."

"Is that the only reason?" she said boldly.

"No. I like you."

"I like you too, a great deal. More than anyone, in fact." She looked up at him earnestly. "I do wish you could come to Hampstead with me."

Philip experienced an emotion which was new to him. Not the stirrings of lust that he always felt with Barbara, but a feeling of protectiveness and genuine affection. For a delightful moment he imagined what it would be like to spend a few months alone with her in the little village of Hampstead. Hidden from the world, and no part of its problems, he could perhaps discover the delicious joy which love could bring to two fifteen-year-olds.

"I can't come, Nell," he said at length, dispelling the pleasant vision from his mind. "Buckingham would soon learn where I'd taken you and he'd come looking for me, Barbara too. How long do you think we would be left in peace?"

"Can Barbara tell you what to do, then?" Nell said, sounding piqued.

"Not exactly, but she's a spiteful bitch and she will make me suffer. That she can do, for she'll wreak her vengeance on you, sweetheart."

"What can she do to me?"

"You jest of course! She can make sure you never tread upon another stage."

"Then I will be an orange girl again," Nell said. "I wouldn't care so long as I could be your mistress."

"Yes, you would. You'd soon grow tired of what little I could offer you." Philip took her hand in his. "You can achieve better things than to be my bed mate."

"It would do for a beginning."

"No, it wouldn't, for if I allowed myself to become your lover I could never advance your interests in the way that you deserve," he said firmly.

"Then don't advance my interests. Keep me for yourself."

"Don't tempt me, Nell. I have great faith in you and I'll not spoil things for you with my selfishness." Philip smiled to think of what Barbara would make of that! "You should be more than just the property of the Earl of Southwick's younger son."

"The trouble is I think I am in love with the Earl of Southwick's younger son."

Philip shook his head. "You are just a little overwhelmed by me at the moment that is all. I am your friend and I will always be your friend. No more than that."

They were already past Gray's Inn and heading out toward the city wall. Philip tapped upon the panel that divided them from the driver.

"You are out of danger now," he told Nell, "so I shall let you go on alone, for I must not be absent from Whitehall for too long. Please remain in Hampstead until I send word that it is safe for you to return." He kissed her fleetingly upon the lips. "Don't brood about me, Nell. It is not an easy thing for me to do to leave you here, but I am sure it is the best thing for us both."

"You really are a most surprising person," Nell said. "I don't pretend to understand you."

"It is not required that you should." Philip swept off his plumed hat and bowed low as the coach moved off without him. "Farewell, Mistress Gwynn, and don't forget to wash your face before you go to bed tonight!"

Philip had a good three miles to walk back, a distance that would not have troubled him under any other circumstances but, after his encounter in Drury Lane, he was wary. He reached High Holborn without encountering a soul and passed through Lincoln's Inn Fields in safety, then turned into Chancery Lane.

"Help me!"

Philip turned in the direction of the sound.

"For God's sake, someone help me."

A man staggered from the shadows toward him and Philip instinctively held his hand ready on his sword. "Stay where you are," he warned. "What do you want?"

"Your pity." The man came closer to him and fell down upon his knees in supplication. He was grey-haired, about the age of Philip's father, and looked weak from sickness. "Help me, if you have any Christian charity, good sir."

"What can I do to help you?" Philip said. "I have no food."

"I have the fever, sir, I need the physic. They make it at the pest house."

"I don't even know where the pest house is." Philip recoiled as the man held out a hand as though to grab him.

"It's not far. Help me, I beg you, for I shall be killed if you leave me here."

Philip thought back to the two desperate ruffians who had attacked him and he understood the stranger's fear. "Go back to your home and I will find the medicine you want and bring it to you," he offered.

"I have nowhere to go. My neighbour's house was looted

when he died and then the bastards turned me out of mine. I shall die here upon the streets."

Philip, with sudden decision, reached down and yanked the fellow to his feet. "No, that you won't. Direct me where to go."

It was, as the sick man had said, not far and yet it was a walk that Philip was never to forget. The few faces he saw told plainly of the horror that was all about him. One man staggered up to them, sores running upon his face and arms, and tried to speak, but he collapsed before he had uttered a coherent sound.

The only cheerful voices that he heard were those of three drunks who rolled along the street singing as loudly as they could. Philip stood aside and watched them pityingly, for he knew their jollity would be short-lived. In a few hours they would be sober once again and still trapped in the city of the living dead.

The old man was leaning heavily upon him now and Philip was relieved when they finally arrived at the pest-house. An Anabaptist preacher stood on the steps canting to any that passed by, though none seemed much inclined to listen to him.

"To be thrown like so much dung onto a cart and buried in an unmarked pit," he cried out. "Is this the way a man should end his time on earth? And where is our king when his subjects are suffering? I'll tell you, good people, he has left London and all the Court with him. He heeds not the word of the Almighty but the advice of his whore, Castelmaine, and such fornicating wastrels as the Duke of Buckingham."

Philip knew this was no time to be defending Barbara but, despite his own differences with Buckingham, he could not stand by and hear him insulted by such a man.

"You will have a care, sir, before you abuse the noble name of Buckingham," he said warningly," or I shall feel the need to teach you a lesson."

The preacher regarded him cautiously. "Are you a friend of royalty?"

"I am a friend of Lord Buckingham, in fact he is the best

friend I have in this world," Philip said, "and I will dispatch upon my sword whoever speaks ill of him."

He spoke impetuously but he meant every word. The preacher must have guessed that too, for he backed away and ran off down the street. He looked back once but Philip had more pressing things upon his mind than following him. The old man had practically lost consciousness and Philip was bearing his full weight.

He lifted him fairly easily and carried him inside, then looked about for a place to set him down. There were people lying everywhere, some in beds but most stretched out on blankets on the bare floor.

An old woman shuffled toward him. Her dress was streaked with sweat and, as she came closer, Philip reckoned her to be the foulest-smelling creature he had ever had the misfortune to be near.

"Are you the nurse?" he asked in disgust.

"That's right." She grinned, showing blackened teeth. "Who's this, your father?"

"No, of course not. Can I put him down?"

"If you can find a space. Here's one." The nurse indicated a motionless figure lying on the floor a yard away from where they stood. "He's gone, I reckon. Riddled with the pox anyway, that one. They catch it on purpose, for they think it will prevent them getting the plague. The brothels are full of the fools."

She rolled the naked body off the blanket with her foot. Philip noticed that she wore boots which were considerably too large for her and he guessed she had taken them from another corpse. He noticed something else too. As well as the syphilis sores there was a huge swelling on the dead man's groin.

The nurse followed his gaze. "They all have that. It's one of the first signs, and then their skin starts to burn. Some throw themselves into the river when the fire inside them gets too hot to bear."

Philip laid the sick man down upon the blanket that had just been vacated and the hag pulled the old man's hair back from his face and pointed to the pustules forming on his skin. "He'll not last long."

"He said you had some potion that would cure him. That is why I brought him here."

"You need to see the doctor for that."

She pointed to a small room at the side, where he found a tired-looking man preparing a jug of what Philip guessed must be the potion.

He looked at the turgid mixture dubiously. "What's in it?"

"A handful of mandragories and the same of rew, then featherfew and sorrel burnet, with a quantity of the crops and roots of dragons."

"Does it work?"

"I pray it does, for it is all we have." The doctor's eyes met his for an instant and Philip could sense his helplessness. "Take this to the patient and make him drink it."

Philip stared at him aghast. "Surely that is your job, not mine."

"Pardon, sir, you brought him in."

"I brought him in that you might care for him."

"I have not the time to care for him," the doctor said. "Force it down him if you must."

"But I am not a medical man," Philip protested, horrified at the prospect.

"Even if you were, sir, you could do no more. By the by, you ought to take some of the physic too, it may protect you from infection."

Philip seized the jug and poured two measures from it. The first he downed himself, grimacing as the bitter liquid touched his tongue, then, taking the other, he went to find the wretched creature that he had committed to this awful place.

He found the old man staring at the ceiling with glazed eyes. Philip knelt beside him and held the physic out to him. "Here, I have it."

There was no sign of recognition and, as Philip held the cup up to the man's cracked lips, he seemed incapable of drinking. Philip raised the fellow's head slightly and succeeded in forcing most of the liquid between his teeth, then laid him down upon the floor again. He understood the physician's words better now. There was nothing more that he could do. Nothing more that anybody could do.

He felt, suddenly, very young and very helpless. There had never been anyone but Nanon to whom Philip could turn for comfort, even as a child, but there was one person who had shown him nothing but kindness since he had come to London, and had done his utmost to protect him from the harsher realities of life, and that was Buckingham. Philip felt he would give the world to see the amiable duke just then.

He was glad to get out into the street again. After the fetid stench of the pest house the air smelt good, stinking though it was from the piles of refuse rotting in the hot sun. He wanted nothing more now than to get back to Whitehall, but he had no sooner set off in the direction of the palace when he heard the sound of approaching horse's hooves.

If Philip had learned anything that day it was to avoid strangers, and he pressed himself back tight against the wall of a building. As the rider came into view he recognised him. The Duke of Albemarle.

"Blast it! He is all I need just now," Philip muttered. He started to edge his way around the corner and was in an alley that ran along the side of the building before he could have been spotted. He was about to break into a run when he heard a shout behind him. Looking over his shoulder he saw three ragged ruffians surrounding Albemarle and dragging him from his horse.

Philip cursed, but he knew what he must do. Drawing his sword, he rushed back along the way he had just come.

Albemarle was pinned to the ground, unable to reach his weapon, and Philip saw the sunlight glint upon a knife that one of the attackers held aloft.

There was no time to think. He aimed his own blade at the hand that held the knife. There was a dreadful scream as the man staggered to his feet, deathly white and with blood spurting from the stump which once had been his wrist.

Albemarle was quickly on his feet and thrust his sword into the injured man's gut.

The remaining two assailants turned to flee. Albemarle hamstrung one before he could get far then brought his weapon down on the fellow's head, splitting his skull.

Philip, who was fast, caught the third man and threw him to the ground, then rendered him unconscious with a savage blow of his fist.

He knew that he should finish him. He had killed the two men who had tried to rob him earlier without a qualm, but this was different, for the man lay defenceless on the ground. Philip hesitated for an instant then resolutely sheathed his sword. He had seen enough of death and dying for one day and the prospect of deliberately taking a life sickened him.

Albemarle's horse was across the street and Philip called it. The animal came to him and he led it back to the Duke.

"That was close. I owe you my life, good sir, and my thanks, whoever you are." Albemarle put away his sword and, for the first time, looked him in the face. "You!"

Philip was certain now that Albemarle's gratitude would turn to anger. "I did not come into the city to defy you, my Lord, but upon some personal business."

"Did you take someone to the pest house?"

"Yes, I did, but that was not the reason I came." Philip ran a hand across his brow. The last few hours had been extremely testing for him and he was in no mood to be cross-examined. "What should we do with them?" He pointed to the dead bodies on the ground.

"Why nothing. The carts will collect them when they come this evening. What are two more amongst so many?"

"Then, if your Grace will excuse me, I'll be on my way."

"Hey, not so fast, young man," Albemarle said, walking along beside him, leading his horse. "I care not why you're here but, by God, I'm thankful that you are, just as I am thankful that I misjudged you before. You are not as delicate as you would have us think. Are you a swordsman too, I wonder?"

"Signor D'Alessandro says I am."

"Who paid for you to learn with him? Buckingham. I'll wager. You would need his name and money to be accepted as a pupil with the famous Signor D'Alessandro."

"Yes. I know I owe Buckingham a lot. Although," Philip added hastily, seeing Albemarle smile, "I don't know how I can ever forgive him for depriving me of the opportunity to go to war."

"Not even when you remember Francis and the way he died?"

"Francis?" Philip said.

"Aye, his brother."

"I did not even know he had a brother."

"No, I don't expect you took the trouble to find out anything about him, did you? You would only have done that if you cared about him, and to you George Villiers has been nothing but a convenience and a provider."

Philip did not contradict him. It was the truth, although he felt ashamed of it. "What happened to his brother?"

"When the Civil War broke out both brothers were at Trinity College but George was so fired with loyalty to the Royalist cause that he ran away, persuading Francis, who was younger, to go with him and they joined the King's army at Litchfield. Their mother was outraged when she found out and she sent them away to Italy but they returned and George persuaded his brother once again to take up arms.

The King was a prisoner in the Isle of Wight by then and any but a courageous madman like George Villiers would have plainly seen that all was lost. He joined the Earl of Holland's troop but they were defeated and the Villiers brothers were attacked as they made their escape. Francis was killed and George saw him fall. He knew that his brother would never have been in the fight, but for him. Francis Villiers was only nineteen when he died, and your age when he first rode into battle."

Philip had listened to the tale without a word. "Thank you," he said now. "Why could he not have told me this himself?"

"Because your kind hide their feelings. Me, I am a plain and simple man, thank God, not well bred or refined. In my family we always said exactly what was on our minds."

"So what did your father say when you first joined the army, my Lord?"

Albemarle laughed and swung himself up onto his horse. "He couldn't say too much, since it was on account of him that I had to leave the county of Devonshire."

Philip raised an enquiring eyebrow and Albemarle leaned down. "I cudgelled an under-sheriff who arrested him! Good day, your Lordship. Doubtless we shall meet again, though not, I trust, in this plague-ridden city."

Albemarle tipped his hat and galloped off leaving Philip alone, truly alone it seemed, for there was not a soul about, nor any sound save for the ringing of the death bell.

Philip's head was throbbing in time to it as he slowly made his way toward the Mall. He had lost his hat in the last affray and the hot sun beat down on him relentlessly. As he drew nearer to Whitehall he considered his appearance. He could never enter the palace in such a dusty and dishevelled state, not without attracting attention which, for once, was the last thing he wanted.

He still had some clothes left at Wallingford House and thought he would risk going there instead, although he was hoping no-one would be home to see him. He had resolved to take Albemarle's advice and try to be reconciled with Buckingham, but he had not yet decided how he would go about it.

As it happened matters were taken out of his hands. The first person he encountered as he entered was Buckingham himself on his way out.

Buckingham stared at him. "Philip! What the devil has happened to you?"

Philip did not answer right away, partly because he had not decided what he was to tell him and partly because Buckingham's image seemed to be shifting slightly, becoming more elusive the harder he tried to focus on it.

He was utterly exhausted and he had walked a long way in the sweltering sun with no hat, but Philip feared there might be a more sinister reason for the dizziness that was engulfing him.

Buckingham, with a look of concern, started toward him but Philip held his hands out in front to stop him coming closer.

"Don't come near me. I've been in the city."

"Did you see any with the Black Death?"

"Several and I touched one."

Buckingham regarded him with dismay. "Are you ill yourself?"

"I don't know." Philip confessed. "I do feel strange, light-headed and my throat is dry. I never should have come here."

He turned around, fully intending to leave, but Buckingham caught him by the arm and held him firmly.

"Don't be a fool. Where would you go? Your home is here and if you are ill then it is here you will be tended. Now do as you are told for once in your damned life. Go to your room and take off your clothes, they should be burned. Don't argue, go immediately."

Philip had neither the strength nor the will to argue. By the time he had climbed the stairs his legs seemed to have turned to jelly and he had to sit upon his bed in order to undress. He had no sooner done so than two servants carried in a bath and filled it with cool water, then disappeared as swiftly as they had come, bundling up his clothes in a sheet.

The water felt good and, as Philip soaked himself, he looked for any signs of blisters forming on his skin but he saw none, although his head pounded fiercely.

By the time Buckingham came in to see him he was in bed with his eyes closed. "Does your skin burn?" Buckingham said.

"No, not at all. I don't believe I have the Black Death. I have no sores or any swelling on my groin."

Buckingham scrutinised him closely and looked relieved to see none of the dreaded symptoms. "Why ever did you go there?"

"I wanted to save Nell."

"For God's sake! Your orange wench? You risked your life for her?"

Philip had not considered the matter in quite that light before. "Yes, I suppose I did. She'll be in Hampstead now and safe, if your driver earned the bribe I gave him, but there are so many other people who have none to help them."

"You've had a frightening experience," Buckingham said, with surprising gentleness. "Tell me all about it later. You should rest now."

"I never meant to inflict this trouble on you," Philip said truthfully.

"Hush. I have sent a servant to find you a physician, if there is one to be had at such a time. Until he comes you had best stay here quietly. I shall be close by if you need anything."

Philip reached out and grasped his sleeve as he turned to go. "My Lord, there is something I must say to you whilst I can find the courage. I have behaved badly toward you and I am sorry. You mean a great deal to me."

Buckingham beamed at him. "There is nothing you could tell me that could please me more. Are you coming back to me?"

"If you will take me back."

"No question of it, none at all, dear boy." Buckingham laid him back onto his pillows. "Try to sleep now."

Philip did drop off to sleep straightaway, and he was still sleeping when the physician arrived some hours later.

"I wouldn't worry overmuch," the physician told him when he had completed his examination. "You have no signs of the plague but I suspect your blood is overheated, so I shall bleed sixteen ounces from you, and then make an issue in your arm to draw the poisons out. That should cure the dizziness. As for your sore throat, swallowing a silk thread dipped in mouse's blood may help."

"Do what you must," Buckingham said quickly, as Philip was about to protest. "I want him well enough to travel to Salisbury!"

SEVEN

Philip and Buckingham eventually joined the rest of the Court at Oxford, for Charles decided that the air of Salisbury was unhealthy. The sickness had left the city by the end of the year so they returned to London shortly after Christmas, a splendid Christmas spent with Monmouth as guests of Lord Arlington at Saxham Hall.

In January Buckingham was summoned to attend an urgent meeting of the Privy Council to discuss the war with Holland. The dispute was by no means ended, even though the pennants from the captured Dutch ships fluttered from the ramparts of the Tower.

"We are at war with France," Buckingham announced when he arrived home. "They have joined with the Dutch against us."

"Surely not!" Philip cried.

"They have no choice. It appears they are bound by some old treaty with the Hollanders and they must honour it. I wouldn't take it too much to heart, though. I don't believe King Louis wants to fight us at all, in fact it's my opinion he will keep as far away from our ships as possible."

Philip was upset at the news nonetheless. Being half-French, he could not regard France as his enemy, and never would.

He went to fetch Nell back from Hampstead before the Winter was over. The country air had done her good. Her eyes were clear and sparkling and her skin had a healthy glow that Philip found most becoming. Buckingham had laughed at him for not taking advantage of her willingness when he'd had the chance and she looked so pretty now that, despite all he had said to her before, he was very tempted to do just that.

"Did you stay with Lady Castlemaine when you were at Oxford?" she wanted to know as they strolled across the Heath together, his arm around her slim waist.

"Hardly! Buckingham and I stayed with Monmouth at Corpus Christi College and Barbara was at Merton with the Queen. Besides, she gave birth to yet another of Charles' bastards whilst she was there, their fifth, I think!"

Although Barbara still fascinated him, Philip was becoming increasingly aware of the effect he had upon other members of the female sex. He knew that this was not attributable to his wit but, if his conversation could not rival that of Buckingham or the Comte de Grammont, he had few rivals when it came to looks and he was learning to use his charms to their fullest advantage.

"You must have visited her."

Philip smiled at her directness. "She did summon me from time to time. Don't tell me you are jealous, Nell!"

"Why should I be? You've made it very plain that you don't want me, and I don't blame you in the least," she added as he was about to protest. "After all, why should you want to sport with such an ill-bred creature as myself when you can take a countess any time you choose?"

"Any time *she* chooses," he corrected her.

"What does it matter? I am trying to show you that I understand you better now. You see I've had a good deal of time to think and I have decided that you were right in what you said about me. I should not be content too long to be your mistress. There are so many things I want – I want to be a famous actress on the stage, I want to be admired by rich and fashionable men, but most of all I want to attract the notice of King Charles."

"Are you telling me that you no longer have aspirations of becoming my lover?" he said slowly

"That is exactly it. I am extremely grateful to you for dissuading me from abandoning all my ambitions. I promise I shall never pester you again with my attentions, for I know they are unwelcome. We shall remain just friends, no more than that, exactly as you said."

Philip studied her for a moment, and then burst out laughing as he considered the irony of the situation.

Nell laid her head against him affectionately. "It's good to hear you laugh, Philip, and to know it is I who have made you happy. You are happy, aren't you?"

"Yes sweetheart." He kissed her on the forehead, wondering what Buckingham would say if he ever he found out. "Ecstatic!"

The Summer that followed was one which, despite the war, Philip was to remember as one of the most carefree of his life.

So many of the waterman had been pressed into service in the navy that there were scarcely any boats to be hired upon the Thames, but this did not trouble the Court. When the heat and dust of August prevented the taking of promenades in Hyde Park they took to the water in the fleet of palace boats, which set sail from Whitehall steps. Philip spent many a happy day upon the River Thames listening to the gentle strains of the musicians and whispering romantic words into some lady's willing ear.

It was a thoroughly self-indulgent time for him, filled with the excitement of pursuit and the satisfaction of conquest, but he could not ignore the battles that were being fought at sea and went regularly to the Royal Exchange, where there was always some news to be heard.

Barbara was surprisingly tolerant of his behaviour, so long as he still made himself available to her, for it diverted attention from their own relationship. They had managed to keep that a secret, for both their sakes, although Barbara took chances which dismayed him at times, even wearing a bracelet made of his hair. It was common enough for lovers to have these tokens made for each other but Philip's hair colour was so distinctive that he feared for their discovery and cringed each time he saw her wear the gift that she had persuaded him to give her.

They often conversed together in public now and were even in the habit of gaming sometimes at the same table.

One Sunday evening in September they played cards in the company of the Comte de Grammont and Lord Rochester, a man of sharp perception who had only recently arrived at Court. He had already made a great impression, partly on account of his womanising and partly for the daring and witty scandal sheets which he composed about everyone at Court, and frequently even about King Charles.

"Has anyone heard more news of the fire that started in the city this morning?" the Comte de Grammont said, during a break in play.

No-one had. The only reason Philip knew of the fire at all was because Charles had gone to inspect it that afternoon, which had given him a pleasurable hour or two with Barbara.

"I'm sure it's nothing to worry about," Barbara said.

"I recall you said that about the plague," Philip reminded her.

"Well this time there's no doubt. Charles and James have viewed it from their barge and they reckon there was scarcely anything to see."

"According to Samuel Pepys there was great deal to see," Rochester said, "and he lives but a quarter of a mile from where it started. I understand it was he who brought the news to the palace this morning."

"But surely the loss of a few houses in Pudding Lane is of little consequence to any save the residents," Barbara said dismissively. "Charles has more pressing matters on his mind."

Philip knew that she was talking about the war, and the conversation turned to the Dutch, as it so often did, especially since they had destroyed half the English fleet at Ostend a few weeks before. The two and half million pounds which Parliament had voted for the war was nowhere near enough and, besides, the Treasury had not yet received them.

"Buckingham thinks that Charles is going to have to bear the cost of re-equipping the fleet himself," Philip said.

"Then I doubt he can afford to continue this war," de Grammont said. "It is rumoured that even the postilions who ride before his coach are three years in arrears of pay!"

Buckingham joined them then and said there was a good view of the fire to be had from the windows facing the river.

Philip went with the rest and looked at it in horror. A great arch of flames showed against the night sky. "What is it?"

"The bridge," Buckingham said grimly. "It's all alight and every house from Tower Street to Cornhill, so they say."

"That's bad news for the merchants," Rochester said.

"And it is especially bad news for me," de Grammont said quietly to Philip.

"For you, Comte? Why is that?"

"Who do you think will be the first blamed for this?"

"I thought it started in a baker's oven."

"I did not ask who started it but who would be blamed for it. The Papists, that is who."

Barbara shuddered, and Philip knew why. She had converted to Catholicism that year. "Surely not."

"This will be blamed in equal parts upon the Catholics and the French," de Grammont predicted. "Since I qualify for condemnation upon both counts I believe it might be best if I lay low for a while. Good night to all of you."

"What exactly has been done to halt the fire?" Philip asked Buckingham as they stood together watching the compelling sight.

"Charles ordered the Lord Mayor to pull down some houses to stop the spread of the flames but, apparently, he has hardly anyone to help him, it being a Sunday."

"Personally, I hope it lasts a week," Barbara whispered to Philip. "If Charles goes to inspect it every day then you and I can have more opportunities to be together."

By the next morning the fire extended half a mile and it looked as though Barbara would have her wish.

Charles summoned Buckingham and the rest of the Privy Council and within the hour Lord Ashley, together with Lord Belasyse and the Earl of Manchester, had established headquarters at Ely House. Fire posts were set up, with bread and cheese to fortify the fire-fighters, and the parish constables were ordered to provide a hundred men, with the promise of a shilling to any man seen to be diligent.

The militia were called in from the neighbouring counties and Charles set off into the streets himself, with his brother at his side and as many courtiers as he could rally to assist him.

Philip was awakened by Monmouth bursting into his bedroom and pulling him out of bed.

"But where are we going?" Philip asked as Monmouth, talking excitedly, dived into his closet and threw him some clothes.

"I've just told you, to fight the fire."

"What ourselves?"

"Yes, isn't it a lark? Everyone is helping, even the seamen from Woolwich and Deptford have been called in to blow up whatever properties must be demolished. What's that on your shoulder?" He pointed to a livid mark, a souvenir of Philip's most recent encounter with Barbara.

"Never mind that." Philip took the shirt Monmouth was holding and quickly put it on. "But what are we to do? I've never put a fire out in my life."

"Nor I, but it will be a fine adventure, won't it?"

Philip knew that to Monmouth everything in life was an adventure, one he wished Philip to share with him. "Well I suppose I should be grateful," he said as Monmouth pulled his boots on for him. "After all it is not every day I have a duke to help me dress!"

"Should we go to waken Lord Rochester, do you think?"

"Are you mad? It's bad enough that you have woken me," Philip said as he was dragged downstairs, still fastening his coat.

Despite his protestations, he was willing enough to assist in whatever way he could and, once outside, he better understood Monmouth's urgency.

Although the fire was more than a mile away from Charing Cross they could feel the heat as it carried toward them on a fierce easterly gale, which was whipping the flames to a frenzy. As they hurried closer they heard the crackling of the flames and the shrieks of people scurrying this way and that with bundles of belongings, all making for the river.

The whole city had taken fright. As they neared Worcester House they saw that Lord Clarendon's possessions were being thrown into a fleet of lighters. The Thames was cluttered with craft of every size and shape. Some were over laden and Philip saw one capsize into the murky waters, losing forever the precious bundles which contained all that their owners had managed to salvage of their worldly goods.

There were frequent explosions of gunpowder and the sky was suddenly peppered with sparks from collapsing masonry as the seamen did their work. Soldiers were clearing the old wooden wharves along the sides of the River Fleet, whilst others were hollowing out the trunks of elm trees to carry water from the river.

All around was feverish activity but, even as Philip and Monmouth wondered where they should first begin to lend a hand, they saw Charles himself. He was on horseback, riding with his guards through the very middle of the chaos, stopping to encourage workers in their efforts and, from time to time, tossing golden guineas amongst them from a leather pouch slung across his shoulder.

He caught sight of the pair and beckoned them over. "Thank you both for coming to help. London needs you."

"Is much lost?" Monmouth asked him.

"Yes, I fear so. The Waterman's Hall is gone and the Post Office. The blaze has now reached Guildhall and we cannot save the Royal Exchange."

Philip was particularly sorry to hear of the loss of the Royal Exchange, for the 'Change, as it was known, was the gathering place of fashionable folk and Philip had spent many a happy hour there selecting laces, gloves or buckles for his shoes. So much had been destroyed already and he realised, suddenly, that the London he had come to know would never be quite the same again.

They hastened toward Guildhall but at Cripplegate they encountered a small force labouring hopelessly against the flames that were lighting the overhanging wooden gables all along the street and they decided to lend a hand there instead. They helped form a chain to pass buckets of water along to those who manned the fire squirts, but the squirts held nowhere near enough and were slow to fill.

Each church was intended to carry a supply of ladders, axes and fire hooks so Philip took some men to the nearby church of Saint Sepulchre's but the provisions had been neglected and the church had nothing save a few leather buckets. They took these but Philip thought how much more useful it would be to have iron hooks to pull down the fiery gables.

It was many hours before the fire was out in Cripplegate. Philip and Monmouth worked harder than they ever had in their lives. They were both filthy dirty and soaked through to their skins. Cheapside was still engulfed in flames so they set to work again. Night came but, just before midnight, the sky seemed to become as light as day when the great cathedral of Saint Paul's became a fiery torch, its flames rising higher than the rest.

Images flashed through Philip's mind as he worked. He recalled the day when he had bought a bunch of lavender upon the steps of the cathedral and looked down Ludgate Hill, amazed at the sights and smells and sounds of the bustling city street. Now it was all gone.

Charles rode by in the early hours of the morning and stopped to talk to them. His face was black and he was as wet and dirty as they were.

"You have done well," he told them, surveying the smouldering remains of Cheapside. The wind stirred the ashes and a flame darted up, but Charles held up his hand as they both made a move toward it. "No more. Let others do it now. Go home and get some rest."

"Should you not rest too, father?" Monmouth asked him.

"I cannot rest," Charles said, "not whilst my people suffer and my capital is destroyed. The homeless are encamped at Moor Fields and I must visit them to give whatever comfort I can."

"We'll go too," Monmouth offered. "Shall we Philip?"

"Yes, of course, if it will help." Philip wearily pushed a muddy lock of hair out of his eyes. He was aching in every muscle but, like Monmouth, he still had the spirit, if not the strength, to continue the fight.

Charles smiled at them. "Wait until the morning. Sleep, refresh yourselves and you'll be worth a dozen of the men you are now. Those are my orders and you must obey them!"

Monmouth lodged in King Street, nearby, and he insisted Philip came home with him. They stripped off their sodden clothes and threw themselves on his bed, utterly exhausted but content in the knowledge that they had done their very best.

"I am glad that you were with me, Philip," Monmouth said impulsively. "I've never had a proper friend before, have you?"

"No, I haven't." Philip felt a little guilty as he said it, for he had not forgotten John Bone, but times had changed for him. His associates now were dukes, not farm labourers.

"Shall we vow that we will always be good friends?"

"If you like." Philip closed his eyes and let the weariness flow over him, turning his limbs to lead.

"And shall we promise we would die for one another."

Philip struggled with the delightful, drifting sensation that was already numbing his brain and fought his way back to consciousness. "What?"

"I said let us pledge that we would die for one another."

"Really, James!"

"Wouldn't you die for me, then?" Monmouth sounded disappointed.

"Yes, I suppose I would, but I can scarcely ask that you do the same for me, now can I? You are the King's son, after all."

"Then you can promise you would die for me and I will promise to always do my utmost to protect you." Monmouth said brightly. "Shall we take an oath on it?"

Philip was more tired than he had ever thought he could be but he knew how much the oath would mean to his earnest friend and he smiled at him fondly. "If you like."

There was no way he could have predicted what fate had in store for both of them.

EIGHT

"What's happened?" Philip asked Buckingham, for the Duke looked unusually serious.

"I have argued with Charles," Buckingham said. "I cannot agree with his decision not to equip the battle fleet. He wants to follow Lord Clarendon's advice and sue for peace with Holland but I told him I would rather encourage the troops to mutiny than force the country to submit to such an ignoble peace."

Philip was horrified. "Why did you do that?"

"Lord Ashley suggested it might bring him to his senses."

"I knew it!" Philip cried. "A pox on Ashley! I am growing sick and tired of hearing about that man, from you and Monmouth. I beg you to be careful, George. Remember you are hazarding much more than Ashley; your lifelong friendship with Charles for a start. Charles doesn't trust him, does he? That is why Ashley needs your good name to advance his interests."

Philip thought it unlikely that anything would really happen to Buckingham, for Charles had forgiven him much in the past, but this time the Duke seemed inspired by a fierce zeal that was not truly in his indolent nature.

Matters came to a head one stormy March afternoon. Philip returned to Wallingford House to find Buckingham dressed in his greatcoat and with a portmanteau packed ready for a journey.

"Philip! I'm so glad you're here in time to say goodbye to me."

"Goodbye?" Philip looked at him blankly. "Where are you going?"

"To Westhorp." Westhorp was Buckingham's house in Yorkshire. "After that who knows? There is a warrant out for my arrest."

"Again?" Philip was unimpressed. Buckingham had been a prisoner in the Tower on two occasions during the previous year, once for challenging Lord Ossory to a duel and a second time for striking Lord Dorchester during a debate in the House of Lords!

"This is different. I'll be charged with plotting against Charles. That's treason and the punishment is death."

Philip regarded him sadly. Buckingham had gone too far this time and was paying the penalty. They had grown even closer since their estrangement and Philip could not bear to think of what might happen to him.

"This house is your home for as long as you wish to stay. I have instructed my wife to furnish you with whatever money you need."

"Don't worry about that. I'll manage," Philip said.

"No, you won't. Your father would never pay your gambling debts, much less your tailor's bill! Don't play at cards too often with de Grammont and stay clear of trouble, if you can."

"That's very fine advice to come from you!" Philip retorted.

A few days later Philip was summoned to appear before Charles. He was not entirely surprised; indeed he had been expecting it, but he was a little apprehensive all the same.

"Well, Lord Devalle," Charles began formally. "You no doubt realise why I asked you here."

"Yes, your Majesty. You wish to know if I have information that could be used against the Duke of Buckingham," Philip guessed.

"Well, have you?"

"No, your Majesty."

"And if you had information would you tell it to me?"

"Since I have not there seems but little purpose in your Majesty's question."

"Yet I asked it. Answer if you please."

"Then I must answer no," Philip said unhesitatingly. "I would never speak against the Duke of Buckingham."

"Because you share his sympathies?" Charles said sharply. "Because you, too, would stir the people up against me and attempt to raise mutinies amongst my troops?"

"I would play no part in treasonable activities, your Majesty, and nor, I'm sure, would Buckingham."

"You defend him? That is unwise," Charles warned. "He stands condemned by those in the highest authority."

"He stands condemned by those who hate him and will gladly listen to any accusations that might blacken his good character and lower him in your Majesty's esteem," Philip said loyally.

"And why should these people condemn him?"

"Because they fear him, and it is easy to see why," Philip said. "He has a gift of oratory and a quick intelligence that puts them all to shame. If he applied himself wholeheartedly to the task then I believe he could be the greatest statesman in the country."

Charles studied him for a moment without speaking and Philip was afraid he had said too much but when Charles did speak again his voice was gentler.

"Yes, I think so too, but what if these gifts of statesmanship are used against me rather than for me? Do you think Buckingham might apply himself more wholeheartedly to that?"

"No, your Majesty. Frankly I don't think he could apply himself to anything for very long. It is his nature to grow bored and need to seek diversion. If he set out to storm this palace he would likely pause halfway along the Mall to lay a wager on a cockfight!"

Charles laughed at that. "You are astute, Lord Devalle, and I suspect you love him nearly as much as I do, but, much as I want to believe in his innocence, the information I have received shows clearly that he is guilty. I think he has allowed his name to be used by more unscrupulous men in order that their cause might have some substance, but I must know the truth. If he submits himself to my authority I shall deal fairly with him, as I have done before. Tell him that if he should contact you."

"I will, your Majesty."

"By the way, Philip, you should know that I have observed you very closely since you came to Court."

"I trust your Majesty has no fault to find with my behaviour." Philip was a little uncertain as to what might be coming next. Barbara had insisted on dancing with him at the Queen's birthday ball and, although he had obliged for fear of her making a scene, he had thought it a bad idea.

"I have no fault to find with you, but rather the contrary," Charles said. "You are a good companion to my son and appear to be popular at Court. The ladies, in particular, seem to like you. There is one, frequently in my company, who lately can talk of no-one else."

Philip froze. Here it comes, he thought. "And who is that, your Majesty?"

"A lady very dear to me." Charles paused for an agonising second. "I trust you will not take this as a reproach but I am requesting that you have a care, for she is very young and inexperienced."

Philip was confused now. "Your Majesty?"

"I am referring to Anna, the Duchess of Monmouth," Charles said, with a hint of a smile.

"Anna!" Philip said, relieved. Monmouth and his young wife had been married when they were children and, although her husband did not appreciate her, Philip found her pleasing company and such an excellent dancer that he often partnered her. "She has developed a slight infatuation for me, I'm afraid, your Majesty."

"And you have given her no encouragement, I suppose?"

"A little," Philip admitted.

"Quite a lot, I'd say, but there, I cannot blame you. She is a lovely girl and my son takes not the slightest notice of her so there is little wonder she enjoys the attentions of his handsome friend." Charles' eyes were twinkling and Philip knew it was not really a rebuke, but the King's next words shook him a little. "There are plenty of ladies at Whitehall who you may pursue to your heart's content and some, of course, who you may not, not unless you are prepared to face the consequences. I'm sure you understand."

Philip was in no doubt that it was not Anna but Barbara who Charles was referring to now and that Charles suspected them. He had received a gentle warning, but a warning nonetheless, and one he knew he would be a fool not to heed, not unless he wished to find himself, like Buckingham, escaping from Charles' wrath!

He was pondering on this as he walked down the corridor and did not notice who was approaching him.

"Lord Devalle, I would have a word with you."

Philip found himself confronting none other than Ashley.

"Well?" Philip really did not see why he should exchange pleasantries with the man who had caused Buckingham so much trouble.

"Not here, in my office," Ashley said. "Follow me."

Philip did not move. "Is that an order?"

Ashley may have been used to giving orders, and to having them obeyed, but Philip was not used to being obedient.

"Not an order, my Lord, merely a request." Ashley smiled disarmingly. "You must forgive my manner but I am extremely upset over what has happened to our mutual friend, the Duke of Buckingham."

Philip had no wish to converse with him upon the subject of Buckingham or anything else, but he was curious as to what he wanted. "Lead on then."

Ashley led the way to his office. "It is of Buckingham that I wish to speak to you. May I assume that King Charles also wanted to speak to you about him?"

"You may assume so."

"Then I must know what you told him."

"None of your damned business!"

Ashley confronted him angrily. "Don't play games with me, my Lord, for I am equal to the best of them and I most certainly can better you. What did you tell him?"

Philip looked fearlessly into the hard eyes, which glittered as Ashley glared at him. "I told him all I knew," he answered coolly.

"What?" Ashley seized him by the arm. "You disloyal wretch! Would you turn against the man who has befriended you and betray his associates?"

"I have betrayed no-one." Philip shook him off, for he could not bear to be handled. "I said I told him everything I knew, which is nothing. Buckingham did not make me privy to his business with you, thank God."

"Then why the devil could you not have been direct" Ashley snapped.

"I don't know why I'm even here, or by what right you speak to me as if I were your servant," Philip said. "Furthermore, since this is the first time I have properly spoken with you, neither do I know how I have managed to offend you, but I evidently have."

"I'll tell you why. You have tried to turn the Duke of Monmouth against me."

"Has he said so?"

"No, but he is very much influenced by you, and when he has been any length of time in your company his attitude toward me is colder. To what other reason should I attribute this? I'll be honest, Philip Devalle, I do dislike you. I think you could be a trouble-maker and that you are no fit companion for Monmouth."

"His Majesty would not agree with you, Lord Ashley," Philip said, controlling his temper with difficulty, "and it is his opinion that counts."

"The King's opinion can be changed," Ashley warned. "If he was to suppose, for instance, that you were implicated in this trouble of Buckingham's he might forbid you the company of his son."

"Are you threatening me?"

"I am suggesting that you, of your own accord, cease your friendship with the Duke of Monmouth."

"Go to hell!"

It was clear that Ashley was not used to people standing up to him, but Philip was not easily intimidated.

"You are not too civil a person for your age, Lord Devalle," he said quietly. "You would be wise to recollect that, now the Duke of Buckingham is escaping from the law, you have no protector here."

Philip turned to go, for there seemed little point in continuing the conversation. "Then, my Lord, I shall manage without one."

When Monmouth came to visit him later that day he decided to tell him nothing of his encounter with Ashley.

"Shall we play a game of tennis?" Monmouth suggested.

"Not this afternoon. I must go to the theatre, for I have not yet seen Nell play in 'The Maiden Queen', and I am told she does it very well. I'll join you later," Philip promised. "Do you sup at Chatelain's tonight?"

Monmouth, who was usually in debt, laughed. "Well I should say so, now that my credit is good again! I've been awarded three year's advance upon my allowance, so tonight we'll eat the best food in the house!"

'The Maiden Queen' was a new play written for the King's House by Mr. Dryden and one of which Charles was very fond, for he himself had suggested the plot. He took pride in calling it his play and had pronounced it an excellent production. This pleased Philip, for Florimel, the most comical woman's part, was played by Nell.

She was superb, although Philip thought that the looks which Florimel exchanged with her lover, Celadon, played by Charles Hart, were perhaps a little too convincing. Hart was a handsome man, whose looks were so delicate that he had always taken women's parts in the days before actresses were employed, and Philip feared Nell might have fallen for him.

There was no doubting that the audience loved Nell, however. In one act she appeared in male attire, with every mannerism of a young gallant, and they applauded her wildly.

Sitting next to him, as enthusiastic as the rest, was Samuel Pepys, the Clerk of the Acts at the Navy Office.

"Is she not an actress of exceptional talent?" Philip asked him proudly.

"Indeed she is, my Lord. This is the third time I have seen the play and I am certain it would be impossible to have that part played better than by her."

Philip said no more to him, in fact he did not particularly like the man, and in this he was not alone. The scandal-mongers claimed Pepys had amassed a huge personal fortune by his clever management of Admiralty affairs. Certainly, he had far too great a notion of his own importance, in Philip's opinion, for he drove in a gilded carriage and put on airs about his valuable collection of plate and fine library of rare books when there were many who thought he would have been better advised to keep silent!

When the play was ended Philip went into the alley which led to the door that the actors and actresses used. He intended to visit Nell in her dressing room to congratulate her but before he reached the doorway he heard footsteps behind him. He spun round quickly, but it was too late. Three men stood shoulder to shoulder, spanning the narrow alley.

It was not yet dark but none could have seen them from Drury lane and Philip knew he was their mercy.

Two grabbed him before he could make a move and, holding him by the arms, pinned him against the wall. The third, the largest of them, raised a mighty fist and punched him in the stomach.

Philip's legs gave way completely as he doubled up in agony, winded from the blow, but the two men still held him firmly. His ordeal was not yet over. Twice more his assailant hit him then they let him go and he collapsed upon the cobbles.

"This is to be a warning, my Lord," he heard a rasping voice say. "You would be wise in the future to be careful of who you displease."

Philip was incapable of making any reply, for he could scarcely even breathe, and the next second he was kicked full in the ribs before the three men ran off into the darkening shadows.

Through a mist of pain Philip became aware that the theatre door had opened and he heard a scream. He saw faces above him, blurred faces that swirled about like birds wheeling in the sky.

"It's Lord Devalle! Fetch Nell," he heard someone say and then she was there, kneeling in the dirt beside him, her face white with fear.

"My God! Is he dead?"

"No, No." He managed to raise a feeble hand and grasped hers. "They haven't killed me, sweetheart, but I am hurt. Can you get me to your lodgings?"

Now that she was a successful actress, Nell had moved to the more fashionable Covent Garden end of Drury Lane, so it was not too far to take him and he managed it with the help of some members of the cast, for he could hardly walk.

"Where do you hurt the most?" she asked when he had been laid upon her bed and everyone else had gone.

"My ribs. I think they're cracked. Can you bind them for me?"

"I'll try." Nell removed his shirt. He was badly bruised, although he suspected she was more horrified by the sight of the old scars on his back, which she had never seen before. She tore a sheet into strips and bound his ribs firmly, then bathed the purple bruises on his stomach with cold water.

"Is that better?" she said anxiously.

"Much." Philip lay back gingerly, for it felt as though every part of him was sore. "You're a darling."

"It's the very least I can do for one who protected me during the plague."

"What a pity I cannot look after myself a little better," he said ruefully. "Would you send a message to the Duke of Monmouth? He will take me home in his carriage."

"You can stay here with me as long as ever you want," Nell said eagerly, but Philip shook his head.

"I shall not compromise you, Nell. You have already done me a great service. But for you I might be still lying in the alley. Are you crying?" he asked, putting his hand to her cheek.

"No," Nell sniffed, brushing away a tear. "Why should I cry because the best friend I have has been set upon by footpads?"

"Footpads?"

"Weren't you robbed then?"

She looked so troubled for him, yet Philip knew she would worry a great deal more if she knew the truth.

"Yes, I was robbed," he lied.

"Oh, Philip, stay here just one night," she pleaded. "We'll be very comfortable. Monmouth can take you in the morning."

The prospect was tempting. Philip felt weak and every movement caused him pain. "He is awaiting me at Chatelain's. At least he ought to know."

Nell threw open her window and looked out over the street. "Hey, boy!" She beckoned the link boy, who stood with his taper, waiting to light folk home and earn a penny. "Go find the Duke of Monmouth at Chatelain's and bring him here."

She tossed a shilling down to him and then regarded Philip pertly, with her hands upon her hips. "Now there's a sight I never thought to see - Philip Devalle in my bed!"

He smiled wryly "And never so incapable as he is now!"

Monmouth came straight away and he was every bit as concerned as Nell. "My dear fellow, who has done this to you? They shall be punished, I swear it."

Philip looked into his worried face and sighed. He knew there was no way he could tell Monmouth that his attackers had been dispatched by Ashley, though he himself was certain of it. "They were only common ruffians, set on stealing from me. Don't trouble yourself on my account, for I am in good hands, but I would have you send your carriage for me in the morning."

"Whatever you wish. You know there is nothing in the world I would not do for you." Monmouth pressed his hand, still looking most upset. "It's mighty good of you to care for him, Mistress Gwynne. You are most kind."

Nell blushed. She had never actually spoken with Monmouth before. Philip watched them as they talked. Monmouth, graceful and good-looking, was perched upon the bed sipping the wine she had brought him and eyeing her admiringly. Philip wondered why he did not feel more pleased.

"I don't know why you want to go home when you have such an excellent nurse to tend you here," Monmouth whispered to him as he took his leave. "My father says she is the prettiest thing upon the stage and it is plain she cares about you."

"He is charming," Nell said when she and Philip were alone again.

"He'd bore you very quickly," Philip told her. "You would like his father better."

"So you say but I've never met the King, nor is it very likely that I shall."

"That's all you know! You've caught his eye already." Philip repeated what Monmouth had just told him. "Soon you will have everything you've ever wanted."

"All I want right now is to care for you." Nell snuggled up to him, taking care not to hurt him.

"But I could never satisfy your ambitions," he reminded her, although he was enjoying her nearness all the same.

"My ambitions? Huh! Sometimes they eat at me so fiercely I can scarcely breathe and then, at other times, they seem completely unimportant.

"What other times?"

"Mostly when *you* are near. Don't lecture me," she begged, kissing his bare shoulder. "I know exactly what you're going to say but, in truth, I can't help it. All my resolutions come to nothing when I am with you."

"In that case," Philip said sternly, "it is fortunate that I am leaving in the morning!"

He hoped to hear some news of Buckingham when he returned to Wallingford House but there was none, save that soldiers had been sent to Westhorp to arrest him. The Duchess of Buckingham had outridden them to warn him, arriving only a quarter of an hour ahead of the troop, but where Buckingham was now Philip had no notion. His interest was not entirely unselfish, for he was well aware that his own position would be less perilous if his protector was once more a free man.

His first visitor when he got home was Barbara. Philip regretted not swearing Monmouth to secrecy, for he guessed that news of his condition had now been broadcast throughout the Court.

"My poor darling!" She hugged him to her, which did him very little good for his ribs still felt tender.

"Isn't this risky, you visiting me here?" he asked, holding her at arm's length. "Charles suspects us, I am certain."

"Don't worry. Buckingham's wife is still away saving her worthless husband, even though he does not care a fig for her, and I came in a plain carriage so no-one will even know I'm here. Unless, of course, you have invited someone, like that orange seller, perhaps, with whom I hear you spent the night."

"I really think you should acknowledge Nell to be an actress now," Philip said heavily, "and if you've come here merely to rail against the person who showed me such kindness after I was attacked then you may leave."

"I haven't come for that. I've come because I care about you." Barbara sank her head into her hands. "It seems of late we can hardly talk without we argue."

"Perhaps we've been together for too long," Philip said quietly.

"Do you mean you're tired of me?" Barbara raised her head and looked at him.

Philip recalled the way she had stirred his passions when he had first come to Court. She still affected him but not, if he was honest, to the same degree.

"I'm not tired of you, my lovely, but I fear our relationship has run its course."

Barbara looked upset. "But I still desire you."

"I desire you too, for you are an incredibly beautiful woman," Philip said truthfully, "but I think it would be wiser for us both if we discontinued our association."

"No! You must promise you will never leave me," she said.

"I can't promise that."

"Of course you can. It would be greatly to your advantage," Barbara said. "Pledge yourself to me and I'll take care of you. What would you have? A career in government perhaps?"

"Good Lord, no!"

"Then tell me what you do want. Charles will refuse me nothing; favours, money, property. I can buy anything I want."

"You can't buy me," Philip corrected her.

Barbara smiled confidently. "We'll see, and we'll see how well you manage without Buckingham to look out for you. You were not attacked by any thieves, were you? You have fallen foul of Ashley, I'll be bound."

"How did you guess?"

"I watch what's going on. You see you do need me," she said, "Unless you propose to skulk here in this house forever, for it is the only place where you'll be truly safe from him."

Philip was saved from replying, for the sound of voices in the entrance hall below told him that he had another visitor.

"Wait here, I am expecting someone, and from the King's House," he added wickedly.

"Surely that common little orange girl - sorry, actress, would not have the brazen nerve to call upon you here?" Barbara was flushed with indignation.

"I doubt that. It is Hart I have invited."

"Charles Hart, the actor? Well, that's different." Barbara primped herself before one of the many mirrors that adorned the walls of Philip's room. "I think he's mighty handsome. Let him come up when you have done with him, for it hardly matters if *he* finds us here together."

Her cheeks had grown quite pink and Philip watched interestedly as she tugged at her revealing bodice to make it even lower. She was evidently excited at the prospect of meeting with Hart and Philip knew he should be jealous, but he wasn't.

"Lady Castelmaine would like to meet you," he told Hart, "but let us get our business settled first. It won't take long. Is Nell your mistress?"

"Really! I don't see that is any of your affair, my Lord," Hart protested.

"Is she your mistress?" Philip repeated.

"No."

"That's good. I trust if I should ask that question again in the future you will be able to give me the same answer?" He glared at Hart in a way he fully intended to be intimidating. It worked.

"Yes, my Lord. I understand."

"I'm sure you do." Philip took the actor back to where Barbara waited. "I have finished with him, sweetheart. He is all yours."

Barbara gave him a dirty look, then beamed at Hart. "Mr. Hart, this is an unexpected pleasure which has brightened up an otherwise dull morning," she said pointedly. "Do you have a carriage or may I offer you a ride?"

As Philip watched them leave together he realised that the last of his affection for Barbara had gone. Only a week before he had watched her ogle a rope dancer and heard her remark upon how his muscles rippled through his tights and now she had practically thrown herself at Hart.

"She is nothing but a whore," he said to himself, "and the sooner I am free of her the better."

Philip wondered if he should not leave London for a spell. He was to get the opportunity sooner than he expected.

At the end of April, the Dutch fleet sailed up the Firth of Forth and word came from Amsterdam that another eighty men-of war were on their way toward the English coast. Charles' desperate hopes of peace disappeared. The Dutch were planning an invasion.

There was no battle fleet to dispatch to meet them on the sea, for there was no money to equip it. All that could be done was to defend the coast. Plymouth and Portsmouth were quickly fortified, whilst the Duke of Albemarle and his militia took the guns from the abandoned men-of war and set them up along the shores of Kent. Even then he was hard pressed to find enough men to fire them, for the army, as well as the navy, was in arrears of pay and Albemarle could offer them no reward but glory.

Monmouth was made Captain of Horse. He was ordered to Harwich and his father requested him to take as many of his friends as he could muster.

"Shall you ride with me?" he asked Philip, who had recovered from his beating.

Philip smiled as he thought how well the trip would suit his plans and how furious Lord Ashley would be to learn that he had accompanied Monmouth. "I most certainly will!"

A great troop rode to Harwich, mostly formed of gentlemen and nobility, and Philip, for the first time, experienced the camaraderie of war as they set about urgently making preparations for defence. He enjoyed himself immensely.

His respect for Monmouth increased considerably as he observed him now for, despite his dullness in some other ways, the young Duke seemed in his element in a position of military command.

Even so, the task of defending England without a navy was a hopeless one.

Sheerness was stormed and twenty of the Hollanders sailed down the Medway toward Chatham, their guns blazing. Philip, Monmouth and his troop rode furiously the fifty miles to Gravesend, for it was feared the Dutch were impudent enough to attempt to reach London itself.

The city was in a panic. All day and night there could be heard the sounds of Dutch artillery firing on the Gunfleet. Charles ordered merchantmen to be sunk at Barking Creek to block the river and posted the militia on Tower hill in case they managed to advance that far, but the Londoners were afraid the capital would be taken all the same. No enemy had ever dared to come that close before.

There was a chain laid ready across the Thames estuary as protection against invasion and, since there was no ammunition for the guard ships at Chatham, Commissioner Pett gave orders for it to be heaved into position. The chain was heavy and sank time and again into the mud. Pett looked on helplessly as the Dutch broke through and seized the flagship, the 'Royal Charles'.

There was not a man on board her to offer resistance. It took a boat with only nine men to take the pride of the English fleet in tow. Albemarle quickly scuppered the 'Royal James', the 'Royal London' and the 'Royal Oak', then cut loose all the rest.

The Dutch sailed for home, towing their prize behind them and firing their cannons in triumph.

The guns stopped. It was over. Sixteen men-of-war lay grounded on the mudflats and five magnificent ships blazed in the docks. London was safe but England had suffered a bitter defeat.

NINE

The first news which awaited Philip on his return to London was that Buckingham had surrendered himself into custody. Tired of playing the fugitive, Buckingham had gambled his uncertain freedom against Charles' affection for him, and he had won.

Charles had found it hard to believe that a man who had served him so well in the past could be capable of treason. Buckingham was finally condemned upon no greater charge than having made an attempt to win the favour of the people.

He was committed to the Tower once more, but it did not come as a complete surprise to Philip that Charles ordered his release after only a few days.

Buckingham soon received a visit from Lord Ashley, the one man in England who was rejoicing at the impudence of the Dutch.

The nation will need a scapegoat now," he reminded Buckingham, "and who better than Lord Chancellor Clarendon? He cannot manage Parliament and he could not manage the war. The man has no allies left, save for the King."

Ashley chose to forget that it had been Lord Clarendon who had recommended him for the post of Chancellor of the Exchequer.

Buckingham had his own grudge against Clarendon now, since it was he who had brought the accusation of treason against him. "If Charles could be persuaded to turn against him then he must fall."

"And who is more fitting to be given the Great Seal than myself?" Ashley said. "All England will then dance to the tune I pipe."

"Have a care," Buckingham advised. "I have lately learned that Charles will not be pushed too far. By the way, I understand that Philip was set upon by some of your 'brisk boys' while I was away.

"He annoyed me."

"How?"

"He is too full of himself by far. Besides, I do not trust him."

"Philip belongs utterly to me," Buckingham said. "I will vouch for him."

"You've told him nothing of our plans, I hope?" Ashley said sharply.

"Nothing whatever, but he'll join us when the time is right. Until then let him continue to win the Duke of Monmouth's confidence."

"He's not the right one," Ashley said. "Lord Grey is far more compliant. This Devalle whelp has defiance in his eyes, and likely a tinge of his family's madness in his head."

"Trust me, he's worth ten of Grey, and Monmouth adores him."

"It is difficult to trust the judgement of a hothead who will hazard the chances of such a bold plot as ours over some petty issue of principle and conceit, the way you did," Ashley retorted. "Very well, I'll leave him be, but keep him out of my way or I will not be answerable for my actions."

He made to leave but Buckingham stood in front of him. A much taller man, he was an immovable object to the lightly-built Ashley.

"You will not harm one golden hair upon his head," Buckingham warned him. "Not if you want my support and my name to add substance to your scheming. Do I make myself clear?"

"Completely," Ashley muttered sourly.

"That's good." Buckingham stood aside to let him pass. "It wouldn't do for there to be any misunderstanding between us two, now would it?"

"What did Ashley want with you?" Philip said suspiciously as they walked in St. James' Park together later.

"Merely to congratulate me on my freedom, that is all. It's good to be in your company again, dear fellow. I've missed you."

Philip knew that he had deliberately changed the subject. "I've missed you too."

They encountered Barbara in the park, conversing with Lord Buckhurst in a most animated fashion. She hailed them both with obvious delight but Buckhurst beat a hasty retreat and looking, Philip thought, quite uneasy, although he could not imagine why.

He soon learned.

"Philip, you will never guess! Lord Buckhurst has taken a new mistress," Barbara told him excitedly. "He is purchasing a house for her in Epsom this very day."

"I fail to understand why that should be of so much interest to me," Philip said, a little puzzled, for he and Buckhurst had never been particular friends.

"You will understand when you hear who she is." Barbara's lip curled maliciously. "She's an actress, someone you know very well, for it was you who started her upon the stage."

Philip looked at her in horror. "Not Nell?"

Barbara laughed. "Yes, Nell Gwynne, your little orange girl. It seems your efforts for her were in vain. She is handing in her parts and leaving the King's House just as soon as she has finished this afternoon."

"I don't believe it." Philip turned to Buckingham, "She wouldn't"

"I'm afraid she has, dear boy. I'd heard it rumoured but I wasn't going to tell you in quite this way." He glared at Barbara.

"What does it matter how he knows?" Barbara said airily. "He always claimed to me that he had no feelings for the slut."

"Well I have, but not the kind of feelings you would understand," Philip said. "I am going to see her. Maybe I can bring her to her senses."

Nell looked apprehensive when he arrived at her lodgings. She had obviously been expecting him.

"Is it true?" he demanded. "Do you really mean to take up residence with Buckhurst?"

"Yes," Nell said in a small voice.

"You can't be serious, Nell! I never would have introduced you to him if I'd known where it would lead. I'd set you up for a higher target than Buckhurst."

"Don't be angry with me, Philip," she pleaded. "I know how you have tried to help me and, believe me, I am not ungrateful but Lord Buckhurst is a good man and he cares about me."

"He is using you."

"What if he is? There is no disgrace in what I'm doing for, after all, I was brought up to be no better."

"I am not concerned with your morals so much as your choice," Philip said. "Can you not be patient for a little longer?"

"No, I can't. The King has paid me no attention yet and he's had ample opportunity. It's all very well for you to talk, Philip, in your fine clothes." She indicated the scarlet brocade coat he was wearing, which was a new one, cut in the latest straight fashion and edged with silver lace. "You're respected with your title and your money. No-one looks down on you. Well, no more they will me when I am supported by one of your own kind."

"Yes, they will. They'll treat you like a common whore and laugh at you when he deserts you, which he will. I know him."

"You're being very cruel."

"I'm trying to bring you to your senses. If you must become some rich man's mistress then at least choose one who will be discreet."

"Would you keep me then, Philip," Nell said hopefully.

Philip shook his head. "No, I wouldn't and I am not as rich as you seem to think, at least not on my own account."

"Is that the reason or is it that you are afraid of Barbara?"

"A pox on Barbara! What has she to do with this?"

"It seems that, for all you say, she still owns you and the King as well," Nell cried passionately. "That woman stands in the way of all I want."

"You could take Charles away from her like that." Philip snapped his fingers. "He is tired of her. That is why Barbara has become so possessive over me."

"Well she can keep you both. I'm going to Epsom with Lord Buckhurst," Nell said defiantly.

Philip sighed. He knew that she was making a mistake but there was nothing he could do to stop her.

"Oh, Philip, can't you be just a little pleased at my good fortune," she pleaded.

"Is that what you call it? The renouncement of a promising career? No, Nell, I cannot."

"But it will be so good to be out of London. The Londoners have never liked the players, you know that. If it were not for the patronage of the Court the theatres would never survive."

"Since you must always portray the citizens of London as either fools, cuckolds or both it's not surprising that they do not like you," Philip reckoned, for such was the trend amongst the playwrights and the Londoners, understandably, took exception to it. "As if that was the reason for your decision. You will be telling me next that you are going in order to take advantage of the Epsom waters!"

"It is fashionable," Nell said weakly.

"To take the waters or to become a whore? You must not do it, Nell."

"Well I shall," she said stubbornly. "Just because you gave me money one May Day upon Strand Bridge it does not mean you own me."

"I have never claimed to own you, you obstinate jade, but I have tried to guide you."

"Aye, into the King's bed, doubtless for your own advantage. Does he pay you well to pimp for him?"

Philip stared at her disbelievingly. "What did you say?"

She backed away from him, looking scared. He guessed the words had come out in haste but they were nonetheless hurtful for that.

"You bitch! Do as you please. From this day on I wash my hands of you."

⁓

Lord Clarendon was blamed for the humiliation of the Medway, just as Ashley had predicted.

He had presumed that the Dutch could not afford a war, especially one across the sea whilst King Louis was encroaching upon their boundaries in the Spanish Netherlands. He had been wrong and the peace treaty which Charles' ambassadors had been forced to conclude in Breda had brought no satisfaction to the English.

Clarendon had been Charles' strength in exile and had united the country at his Restoration but the Chancellor was an old man now, crippled with gout and unpopular with the new members of the administration, who considered that he belonged to the past and not the future. Charles was forced to agree with them.

Buckingham was overjoyed. His old enemy was finished at last. "Charles has sent Albemarle and York to relieve him of the Great Seal," he told Philip.

Philip was not surprised, although he did wonder at Charles sending the Duke of York to do the dirty deed, for he was Clarendon's son-in-law.

In the event, Clarendon refused to relinquish his seal of office to any but the King himself and a crowd of courtiers gathered to watch his arrival. To them the strait-laced old Chancellor was little more than a joke and they were relishing his downfall.

Clarendon had never made any secret of his disapproval of Barbara. He had not even allowed his late wife to visit her, and she and Buckingham were the most jubilant of all, united in the downfall of a common foe. Philip stood back apace and watched them as they both jeered him and shouted insults, for all the world, he thought, like silly children.

Clarendon bore it all with dignity but his step did falter when he drew level with Ashley.

Ashley said not a word. His talking had all been done and he made no display of exaltation, but Clarendon would have known that this man was his real enemy and far more dangerous than the noisy horde who mocked him. They looked at one another and Philip saw Ashley smile.

Monmouth, who was holding onto Philip's arm, saw it too. "I wonder why Lord Ashley is not shouting with the rest."

"He has too much sense." Philip could admire the man for that if nothing else. "Has Ashley talked to you about Clarendon?"

"Oh yes. He feared that if Clarendon was allowed to remain Lord Chancellor there would be insurrection in my father's capital."

"I meant has he ambitions to succeed him?"

"How should I know?" Monmouth said. "I suppose he has ambitions to serve the country in the best way that he can. Isn't this exciting?"

Philip regarded him with exasperation and a measure of disgust, in fact he suddenly felt disgusted with all of those around him who, in his opinion, demeaned themselves by gloating at a defeated man.

He noticed that Albemarle stood alone, as if he wished to disassociate himself from all the rest. Philip had great respect for him and thought he could do no better than to do the same.

Philip paid a visit to the theatre that afternoon. He had not been able to bring himself to go since Nell had left but he felt in need of some diversion away from Monmouth, Barbara and even Buckingham.

"Well, if it ain't our handsome Lord Devalle back amongst us once again!"

Philip found himself confronting the buxom charms of Orange Moll, the leader of the orange girls.

He tossed her a coin and took a fruit from her tray. "Hello, Moll. What's the news?"

She laughed. "What news is there when you're away from us, my Lord? You've heard what's happened to poor Nell, I suppose?"

"To Nell?" Philip said, alarmed. "What is it, Moll?"

"Why, she's been left already by Lord Buckhurst and, what's worse, he now makes sport of her." Orange Moll began to laugh again, but she stopped when she saw Philip's expression.

"Is this true?" Philip demanded, for the orange girls were notorious for their gossip.

"I swear it is, my Lord, upon my honour."

Philip raised an eyebrow at this expression, quaint upon the lips of one whose honour was not considered prominent amongst her attributes. "Do you know where she's lodging now?"

"I don't, but even if I did I wouldn't tell a soul. She's turned her back on all society, she says."

"But not on me Moll. She wouldn't mean me."

"Especially you, she said, my Lord. To tell the truth I don't think she can face you. She told me how you parted and, as I stand here, the tears were running down her face. I reckon losing you upset her more than losing Buckhurst."

Philip would have engaged her longer but another customer was approaching, one who would be sure to want to hear the tale, for it was Samuel Pepys. There were ten minutes remaining before the commencement of the play so Philip went backstage.

Beck Marshall was standing in the wings, resplendent in her make-up and her costume. "Where's Hart?" Philip asked her.

"He's still dressing, but I wouldn't see him now," the actress warned. "He gets very temperamental before a performance."

"Does he now? I wonder how he fares before he visits Lady Castelmaine!"

Hart looked wary when he recognised his visitor. Philip, however, could not resist a fleeting smile when he saw that Hart was wearing one of his own cast-off coats. In common with many of the courtiers, Philip often donated his ornate clothes to the theatre when he tired of them.

"Most becoming," he decided, "though it is a trifle long for you. No matter, it is you I came to see and not my coat."

"My Lord, to what do I owe this most unexpected and, if I may say so, ill-timed delight?" Hart asked him nervously. "I must be in front of the curtain in a very few moments."

"What I have to say will take no longer," Philip said. "You can, perhaps, guess why I am here."

Hart swallowed. "Yes, my Lord. It is about the Countess of Castlemaine, is it not? I swear to you that it was she who led me on and not the other way about. Rather than risk your displeasure I will gladly pledge here and now to have no more to do with her."

Philip laughed out loud to hear his ardent successor so eagerly promising to desert Barbara in order to save his skin.

"As for Castlemaine, Hart, why you may keep her, and I wish you all the luck which you will need. I would as soon own a scorpion as that virago! It is on account of Nell that I am here."

"Nell?" Hart looked considerably relieved. "That slut! I pray you, Lord Devalle, not to mention her to me."

"You do know where she is?"

"I know. She sent a message to me yesterday, but she shall never come back here."

"Were you in love with her, by any chance?"

Hart was silent.

"Answer me, were you in love? Is that what causes you to speak so bitterly of one you were once proud to number amongst the players of the King's House?"

"What did she care about the King's House?" Hart retorted. "She was quick enough to turn her back upon us all for

Buckhurst. Yes, my Lord, I was in love with her and I did teach her all the art she knows, and fine repayment the ungrateful bitch gave me."

"Man, you taught her nothing. Nell was born an actress," Philip said. "If you can take any credit then it is for the parts which, through your preference, she obtained. What if she went to your rivals at the Duke's House instead? Would you want her playing there?"

"They'd not take her either, I've made sure of that. Nell Gwynne will never act in a patented house again. Let her seek employment at Sadler's Wells if she wants to go back on the stage."

Sadler's Wells was an unlicensed theatre, frequented by only the coarsest audiences.

"She will act here," Philip insisted.

"She will not." Hart faced him defiantly.

Philip had already decided how to play this. He tossed his curls. "Very well, Hart, have it your way. You are not a gentleman by birth but I will allow you a gentleman's death, although I would be within my rights to run you through right now. I will meet with you at Chelsea Fields tomorrow at dawn. Be sure to bring your second and a competent surgeon."

Hart stared at him aghast. He had once been a lieutenant in the army but Philip knew Hart would be no match for him in a duel.

"You mean to fight me on account of Nell?" he gasped.

"Not at all. I mean to fight you on account of Castelmaine."

"But you just now said that I could keep her."

"I know exactly what I said, but I have changed my mind." Philip flicked an imaginary piece of fluff from the velvet of his sleeve, enjoying Hart's dismay. "Of course, I might change it again - if you would consider taking Nell back."

"But that is…" Hart sought for the word, "that is…"

"Persuasion," Philip finished for him. "I will give you my word as a gentleman that I shall never trouble you on Barbara's account so long as you allow Nell to remain here."

"It is not entirely up to me, you know," Hart reminded him sulkily. "Killegrew manages the theatre."

"I'll take care of Thomas Killegrew, but he will not agree to anything which would upset you. Can I tell him that you are in accord with this?"

"Tell him what you please," Hart said grumpily. "I'll take her back."

Philp smiled. "I thought you would. Now tell me where she is and I'll relinquish you to your audience."

"The Cock and Pye tavern in Drury Lane. I hear she sings there for her rent."

Philip went directly to the Cock and Pye. Although it was barely four o'clock the place was full. A fiddler played a merry jig and the customers clapped to keep time as a little figure he knew so well danced before them, as lightly and as prettily as she had once danced for him on Strand Bridge.

Philip stood back out of sight and watched her, smiling fondly as she finished her dance and curtsied to her audience, for all the world as though she still stood on the stage of the King's House.

"Tell Mistress Gwynne there is a gentleman to see her," he instructed the pot man.

"Tell her yourself," the man said without turning around.

Philip grabbed him by the collar and pulled him back so hard the fellow all but choked. "Fetch her and fetch her now."

Nell stood stock still when she saw who it was had asked for her. The colour rose in her cheeks and she looked near to tears.

"Hello, Nell."

"Philip! I never thought to see you in a place like this," she said hesitantly. "What are you doing here?"

"Now that's a bloody stupid question if ever I heard one! Come here, you silly bitch, and be forgiven."

Nell gave a little cry of joy and ran headlong into his arms in full view of the company. "Oh, Philip, why are you so good to me?"

"I really don't know." He steered her away from the crowd of gawping onlookers. "Take me to your room. We can't talk here; much less may you embrace me!"

Once alone with him the tears came and she clung to him. This time he did permit it, smoothing her untidy curls while she cried upon his shoulder.

"I have undone all the good you tried to do me," she gulped between sobs.

"Not at all."

"I have. I am a worthless and ungrateful jade. You should have let me die of the plague instead of risking your own life to save me."

"Surely I should be the judge of that, since it was my life," Philip said. "Here, see what you've done to my coat, wench? Your tears have marked the velvet."

Nell managed a smile. "You and your precious clothes. You are as vain as a peacock, Philip Devalle!"

"Since my looks are the greatest asset I possess I am bound to be," he said matter-of-factly. "You, now, have no clothes sense whatsoever. Even when you're in a decent dress you wear it carelessly and, like as not, have the sash undone or the buttons fastened wrongly. I believe the time has come for me to take you seriously in hand if you are ever going to amount to anything!"

"Does that mean you're going to take me for your mistress after all?" Nell cried, brightening at the prospect.

Philip looked into her pretty face, full of adoration for him. It took all his resolve to turn away. "No, it does not, and you know the reason why."

She sighed. "It's because of Buckhurst I suppose. You will not have it said that you took his discarded mistress."

"The point is not whether I would take his discarded mistress but whether the King would."

"The King?" Nell laughed mirthlessly. "That dream is over for me now. I've ruined it. Besides, I'd rather have you." She laid her head against his chest. "It's always been you I wanted most."

Philip struggled with his good sense. "We've been over this. I can't afford to keep you, Nell," he admitted. "Not in the way you want or you deserve. I am still dependent on my father and the Duke of Buckingham and neither, I fancy, would grant me an allowance to keep a mistress! Do be sensible."

"What if I kept myself?" she suggested. "I'll earn my living somehow and I won't ask anything of you, I promise, save that you visit me from time to time."

"No," Philip said resolutely.

"Is it because of the dreadful things I said to you before I went to Epsom?" Nell said. "You must know that I never meant them. I tried to shout down to you as you left but I couldn't get the damned window open quickly enough, and that's God's honest truth. You've never acted as though you owned me, though I have often wished you would, and as for the name I called you…"

Philip kissed her, partly because he wanted to and partly to silence her. She responded to him with a passion that fired his own and, for a delightful moment, he allowed himself to succumb to the desires she roused in him. He would have taken her that day at Hampstead, so why not now? Even as he reasoned with himself Philip knew it was no use. This was not Barbara, nor was it some hardened little coquette from Court who he could use to gratify his sexual cravings. This was a person he might hurt, one he cared about and who cared for him, and that thought was altogether too daunting for him.

"This was not why I came," he protested, pushing her away, although it took all of his resolve. "Believe me there is nothing I want more right now than to throw you on that bed and make you mine, but I shall not do it, Nell, and you must not expect it of me. If you really want to please me then you must go back to where you belong, on the stage of the King's House."

Nell's face fell. "I am never to be taken back there."

"Nonsense! You are to return right away."

"Would that I could. It's Hart. He'll never agree to take me back."

"On the contrary, he has already agreed," Philip assured her.

"You talked to Hart?"

"This afternoon. He earnestly awaits your most welcome return."

"He never said that!"

"Well, no, not exactly," Philip confessed. "But he has agreed, although I fancy he will make you take some minor roles at first to salve his pride," he warned.

"I don't mind that. Oh, Philip, you are marvellous." Nell hugged him. "I don't deserve a friend like you, for I have disregarded all the advice you have given me."

"You are not going to do so anymore," Philip disengaged himself and sat her opposite him. "In future you will do exactly as I say, is that clear?"

"Perfectly," she said demurely.

"Not because I think I own you," he stressed. "To my mind possessiveness is an ugly thing. I simply regard myself as taking care of Charles' property until such time as he has sense enough to claim it."

"That again?" Nell cried despairingly. "He will never take me now that my affair with Buckhurst was made so public."

"Yes, he will, and I intend to see to it. I'd best go now and visit Thomas Killegrew."

"What shall you say to him?"

"Why, simply that Charles Hart insists on your return! After that I will have some quiet words with Buckingham. For reasons best known to himself he has been encouraging Charles in the ridiculous passion he has conceived for Moll Davis who, to my mind, is an ordinary little thing."

Moll Davis was an actress with the rival Duke's House.

"Ordinary she may be yet she has exchanged her rooms in Lincoln's Inn for a house in Suffolk Street and displays a ring

King Charles has given her which, she boasts, cost him seven hundred pounds. I hate her. One night I invited her to sup with me and I slipped a dose of jalop into her pudding." Nell giggled. "That was one night she didn't go to meet the King, nor was she seen by anyone else for several days!"

"I don't believe I wish to hear about that," Philip said severely. "Now I think you should put on your prettiest dress and then go straight round to the King's House and be charming to Hart. Speaking of charm, I shall need all of mine this evening. I have just recalled that Barbara made me promise I would keep an assignation with her at five o'clock. You cause me nothing but trouble!"

It was nearly half past six before Philip presented himself at Barbara's apartments, but he could not bring himself to care. If her exhibition with Hart had destroyed what was left of his affection for her then her exhibition with Clarendon that morning had certainly destroyed what was left of his respect. He had been doing his best to end their relationship for some time but Barbara would not allow it and each time she had managed to win him round. Philip was a slave to his senses and, despite how he felt towards her, she still satisfied his most animal desires. That was how she managed to control him and, at times, he hated himself for his own weakness.

"And where the devil have you been?" she demanded angrily the instant he set foot inside her door.

"I went to the theatre."

"So I am less important than a play?"

"As it happens I did not see the play. I saw Charles Hart, then left before it had begun," Philip told her truthfully.

Barbara stared at him. "You went to see Hart? About me?"

"No. Don't flatter yourself. I wished to talk to him about Nell."

"Nell? Your poxy, jumped-up orange wench?" Barbara was now beside herself with rage. "What's Nell to Hart?"

"An old flame." Philip paused a moment to allow Barbara to digest that piece of information. "I persuaded him to take her back. That is," he added, smiling wickedly, "back upon the stage."

"And how did persuade him?"

"Oh, I think you'd better ask him that."

"I will, but if you left before the play began you could still have been here earlier. Where did you go afterwards?"

"That's my affair."

"You were supposed to be with me," Barbara reminded him furiously. "Were you with another woman?"

"Yes." Philip was annoyed by the interrogation. "Yes, I was and there is not a damned thing you can do about it, Barbara."

"You belong to me," she insisted.

"No, I don't, nor ever shall. I'll not be owned by you or any woman."

"I'll have you followed everywhere you go and I'll make trouble for you if you try to leave me," Barbara threatened.

"I'm not going to leave you but I'll be hanged if I shall promise to be faithful when you take the King, Charles Hart and Jacob Hall the ropedancer into your bed in the same week! The King may endure your jealous tantrums but I shall not."

Barbara drew back her hand, clearly intending to strike him, but Philip grabbed her wrist and held it firmly.

"Don't ever do that," he warned her.

She struggled but he only tightened his grip.

"Did you hear me, Barbara?"

"Yes," she hissed. "Let go of me, you brute."

Philip did let her go, then turned away and watched her through a mirror whilst he pretended to fuss with his hair. She sat down on the bed looking so dejected that he felt quite sorry for her.

"Don't be sad." He sat down beside her. "I still want you."

"You've hurt me," she sniffed, showing him the red mark he had made upon her wrist. "No-one has ever done that in my life."

"Then you are very fortunate. You are also very spoiled and very willful. You must learn you cannot own all you want," he told her seriously. "That is why you have nearly lost the King. Would you lose me too?"

Barbara shook her head.

"Then do not let your evil temper come between us."

"Shall you come and visit me tomorrow?"

"I'll come. I cannot stay away from you for very long." He pulled aside the loose robe she was wearing to reveal her plump, white body, so firm and yet so supple. "You are without doubt the most beautiful woman I have ever seen but even were you Venus I would say this - between now and tomorrow afternoon I shall go where I please, consort with whom I please and do whatever I damn well like. Is that clear?"

"I shall know exactly where you go," she retorted with a flash of her usual temperament. "Everything you do will be reported to me."

"You can set as many spies to watch me as you choose only be advised, if you do not like what they tell you then you had best keep silent," Philip said. "If you should presume to criticise my behaviour you will see no more of me. I am not afraid of you."

It was the end of Barbara's rule over him.

TEN

༄

Monmouth went to Paris at the beginning of Winter to visit his aunt, the Duchesse d'Orleans, and he stayed away until Spring. Philip found, unexpectedly, that he missed his company, particularly since the Duke of Buckingham was growing more and more absorbed in affairs of state.

Deprived of them both at the same time, Philip looked about for other diversions but, for once, found few. De Grammont had been pardoned by King Louis, truly pardoned this time, and had returned to live in France. He had finally married Elizabeth Hamilton at the insistence of her brothers, who feared the Comte's ardour was cooling. It had so far cooled, in fact, that they caught up with him at Dover on the very point of leaving the country! He obeyed their wishes resignedly enough, when reminded of his duty, and took Elizabeth with him, which meant that Philip lost two more of his favourite friends.

He found some consolation in the company of Monmouth's lively wife, Anna, and a beautiful newcomer to Court, a rich, Scottish heiress named Henriette McClure, but the plain truth was that he was bored. For the first time since he had come to Court he felt discontented with his lot.

Monmouth returned in March but it was not long before he was once more planning to cross the Channel, hinting to Philip that he had been entrusted by his father with some secret correspondence and that Philip was not to breathe a word of it to anybody, not even Buckingham or Ashley. Philip found the whole thing very tiresome and, what was even more tiresome was that Anna sprained her thigh in May, whilst practising a dance step in her lodgings.

Poor Anna was never to dance again, nor even walk without a limp. Philip rarely saw her after that, for she was forced to take to her bed for several weeks and had a constant stream of royal visitors.

"It is high time I did something with my life," he told Nell when he visited her one morning at the Cock and Pye tavern, where she still lodged. "I am in danger of becoming an aimless fop."

"You could go into politics, like Buckingham," she said.

"Now you're being ridiculous! Perhaps I should propose marriage to Henriette McClure."

"McClure? That haughty bitch! She's not for you."

"She's rich, and in her own right," Philip said. "She's a beauty too, and she earnestly desires a title."

"But you're not in love with her."

"Love one's own wife? What a quaint notion!"

"Don't make jests, it doesn't suit you." Nell was reclining quite inelegantly across a chair and she was dressed only in her shift and petticoat, for she always rose late and Philip had called upon her early.

"I am never going to fall in love," Philip vowed. "I have seen what it does to romantic fools like Buckingham. I wish you wouldn't sit like that." He pulled down her petticoat, which was hitched up to her thigh. "Why can't you learn to dispose of yourself like a lady?"

Nell laughed. "But I'm not a lady, nor shall I ever become one, not even if I should become the King's mistress. Mary Knight did tell me, by the by, that his Majesty was asking whether Hart had taken leave of his senses to keep me confined to such miserable parts when it was plain I had more talent than the rest. What do you think of that?"

"I think it is high time you were once more given the opportunity to display your considerable talent," Philip said.

"Hart is still resentful."

"A pox on Hart! He does not write the damned plays but, thanks to Buckingham, I have the acquaintance of some who do. There's Etheredge," he mused, half to himself, and then shook his head. "No, he's too lazy; or rather he's so busy with the pleasures of the Court that he has not had time to write a play in three years. There's always Sedley."

Nell coughed, a little embarrassed, for Sir Charles Sedley was a friend of Buckhurst and had often visited the couple at Epsom.

"Oh yes, I had forgotten" Philip said heavily. "He'd never write a part for you. In any case, the King's House has only just run his 'Mulberry Gardens'. Wait, I have it - Mr. Dryden!"

"But he has been appointed Poet Laureate now," Nell reminded him. "He'll be much too busy and important to concern himself with me."

"Surely even a Poet Laureate has to earn a living, and I'll warrant he'll not earn too good a living at a Court whose king can't even spare the money to properly equip his navy," Philip said dryly. "I'll see if he will at least listen to a proposition."

Dryden did listen. "Write a comedy expressly to display the talents of Nell Gwynne?" he said when Philip had finished. "My dear sir, it cannot be done."

"And why not, pray?"

"Because to write a play takes time and I am presently engaged in the writing of a tragedy. I'm calling it 'Tyrannic Love or the Royal Martyr'."

"Then set it aside and start another."

Dryden sighed. "You really have no idea what life is like for those unfortunates in my profession, have you? His Majesty the King is gracious enough to give me notions for my plots, notions which I could actually do very well without, but when I ask him for a small subsistence in order that I may compose a classical poem upon the life of King Arthur, then I find the royal purse much leaner than the store of royal ideas!"

"Why on earth would anyone wish to read a poem about King Arthur?" Philip said scornfully. "The public wants a comedy, that's what they come in their hordes to see."

"You're not a member of the literati are you, my Lord," Dryden said with a smile.

"I'm barely even literate," Philip confessed, "but I *am* a theatre-goer, therefore I do contribute in some small way to your livelihood. I am prepared to contribute further to it in the sum of, shall we say, one hundred pounds if you do the thing I ask."

"I'd like to help her, she's the finest little actress I have ever seen, but this play is promised," Dryden said. "Maybe Hart would let her play the lead."

"He might, if I pressed him, but Nell is no tragedian."

"Let her try and I will write for her a special epilogue, a comic epilogue, one that will draw attention to her. How would that be for a quarter of the price you just now offered me?"

Philip put the money on the table before him. "Take it now, while I still have it. My allowance comes but once a month and I am monstrously extravagant. Don't disappoint me, Mr. Dryden. A classical poem indeed," he muttered as he left, "and about King Arthur!"

Dryden did not disappoint him or, indeed, any of the audience who witnessed the first performance of 'Tyrannic Love' a few months later.

Nell made a good attempt at a difficult and unaccustomed part, her first lead for over a year, but Philip knew the best was yet to come.

The house was packed, for her admirers had not forgotten her. Even Mr. Pepys was there, although he had but recently been made a widower, but the most enthusiastic applause of all came from the Royal Box as the bearers prepared to carry Nell off the stage, apparently dead.

Suddenly she sat up on the stretcher and, to the astonishment of her audience, prodded the lead bearer.

"Hold, are you mad? You damned confounded dog!
I am to rise and speak the epilogue!"

The audience broke into laughter and then into further applause as Nell got to her feet and chased the bearers away. After such a heavy play it was an unexpected treat to see her once more as the comic figure they loved so well.

The long epilogue that Dryden had written for her was funny and Nell's delivery was perfect. The applause at the end of it was deafening and Philip saw Charles rise to his feet and bow to her as she curtsied up to him.

Philip's only disappointment was that Buckingham had not been there to witness Nell's triumph but he was pleased to find the Duke home when he arrived back.

"You should have seen her," Philip said excitedly. "She was magnificent, and afterwards she told me that the King had sent for her. She'll be his mistress now for sure."

"Congratulations," Buckingham said dully. "I never doubted you could engineer it in the end."

Philip had been so full of his own news that he had not noticed Buckingham's troubled expression. He was aware now, for the first time that the Duke was not his usual jovial self. "What's happened? Is Ashley worse?"

Lord Ashley's personal physician, John Locke, had performed a delicate operation on him and some thought he would not survive it.

"No, he's much improved."

"What then?"

"The Earl of Shrewsbury has decided to object to my relationship with his wife."

Philip thought that scarcely surprising, for Buckingham and Lady Shrewsbury had become more and more brazen.

"Can you not console yourself with the thought that he has left you undisturbed for years?" Philip said unsympathetically, for he had never liked the Countess.

"You don't quite understand. He has challenged me to a duel."

"You never accepted his challenge?"

"What could I do, appear a coward before the whole Court?"

"But you are plainly in the wrong," Philip said. "Dammit, man, she is his wife."

"I have no choice. The challenge has been made and my honour is at stake."

"Your honour will be forfeit no matter what the outcome," Philip pointed out.

"Will you desert me if I am disgraced?" Buckingham said anxiously. "I value your friendship, you know."

"And you shall always have it," Philip assured him. "Whatever happens, now or in the future, I will stand by you, whether you are right or wrong."

"You are a dear fellow."

"I am a Devalle," Philip reminded him with a wry smile. "We are known for our loyalty and courage but not, regrettably, for our sanity!"

The duel took place the following day at Barn-Elms. Shrewsbury received a wound from which he later died.

Buckingham was condemned by most of the Court. Philip knew he had not deserved to win but he was still glad that he had.

Shrewsbury's death made a considerable difference to Philip, for the Earl had not long been buried before Buckingham moved Lady Shrewsbury into Wallingford House.

Even his staunchest friends were shocked. Philip kept his promise to be loyal and he remained Buckingham's companion but he felt he could no longer reside in the Duke's home and moved into rooms in Whitehall.

He was not the only one to be leaving. The Duchess of Buckingham found the situation even more intolerable. Philip felt extremely sorry for her. The Duchess was the daughter of the Parliamentary General, Sir Thomas Fairfax, who had been granted much of Buckingham's property before the Restoration. Philip suspected that the main reason Buckingham had married her was to get it back, but she loved her husband, despite his brazen infidelities. This, however, was an insult too gross to be borne.

"I'm going to my father's house," she told Philip when they said goodbye. "This fits in too well with my husband's plans, I fear, but there is nothing else that I can do if I am to save my pride." She offered Philip her hand, for they had always been friends. "Take care of him."

"That is a somewhat tall command, your Grace," Philip said. "If he took any notice of me at all then the Earl of Shrewsbury would be still alive and in possession of his whoring wife, but I will try."

"Thank you. It is Lord Ashley who is leading him astray, I'm certain of it."

"Ashley? That name again! It's all I hear from Monmouth lately. I fail to understand how such a small and inconsiderable-looking man can wield such power over all he meets."

"He's dangerous, Philip. My advice is to stay clear of him."

"I have no need to, for lately he stays very clear of me," Philip said, "although I don't know why."

It was the truth. Since the incident in Drury Lane, Ashley had not attempted to make contact with him.

Barbara no longer lived at Whitehall. Charles had bought her Berkshire House, a sumptuous residence and, Philip thought, a parting gift. After she moved he saw less and less of her, for he was not so enamoured that he would take the trouble to leave the palace in order to have the pleasure of her company. Barbara filled her new home with her new admirers, such as the playwright William Wycherley, Hart and little Henry Jermyn, back in favour once again. She seemed to be contented, so that Philip was surprised to receive a visit from her one evening.

"Barbara! It is unlike you to come a'calling."

Barbara pouted prettily. "Does that mean I am not welcome?"

"You are welcome, but you may not stay long. I have promised to meet someone at nine o'clock and it will do my honour no good if I fail to keep the appointment."

"Who is she, then, that will not wait a minute after nine for you?" Barbara asked, kissing him upon the cheek.

"It is a *he*. Lord Rochester, in fact, and I owe him a gambling debt, so you see I can't be late. You will excuse me if I change?"

"Of course. I'll even help you." So saying, she removed his coat and hung it in his closet. "Actually, I only want to talk."

"That makes a change!"

Barbara immerged from the closet carrying, in one hand, a coat of brilliant peacock blue and, in the other, one of rich red velvet. "Which?"

"You choose. Buckingham told me today that Charles wanted to be reconciled with you."

"He does." She laid the blue brocade across a chair. "I like you in this best, it matches your eyes. I'll tell you what he offered me too – the title of Duchess of Cleveland, with all the honours and privileges of the rank, and a pension in order that I might support the dignity of my new position."

Philip raised an eyebrow. "I would say that was a more than generous offer."

"Oh, you would, would you? Well before you judge it so allow me to explain just what he would have in return for this generosity." Barbara picked up the silver brush she had herself given him and commenced to brush his curls. "First, I must forever abandon Jermyn and consent to his being dismissed from Court again for a considerable time."

"And a good thing that would be," Philip said. "Insufferable little puppy! Surely you would not let him stand in the way of your advancement?"

"No, I have already agreed to that. The second condition is that I should rail no more against bloody Frances Stewart, no matter what cause he shall give me."

Frances Stewart was now married and had become the Duchess of Richmond. She still held a place in Charles' affections, though not so dear a place as she had once held.

"You must agree to that as well, if you are not a fool. You must know by now that every time you attack the woman he will defend her."

"Yes, I have agreed to that too," Barbara said sullenly, "but there is yet another condition and I hope I must not agree to that."

"What is it?"

"You."

"Me?" Philip took the brush from her hand and turned around to face her. "What do you mean?"

"You know that he has suspected our association for some time. He says that he intends no punishment for you since, unlike Jermyn, you have been discreet and not flaunted my favours in front of him, but he insists that I have nothing more to do with you. He says that, through you, I am cheapened in the eyes of the world."

Philip was indignant at that. "Are you, by God? And why, pray, should I cheapen you when actors and rope-dancers do not?"

"Because you are younger than me and because you have become such a womaniser. It is your fault," Barbara said peevishly. "If you had stayed faithful to me then perhaps I could have had the title and kept you too."

"Well you can't, and I don't propose to justify myself to you, not for infidelity. As for your title, take it. That is my advice. A duchy, surely, is the highest reward that any royal mistress could hope for."

"He only makes me a duchess in order that he can be rid of me," she said. "This clears his conscience, don't you see? It is no reconciliation. He'll discard me now for Stewart and your precious Nell Gwynne, who, I hear, expects his child."

"I still reckon it a generous offer," Philip said, putting on the coat she had laid out for him, "and you should take it."

"Can you bear to let me go so easily then?"

"I hardly think the little we have left is worth the sacrifice of such an opportunity," he told her frankly, "and, besides, what prospects would there be for me at Whitehall if you refused his offer on my account?"

"You don't need to stay at Whitehall. I might go to France."

"To France? Why should you wish to go to France when everything you have is here?"

"That is all you know. If matters work out then I shall be well set up in France," Barbara said. "King Louis will reward me generously for the way I have served him. See this?" She pointed to a gold comb in her hair. "And this." She lifted up her skirt to show a fine lace petticoat. "Both presents from Colbert. He comes to see me regularly at Berkshire House."

"I fail to see how sleeping with the French Ambassador will incur the gratitude of the French King," Philip said scornfully.

"He does not come to sleep with me but to find out what I have discovered and to advise me what I should tell Charles to do."

"Are you saying you have become a French agent?" Philip found it hard to believe, even though Barbara had become a Catholic. "Why would you do that?"

"Because this is much more important than you could ever suspect. Louis plans to ruin Holland."

"Have we not just signed a treaty with them?"

"Oh yes, but Charles would far sooner be allied to France and he has pledged to aid Louis."

"With what?" Philip asked. "The Cabal would never vote him money for such a scheme."

Charles had not immediately appointed a successor to Lord Clarendon but had decided to rule with the aid of a committee, one whose name happened to incorporate the initials of its members, Clifford, Ashley, Buckingham, Arlington and Lauderdale.

"Not if they knew exactly what he wanted the money for," Barbara agreed, "but he's as crafty as that pet fox of his that the Queen detests so much. He has confided so far only in Lord Clifford, for he is a Catholic and of like mind."

"But Charles is not a Papist," Philip said, a suspicion forming in his mind, for it was already rumoured that the Duke of York had converted to the Catholic faith.

"He's one at heart, and he has promised to declare himself so when the time is right. With Louis to support him he proposes to establish Catholicism here. Does that alter things?"

"It will alter a great deal." Philip was stunned at the possibilities and shocked at the duplicity of a king who, until that moment, he had deeply respected.

"I meant does it alter things between us?"

"Not a bit. Why should it? I am not a Catholic, and I shall not become one for your sake, or for the sake of Charles."

"But you have French blood."

"French Protestant blood," he emphasised. "My mother was a Huguenot. It may well be that I decide to serve France one day, for King Louis seems to be a man I could admire, but I would endeavour to do so only in a capacity which would not be damaging to England."

"But if you stay with me then you will never have to serve Louis or anyone else. I would support you."

Philip shuddered. "You mean become dependent on you? God forbid!"

"But you'd have everything you needed."

"Everything except my dignity if I accepted that proposal."

"Then I will make you a better one. I will marry you."

"You are already married," he reminded her, "after a fashion."

"What if I could persuade Roger to divorce me? You couldn't refuse me then, surely, and King Louis could hardly do less than grant us both a Duchy. You would like that, wouldn't you, my darling, to be a Duke?"

"Barbara stop it, this is madness," he protested. "I am quite contented with the title that I have and, besides, when I take a wife it will be one who…," he paused, searching for words which would convey his feelings without giving too much hurt.

"One who is not older than you?" she finished for him.

"No, I do not care a fig for that. I was about to say one who will not make a cuckold of me before the whole Court. You'll not make a fool of me as you have Roger Palmer."

"But I wouldn't."

"Of course you would! If you could not be faithful to a king it is hardly likely you would be faithful to me, a mere earl's son, no matter what pretentious title you had purchased for me. You're a whore, my love, a beautiful, exciting, eager little harlot. I was proud to be your lover, but I would not be your husband for a kingdom, let alone a dukedom."

Barbara sucked her breath in sharply. "You unfeeling bastard!"

"Not at all. You know you will always be very special to me," Philip said truthfully. "You were my first lover and whoever I eventually do marry will be jealous of you for that. I am not insensible of the honour you have done me in taking me to your bed and the even greater honour you now offer me by wishing to become my wife, but you shall not use me to save your face, Barbara. Better you use your precious little Jermyn for that."

"It is not Jermyn's child I am expecting. It is yours," she shouted back.

Philip stiffened for a moment, and then he laughed. "Now how can you possibly know that? If you are with child again it could be any of a dozen men. What about Wycherley? Why choose me to be its father?"

"Because it was you. A woman has intuition about such things."

"Don't give me that tale! What, shall you go round to each of us in turn until you can find one to accept your offer?"

That was cruel and Philip knew it but, even so, he was unprepared for Barbara's reaction. Screaming with rage, she hurled herself upon him, scratching, biting and kicking him with such ferocity that it took all of his strength to hold her off.

He managed to seize one of her wrists and was about to grasp the other when he noticed something glinting in her free hand. As she brought it round he realised that she was clutching a little pointed knife.

Quick as lightening Philip kicked her feet from under her, so that she landed quite heavily upon the floor. Pinning her arm down with his foot, he wrenched the weapon from her and hurled it, embedding it in one of the bed posts.

He pulled her to her feet and Barbara cringed, as though expecting him to hit here, but he let her go. Her hair had become disarrayed in the struggle and her rouge was smudged. Philip thought, disgustedly, that she looked like a common trollop from the streets.

"You may stay here and repair yourself, my Lady, or should I say your Grace, but I want you gone before I return," he told her, "and I do not ever wish to see you in my rooms again."

The next day, after a troubled night, Philip decided to tell Buckingham all that Barbara had told him.

Before he had begun to speak Buckingham gave him the news that Barbara had miscarried.

"How is she?" Philip said anxiously for, no matter how little he now felt for her, he did not want her death upon his conscience.

"Oh, she will recover. Barbara has the constitution of an ox. Why so concerned?"

"Because it is my doing, I'm afraid."

Philip told him briefly of their skirmish.

"You could hardly have been expected to stand there whilst she stuck a knife in you," Buckingham pointed out reasonably, when he heard that part of the tale.

"Still, I should never have said the things I did to stir her up. If that was truly my child I have murdered it."

"I'm sure it's not the first child you have fathered at Court and it's not likely to be the last," Buckingham said. "What are you trying to do, people Whitehall entirely with your progeny? Besides, if it makes you feel any better, Charles refused to own that brat a week ago. If that is all that's troubling you I beg you put it from your mind."

"Would that it was."

When Buckingham had heard the rest of what Philip had to relate he grew solemn. "This would be the ruination of Ashley's plans. He is proposing to bring in a Union of Protestants."

"You'll understand, I'm sure, if I am but little concerned at the inconveniencing of the person who caused me to spend a most uncomfortable week recovering from the treatment of his agents," Philip said.

"But what about me?" Buckingham asked.

"I would do almost anything for you, and well you know it."

"Then you must go to Ashley with the tale you just told me."

"I have no desire to speak with that man, on this or any other matter."

"But you will, for my sake, won't you?" Buckingham begged him. "It's time the pair of you made friends. I think you may have more in common than you know."

Ashley certainly seemed determined to be friendly when Philip visited him an hour later and recounted the events exactly as he had to Buckingham.

"Would you say there was any possibility of a reconciliation between yourself and Lady Castelmaine?" Ashley said when he had reflected upon the story.

"I would say there was no likelihood of that at all," Philip said. "In any case she's lost the child she claimed was mine, so she has no reason for desiring a reconciliation."

"You could give her another," Ashley suggested.

"What do you take me for, a stud?"

"You've given a fair impression of one up to now," Ashley said. "It is a pity that you had to be so rough with her. Is it your habit to throw pregnant women on the floor?"

"Not unless they have a knife in their hand," Philip said evenly. "I regret I cannot spy upon her for you. I have brought you all the information I am able to obtain."

"Perhaps not. There are other sources you can use for information. Buckingham tells me you were instrumental in procuring Mistress Gwynne a place in Charles' affections. I'm certain she will be grateful to you for such a favour."

"Nell is grateful," Philip said, "but I could not use her to spy upon the King."

"*Could* not? I suspect you *would* not," Ashley stressed.

Philip made no reply. Despite his painful experience in Drury Lane, he had no intention of letting Ashley bully him into doing anything he did not wish to do.

Ashley smiled. "As you please, my Lord. You are a stubborn young man. I fancy I'll do nothing with you."

"Which is fortunate. If I had allowed you to persuade me two years ago to abandon the Duke of Monmouth I would not have learned something which I am now feeling might be significant."

Ashley leaned forward in his chair. "Tell me."

"The King has used Monmouth as a courier to carry messages between him and his sister in France. These messages were so secret that he was not to allow them to fall into the hands of anyone, even her husband, the Duc d'Orleans."

"Monmouth never told me about that!"

"Of course not. Charles expressly forbade him to do so," Philip explained, with considerable pleasure.

"Yet he told you. Buckingham was right, you could be useful to us," Ashley said. "But why did you wait so long to divulge this information?"

"To be honest, I never realised its significance until yesterday. I don't believe Monmouth has a clue as to what is written in the letters that he carries."

"I'm sure he hasn't," Ashley agreed. "Monmouth is a dolt but I fancy you are shrewder. If you should hear anything else of importance I beg you to report it to me - and only to me. Do you understand?"

"You mean without reporting it to Buckingham first?"

"That would be best. He is well-meaning but, alas, a trifle headstrong and inclined to sentiment. How long have you been at Court, Lord Devalle?"

"Almost seven years. Too long, I fancy," Philip said bitterly. He was feeling disillusioned with both the King and the Court.

Shaftesbury nodded, as though he understood. "What you see before you is all light and laughter, but if you look a little closer you discover the darkness that lurks beneath. All is not as it seems."

"I am beginning to realise that now."

"Are you ambitious?" Shaftesbury asked him.

"I used to want to be a soldier. The Duke of Albemarle refused my services during the plague and, on reflection, I believe that he was right but maybe he would have a better opinion of me now if I were to visit him again."

"A soldier's life is hard. A man may make his fortune and his mark much easier if he becomes a politician," Ashley said. "Think on that."

Philip did think on it, but not very deeply. The fact was that the longer he remained idle at the Court the harder it was to motivate himself to do anything at all.

He never paid his visit to the Duke of Albemarle, for Albemarle developed dropsy toward the end of that year and worsened rapidly. He died the following January and when Philip attended the magnificent state funeral held for him in Westminster Abbey he could not help but think, sadly, that England had lost a most remarkable man. A man who's like he would never see again.

ELEVEN

There was little else talked about that spring but the proposed visit of Charles' sister, the Duchesse d'Orleans, known in France as Madame and to her adoring brother as Minette.

Monsieur, the Duc d'Orleans, who had at first refused his wife permission to visit her brother at all, had finally relented, providing that she travelled no further than Dover and stayed for no more than two weeks.

It was said that Charles loved his little sister more than anyone in the world and he seemed beside himself with joy at the prospect of spending time in her company. Philip, in common with Buckingham and Ashley, read a more sinister motive into the visit.

It was no secret that Minette was passionately committed to King Louis and the Catholic religion, and they now had reason to suspect that Charles wanted Louis' aid to conquer the Dutch, who were England's chief rivals in trade, and that the condition of his aid was that England became a Catholic nation.

When Charles led his sister up on deck after they reached Dover it appeared, on the face of it, to be nothing but the most innocent and happy family reunion, but Charles and James had boarded Minette's ship in the Channel and Philip guessed that any private conversations would have been held there.

Minette leaned over the rail to wave to Monmouth and Philip noticed a dark-haired girl standing next to her and talking vivaciously to Charles.

"Who's that with her?" he asked Monmouth.

"Her name's Louise, I met her in France. My father certainly seems to be taken with her."

Philip could not help but wonder if that was not the very reason she had accompanied Minette. If King Louis knew his cousin Charles at all he would have known how susceptible he was to a pretty face, and how useful it might be to have a French Catholic installed as Charles' mistress to watch over France's interests!

Since Minette was not allowed to go to London, Charles had made sure that all the diversions the city had to offer were brought down to Kent, even a play, for the company from the Duke House performed 'The Sullen Lovers' for her entertainment. It was a play based on Moliere's 'Les Facheux' and mocked the French unmercifully but she did not seem to mind. Monmouth was so pleased with the performance of the actor James Nokes that he presented him with his own sword and buckled it on for him himself. Philip privately thought that a little extreme but it was a gesture typical of Monmouth and no more or less than he would have expected of him.

Philip had not forgotten that Ashley had requested him to observe what went on in the royal family but there was nothing to be seen of a secretive nature, indeed it seemed that Charles and his beloved sister were hardly ever alone. There was a constant round of gaiety the like of which the little town of Dover would not see again; ballets, balls, firework displays, parties on land and aboard ships.

Never, even at Whitehall, had Philip known so much activity to be crammed into such a short space of time.

When the moment finally came for Minette to depart it seemed that Charles would never let her go. Tears rolled unashamedly down his cheeks as he three time bade her farewell and then returned for yet another embrace. Sentimental Monmouth wept quite openly at the sight and Buckingham could not hide his own emotion but Philip was unmoved. Charles had lost the lofty position he had once held in Philip's eyes and he would never regain it. Philip considered deceit upon so great a scale as that related to him by Barbara was quite unforgiveable.

It seemed that he suddenly saw deceit all around him. There was Charles planning to deceive his ministers and Minette, who had captivated everyone and yet, Philip guessed, was no more than Louis' agent, come to persuade her brother to bind his unwilling country to a Catholic empire. Even Buckingham, vain and easily swayed by promises of glory, was talking of Charles' promise to him of an army command, should England and France combine against the Dutch, whilst Monmouth, earnest and well-meaning, was relishing the secrets entrusted to him by his father without having the intelligence to properly interpret them, or even, probably, to appreciate their momentous importance if he had.

And then there was Ashley. Reviewing him again, against such a background of perfidy and cunning, Philip began to see Lord Ashley in a new light. Here, at least, was a man consistent in his purpose, which was the very reason, Philip suspected, that Charles did not confide in him.

Philip went to see Ashley of his own accord when the Court returned to London, even though he had nothing of any substance to report.

"They had time to sign a dozen secret treaties," Ashley said. "Charles proposes war quite openly with Holland now, as France's ally, but there is not a damned word spoken of French aid or the fact that he intends to make us Catholic, yet I can think of no other reason for King Louis to help us. He is a clever man, the King of France, make no mistake about that, and a powerful monarch, dedicated to increasing France's glory."

"There seems little wrong in that," Philip said, thinking how Louis contrasted with Charles, who Philip had begun to see as shifty and underhanded. "I think King Louis is a man I could serve."

"Why don't you?" Ashley said. "Monmouth has pledged to join the French army if the Dutch march toward the Rhine. There can be nothing dishonourable in fighting for your mother's country against a common enemy. Buckingham tells me he is soon to go to France to negotiate the terms of the alliance and doubtless he will want to take you with him, since he likes to show you off. If you are as clever as I think you are then you can use the introductions he will give you to do yourself some good. You will also have the chance to find out for me exactly what he is doing there."

"You don't mean me to spy on Buckingham, surely!" Philip was appalled at the thought.

"Why not? You do know, I suppose, that his mother was a Catholic?" Ashley said craftily.

Philip did know, but he also knew that Buckingham had been brought up in the royal nursery after his father had been killed and that his mother had been allowed to have no influence upon her sons. "You may remember, Lord Ashley, that I once refused to inform upon the Duke of Buckingham for King Charles."

"This is different," Ashley said with a smile. "Me you can trust!"

A few days later Sir Thomas Armstrong arrived from France in great haste and rushed straight in to see the King.

Within minutes Charles was in a state of near collapse and the Court was stunned, not wishing to believe the news.

Minette was dead.

"I must protest, Monsieur, and in the strongest terms."

Ralph Montagu, the English Ambassador to France, faced Monsieur, the Duc d'Orleans, angrily.

"Indeed?" Monsieur unconcernedly bit into a piece of marzipan, eating it carefully so as not to smudge the carmine on his lips. "You've always some complaint."

"Apparently you have seized all of Madame's letters from King Charles."

"That's right. She was my wife. Her possessions come to me. The letters are now my property." Monsieur stood up and viewed himself before a mirror, smoothing a wayward ringlet into place. "Is that all?"

Monsieur was a most attractive man. He had delicate, almost girlish features, fine eyes and a well-shaped mouth, which often pouted sulkily. Today, however, nothing would put him out of countenance. The Court was to receive English visitors and he was dressed extravagantly for the occasion in a pink coat, edged with layer on layer of gold lace, pink satin shoes with huge gold buckles and a cloth of gold sash around his waist. He knew that he would be admired, and there was nothing Monsieur liked better.

Ralph Montagu was obviously not one of his admirers. "Those letters were the property of the King of England, and they should be returned to him."

"Well they won't be." Monsieur took another sweetmeat from the dish, for he was a continual eater. "I got them first and, what is more, I intend to have them translated for me. I shall have Monmouth's read as well."

Monsieur had been extremely annoyed at the pleasure his wife had derived from her friendship with her young nephew. At Madame's request his own favourite, the Chevalier de Lorraine, had been banished by King Louis to Italy and, after that, Monsieur had enjoyed asserting his rights as a husband to upset her whenever he could.

"Monmouth's letters are of no concern to me but I have been charged by King Charles to take possession of his correspondence with Madame."

Monsieur filled his pockets with some more marzipan, in case he should be hungry during the Duke of Buckingham's official reception. "Then you will have to tell him that you failed, won't you?"

✑

Philip stood back whilst Buckingham approached King Louis, bowing three times as he did so to arrive at exactly the correct distance from the King, who offered his hand most graciously.

"I crave your Majesty's indulgence to present my protégé," Buckingham said, when all the necessary formalities had been observed toward Louis, the little Dauphin and Monsieur. "Philip Guy Pasquier, Lord Devalle."

Louis smiled. "The son of Madeleine Pasquier? Advance, my Lord, and kiss my hand."

Philip did so, bowing three times, exactly as Buckingham had done, and executing the difficult manoeuvre with no less grace.

Louis looked pleased for, as Philip had been told, he enjoyed all demonstrations of respect, the more so when they were perfectly performed. "You are a credit to your mother, my Lord."

"Thank you, your Majesty."

Philip raised his eyes and studied the man who he was rapidly learning to admire. Although not easily overawed, he was momentarily overcome by Louis' presence, a feeling he had never experienced in the company of King Charles. There was a formality and dignity about this monarch which defied anything but the greatest respect.

Despite his formidable achievements, Louis was only in his early thirties and extremely good-looking, with his dark curls and dimpled chin. Philip noticed that his eyes had no humour in them, unlike those of Charles, and he guessed that Louis was a serious person. All in all, he was not in the least disappointed in him.

No less intriguing was Monsieur. Philip had heard much about Louis' notorious brother, and all of it shocking. He had imagined he would be a rather ridiculous figure but instead Philip thought him very handsome and most stylish.

Monsieur also offered him his hand, which was perfumed. "Charming," he said, studying Philip closely. "Absolutely charming."

Philip had become so used to admiration that it no longer occurred to him to be surprised by it but, even so, he was unprepared for such a frank appraisal of his looks. He treated the Frenchman to his most winning smile. "Thank you, Monsieur. You are most kind."

"Lord Devalle, I trust you will be attending the entertainments to be held tonight to mark his Grace's visit?" Monsieur said.

"Indeed, I am looking forward to them, Monsieur."

"I have organised everything, you know. I always do," Monsieur informed him proudly. "You may sit next to me. That would be quite in order as you are the Duke's guest."

Buckingham registered some surprise at this, for Monsieur was known to be obsessed with matters of social precedence and Philip's rank did not entitle him to such an honour, even as Buckingham's guest.

Philip realised this. "If I am accorded such a privilege as your company, Monsieur, then I am sure this evening will be doubly pleasurable to me," he said, bowing very low.

It was the smooth response of a practised courtier and he saw Buckingham smile with pride.

"You certainly charmed Monsieur," Buckingham said when they were being driven the few miles to Versailles, where the evening's festivities were to take place.

"Yes, I thought that too." Philip had already resolved to make himself as pleasing as he could be to Monsieur that evening. There could be no person, he figured, more conversant with the affairs of the late Madame than her husband, and certainly no more influential person he could use to further his own career in France.

"Do be careful of him," Buckingham warned. "He's nowhere near as harmless as he looks."

Philip laughed at the Duke's concern for him. "Don't worry. Monsieur can hardly do me any harm whilst we are watching a fireworks display!"

As they approached Versailles they saw that a stage was being rigged up in the courtyard in front of the chateau, ready for the opera that was to be performed later.

"This is very grand," Philip said, looking with interest at the chateau that had been built behind and around a little hunting lodge, which had been left intact.

"Louis' father used to come to the lodge to escape from the duties of the Court," Buckingham explained. "Louis has enlarged it and it's his escape now, a place to bring his mistresses and to hold the kind of entertainment he could never contemplate at the Louvre. He'll live here all the time eventually, I reckon, with the Court and his administration."

Although they were Louis' special guests they had to share a small room where there was barely space for them both to dress at the same time, but Buckingham told him they were lucky to have been offered even that cramped accommodation, since most of the other guests would have to travel back to Paris afterwards, if they had not been able to obtain rooms in the little town that was rapidly expanding around the chateau.

"If he intends to move the whole Court here he'll need to make the place a good deal bigger," Philip said, as they changed for the evening. There was no room for a valet to be in attendance so they had to shift for themselves. "I dread to think what they will make of me, for it is so dark in here I cannot even see if I have my patches in the right places."

"You don't truly want a compliment?" Buckingham said, laughing. "Not from me!"

"It wouldn't come amiss on such an important occasion."

"I really don't see that I ought to feed your great conceit, but, if you must know, you are a delight to look at," Buckingham told him as they went to the front of the chateau, where the stage was now ready for the performance.

"So many people," Philip murmured, "And so elegant." He looked enviously at the brightly coloured coats the men were wearing, adorned with bows and embroidered flowers, and glinting with gold and silver lace. By comparison his own outfit was quite plain, although made specially for the visit. "I shall really have to have a coat like that."

Buckingham groaned. "I feared as much! I suppose you'll need high-heeled shoes as well, just like Monsieur's!"

Monsieur was, indeed, teetering on heels so high they looked like stilts. He had a gentleman on either side of him and he was talking animatedly to both of them, so Philip thought he had better not present himself just yet.

Buckingham pointed out Madame de Montespan, Louis' latest mistress, who was also a Lady-in-Waiting to the Queen. Philip thought she was beautiful.

He was admiring her when he heard his own name called and recognised de Grammont and Elizabeth among the guests invited to honour Buckingham.

Philip embraced Elizabeth delightedly. "It's good to see some friendly faces," he admitted.

"Don't tell me you are nervous, Philip?" Elizabeth teased him. "Not you!"

"A little," he confessed, "especially since I have been granted the singular distinction of a place beside Monsieur during the opera and the fireworks, but how do you two fare?"

De Grammont shrugged. "How should I fare? Are there not fifty-two cards in a pack in France, just as there are in England? Before you leave, my friend, I will teach you Lansquenet and Hocca. They are much played here."

Philip laughed. "Still the same de Grammont, eager to take my money! But what of you, Elizabeth? Are you happy with your new friends?"

"Why yes, of course, who could not be happy in Paris?" she said, but Philip noticed she had lowered her eyes and he knew she was lying.

"Truth," he demanded, when the Comte and Buckingham moved out of earshot. "You can tell me."

"Then I will say to you and only to you that I am miserable here," she admitted. "How I wish that you were staying longer. We could have fun, as we used to do. The women hate me here, I don't know why, and they're a vicious bunch."

"But doesn't your husband protect you?"

"I rarely see him, except on these occasions. He gambles all the time and entertains his friends and doesn't care for me too much. To tell the truth I don't believe he wanted to marry me at all," she sighed, "but there, I mustn't spoil things for you tonight with my troubles. Oh, you do look so nice."

Philip kissed her fingertips, thinking of the day he had first seen Elizabeth in her sedan chair on Ludgate Hill and of how ironic it was that she should be the first person to greet him at Versailles, just as she had been at Whitehall.

"I will find opportunity to speak with you again before we go," Philip promised. "Now I had best attend upon Monsieur, for the performance will soon be beginning."

Monsieur's two companions greeted Philip icily as Monsieur introduced them as the Chevalier de Beuvron and the Marquis Pasquierroy, and it was evident that they resented him. Philip suspected that Monsieur might be using him to make them jealous, and that thought amused him far more than the opera, which was 'Alceste', written by Jean-Baptiste Lully, the favourite composer at the French Court. Philip, despite his accomplishments with the guitar, had little real appreciation of music, whilst his love of the theatre was confined to the frothy comedies performed upon the stage of the two London Houses.

He applauded appreciatively nonetheless, which seemed to impress Monsieur.

"Do you dance the ballet, Lord Devalle?" Monsieur asked as they walked together down the long lawn known as the Tapis Vert towards the Grand Canal, where the next part of the evening's entertainment was to be held.

"No, Monsieur." Philip had always avoided taking part in Court theatricals, for he felt them to be somewhat undignified.

"Pity. You would look absolutely splendid in costume." Monsieur looked him up and down. "You have a fine figure, I have noticed that, and the most superb legs."

Philip acknowledged the compliment with a nod of his head. "Thank you."

"And you are tall. I particularly noticed that. I have always wished that I was taller."

Philip guessed that was why he wore the high-heeled shoes, although they seemed to be a lot of trouble to him.

"Would you like to rest for a moment?" he said, for Monsieur seemed to be finding the short walk quite fatiguing.

"It would be better if you offered me your arm," Monsieur suggested.

Philip did so right away and Monsieur rested on it happily.

When they reached the canal, Philip saw that the surface of the water was covered with a fleet of little Galiots and Shallops, their main masts topped with pennants, which fluttered in the mild Spring breeze. They were hung with gaily coloured lanterns which showed up brightly against the darkening sky and it was a dazzling sight.

When all the guests were on the water the firework display began. This was much more to Philip's taste. The noise was deafening and the sky was filled with brilliant flashes of colour. Even the surrounding trees glowed red, then green, then yellow as devices were ignited amongst them. Philip thought he had never seen a more wondrous sight but when he turned to tell Monsieur so he was surprised to find the Frenchman was looking at him instead of the fireworks.

Philip found the intensity of his gaze somewhat disconcerting.

"I can watch this kind of nonsense any time," Monsieur said, by way of explanation, "whereas I rarely get the opportunity to see a man as pretty as you."

"You flatter me, Monsieur."

"I like you." Monsieur drew closer to him to be better heard above the explosions and spoke into his ear. "Attend upon me in the morning and I will personally take you upon a tour around the gardens. Not too early, mind!"

Philip didn't see Buckingham until the evening was over and they were getting ready for bed.

"Monsieur appeared to be taking a good deal of interest in you," the Duke said.

"You don't sound pleased."

"Can you wonder at it? You know his reputation. I would never have brought you here if I had known he would make such a fuss of you."

"But Monsieur is an influential man," Philip pointed out. "One who could advance me with King Louis."

"I can do that," Buckingham said crossly.

"Of course you can," Philip agreed, settling down as best he could in the hard little bed that Buckingham had allotted as his. "But surely the more I have to speak for me the better."

"Even so, I wish you to have no more to do with him," Buckingham said, climbing into his own bed, which was not much softer than Philip's, for all he was such an honoured guest.

"After tomorrow?" Philip suggested.

"Why tomorrow?"

"Because he wants to take me around the gardens in the morning."

Buckingham sat up in bed and viewed him in astonishment. "He must have really taken you to his heart. You'll have to go, but for God's sake be careful."

"Lest he should try to seduce me in the gardens?" Philip said jokingly.

Buckingham was refusing to treat the matter as a jest. "There is no knowing what a man like him may do. It is even rumoured that he had a hand in poisoning his wife."

"I thought Madame died of colic?"

"We will probably never know the truth," Buckingham said grimly.

"He hardly has the appearance of a sorrowing widower," Philip allowed, "but why would he want her dead?"

"It was on her account that the Chevalier de Lorraine has been banished to Italy and those who claim that she was poisoned also claim the poison was Italian."

"Gossip!" Philip said. "Elizabeth told me what a nasty lot some of them are here."

"And Monsieur is the worst of any."

Philip could not believe the agreeable Monsieur could be half as bad as Buckingham was painting him. "Was he not a soldier once?"

"He was, and a brave one too, by all accounts. He distinguished himself during the War of Devolution and then went on to win acclaim throughout the campaign in Flanders."

"Why did he not continue such an illustrious career?" Philip wanted to know.

"He was not permitted to continue it. After the victory the people shouted 'long live the King and Monsieur, who won the battle'. It was the end for him, for Louis would brook no competition from his brother and he made sure Monsieur never got another army to command."

Philip was shocked. He could hardly believe Louis capable of such meanness. "That was unworthy of him," he reckoned.

"Maybe, but their mother is really to blame. Throughout their father's reign their uncle Gaston caused a great deal of trouble and later, after Louis followed his father to the throne, Gaston was the leader of the 'Frondeurs', who caused the citizens of Paris to try and take him out of the care of his mother and Cardinal Mazarin. Louis was only a child at the time but the memory of the Fronde has stayed with him. That is why, to this day, he hates Paris and trusts no-one, not even the members of his own family, and it was why the Queen was determined that Monsieur and Louis should not be rivals. She treated him more like a daughter than a son and, between them, she and Louis have destroyed the man. He has become spiteful, scheming and extremely dangerous. Are you listening to me?"

Philip snuffed out their candle and smiled into the darkness. "Don't I always?"

TWELVE

 ‿∽

Despite Buckingham's doleful warning, Philip presented himself cheerfully enough in Monsieur's ante-chamber the following morning. He had promised Lord Ashley that he would observe what went on all around him and he felt sure that Monsieur was the key to everything he wished to know.

Monsieur greeted Philip happily. "You look divine," he said. "Now, what were we going to do today?"

"You kindly offered to show me round the gardens, Monsieur," Philip reminded him.

"So I did, but not for too long. Fresh air is ruinous for my complexion."

Philip secretly wondered how the air could ever reach Monsieur's complexion, so thickly was the powder applied to his fine-featured face. Once outside he looked rather like a painted doll, yet he seemed content with his appearance as he glanced at his reflection in one of the tall windows along the terrace.

"Now, where shall we go?" he said.

"Anywhere you like, Monsieur. I have never seen the gardens."

"The important thing is not to see the gardens so much as to be seen *in* them," Monsieur said, "and, of course, it matters considerably who you are seen with. It goes without saying that it will do you a great deal of good to be seen with me. Likewise, it will do me no harm to be seen upon the arm of such a personable creature as yourself."

Philip took the hint and swiftly offered Monsieur his arm, as he had the previous evening.

"Since we have already established that the primary object is to be seen together we had best walk slowly," Monsieur said.

They did, down a path that separated two wide beds of lawn and led to a circular pond. Monsieur glanced about to reassure himself that they were being watched.

"There's Villeroy," he said gleefully. "He looks at you with daggers in his eyes. He's jealous. Good!"

And so the tour went on. Philip was quite aware that he was being used to rekindle fire in those admirers whom Monsieur imagined were taking him for granted, but he did not mind. If Monsieur sought to impress the Court by parading him as his newest conquest then let him, for Philip figured it could only add to his own prestige.

Monsieur introduced him to several people. There was not one about whom he had not some piece of scandal to relate after they had gone, but Philip had grown accustomed to hearing Court tittle-tattle during the years he had spent at Whitehall and he found Monsieur quite amusing. He soon forgot Buckingham's words of caution and began to relax and enjoy himself.

He was particularly pleased when they encountered Athénais de Montespan, King Louis' favourite. Philip was on familiar ground here, talking to a beautiful woman, and he made full use of his charm. He thought how much he would have liked to get to know her better, although it didn't seem very likely.

Monsieur watched them good-naturedly. "You are quite a ladies' man," he remarked when they walked on.

"I've had my share of conquests," Philip allowed modestly.

"More than your share, I'd say." Monsieur did not seem put out by that but, if anything, appeared to find it entertaining, for he began to laugh. "There will be plenty of them at the ball tonight, my dear, and all masked too. What fun! Who knows, one of them may even claim you for herself!"

"That would not do me much good, I fear, Monsieur, since I shall soon be leaving France," Philip said regretfully.

The visit was going to be all too short for him, but he knew that Buckingham was even now with King Louis, settling the business upon which he had come. Once that was completed he guessed the Duke would be anxious to go home.

Philip didn't particularly care if he never went back. He felt quite at home here and there were a good many people with whom he longed to be better acquainted. He was also very aware that it would take much longer than two or three days to discover what Lord Ashley desired to know, but there was no way he could stay. The only people he knew in Paris were de Grammont and Elizabeth, and he could hardly impose upon them for very long. Besides, without Buckingham's generosity he would need to live upon his own allowance and he guessed that would not take him too far in this fashionable society!

"Would you like to remain in France for longer, then?" Monsieur said, as though reading his thoughts.

"Very much, Monsieur, but I am somewhat dependent upon the Duke of Buckingham, so I must do as he wishes."

"Pity. Oh well, life is full of little frustrations, and believe me, dear, I know." Monsieur gave him another of his searching looks "Take me back now, there's a sweet thing. If I stay out here much longer I shall shrivel in the sun and be quite worn out before the ball tonight."

Monsieur did not seem worn out, indeed, if anything, he quickened his pace as they returned to the chateau, as though eager to be doing something else. Philip wondered if he had in some way offended him, although he could not see how.

His mind was put at rest on that score as they parted, for Monsieur kissed his own perfumed fingertips and placed them on Philip's cheek. "Until we meet again, my Lord."

Philip decided that Monsieur was an enigma, one that he would probably never understand.

There was, indeed, an abundance of beautiful ladies to be seen that night and, although it was a masked ball, most took great care to be recognisable, despite the dainty, jewelled masks which hid the upper part of their faces. Philip noted them so appreciatively that it was a little while before he realised that Monsieur was absent from the revels.

"He'll be here," Buckingham predicted. "He never misses any entertainment. Perhaps he's here already and we haven't recognised him."

"I imagine Monsieur would make sure he was unmistakeable, even in a mask" Philip said. "He probably wants to make a special entrance, and talking of entrances, just look at that."

The lady who had just appeared claimed everyone's attention, for she was attired in a dress so ornate that it put to shame that of every other woman in the room. It was made from cloth of silver and the skirt and bodice were embroidered all over with pearls. More pearls graced her white throat and dangled from her ears, whilst her dark curls were tied with dozens of tiny silver bows.

"I wonder who she is. A princess at the very least, I should imagine," Philip guessed, watching the unknown lady, who was now the centre of attention.

No-one seemed to know.

"A true Madame La Mystérieuse, but you may discover who she is." Buckingham nudged Philip, whose attention had been drawn to those around him, all busily speculating upon the identity of La Mystérieuse. "She makes for you, I think."

"The devil she does! What shall I do?"

Buckingham laughed. "Why, partner her, of course. This is a ball, after all, and you have partnered most of the ladies at Whitehall. Why should you find this unknown woman so unnerving?"

"Because she is unknown, I suppose. She could be anyone at all, but I fear you're right. It's me she wants."

Philip bowed and offered his hand to the Lady of Mystery, who accepted it with a smile. She certainly appeared to be a beauty, although her cheeks were a little too heavily rouged for Philip's liking and he noticed that her eyelashes were stiff with paint. Even so the eyes behind the velvet mask were alluring and the dainty hand that took his was as white and soft as any he had ever held.

She danced the majestic Coyrante quite superbly, but Philip had expected no less from such an elegant creature. When the difficult dance was done he tried to talk to her, but she only tossed her long, dark ringlets provocatively and blew him a kiss from behind her fan as she left him.

He managed to partner Elizabeth several times and some of the other ladies too, including the enticing Athénais. As well as being lovely, Athénais had a delightful voice and Philip felt he could listen to her forever, for her extravagancies of speech made the most ordinary topic of conversation seem fascinating.

Philip was fluent in the French language, thanks to Nanon and de Grammont, and was confident of his talents on the dance floor so he had a most pleasurable evening. He noticed that Louis himself did not dance, but only sat beside his dull, Spanish wife watching the colourful company benignly.

He was well aware of the honour that the King did Buckingham by entertaining him in such a lavish manner but, even amidst the gaiety, Philip could not forget that their visit had a serious political purpose. He was certain that Buckingham would never, knowingly, be a party to any underhanded treaty, but Philip still very much desired to discover the truth of Minette's secret correspondence with her brother. They were due to leave for England in a matter of days, however, and he had heard that Monsieur would be returning to Paris the next morning, so he feared he would have no more chance to speak with him, much less gain his confidence to the degree that he might obtain any information from him.

Philip was so absorbed in his thoughts that he had not noticed Madame la Mystérieuse heading his way again. He had seen her cast many looks in his direction during the evening, although she had partnered a few others.

As before he offered her his hand and, as before, she partnered him superbly, only this time she did not let go of him at the finish of the dance.

The clocks were striking midnight, the hour when all must be unmasked, and several gentlemen stepped forward, hoping for the honour, but La Mystérieuse shook her head at them and pulled Philip closer.

Then, in front of everyone, she kissed him full upon the mouth.

It was a passionate kiss. Philip, though taken aback, found himself instinctively responding.

The other dancers cheered and Philip, who was growing a little tired of the whole thing now, decided he had better do what was expected of him and get the matter over with.

As he went behind her to untie her mask he caught sight of Buckingham, laughing with the rest, but then, as he removed it, he saw the Duke's expression change. When his partner turned and he saw who he had unmasked Philip realised why.

It was Monsieur.

Philip felt his cheeks grow hot when he heard the laughter all around him and recalled who he had just kissed.

Monsieur himself was giggling like a schoolgirl. "My Lord, I trust that I have given you no offence. After all, you do like the ladies, do you not?"

Philip did not reply. Indeed, he was incapable of forming any civil answer, and the mocking laughter of the Marquis de Villeroy made matters worse.

He turned abruptly and left the room without a word.

"It will not do, my Lord Buckingham, it will not do at all," Louis said quietly. "No matter what idiocy my brother has been at, Lord Devalle may not snub him in this manner. He will need a full apology and, since the slight was made in public, so must the apology be made."

"I'll speak to Philip, your Majesty," Buckingham promised, "but knowing him as I do, I think it most unlikely that he will comply."

"Then you must make him, my Lord. Use every means at your disposal," Louis advised him. "I can make no treaty with a man whose consort has openly insulted my own brother at Court."

The room, meanwhile, was in an uproar. Monsieur burst into tears and all efforts to console him were in vain. The dancers were no longer interested in dancing but stood in groups discussing the unprecedented situation. Most were of a like mind to the King but there were some, Elizabeth and Athénais amongst them, who felt that Philip had been badly used and that, under the circumstances, he had behaved quite understandably.

∽

"No!" Philip said as Buckingham explained what was required of him. "Apologise when I am the injured party? Never!"

"But he is Monsieur."

"I don't care if he's God, I'll not apologise."

"Oh, that's just wonderful! Only this morning Louis presented me with a jewelled sword and a mistress for Charles," Buckingham told him. "Now we are disgraced."

"What mistress has he given Charles?" Philip asked swiftly, his suspicions immediately aroused.

"Why, Louise de Quéroualle, the little Brêton girl who came to London with Minette. Charles took a fancy to her and King Louis requested that we take her back to England with us. What happened tonight could jeopardise that as well as my mission here."

"And a good thing that might be if part of your job is to place a Catholic agent in Whitehall," Philip retorted.

"But failure will bring shame upon me, Philip. Is that what you want?"

"You're being quite unfair," Philip protested. "You know I'm in the right. He tried to make a fool of me and no-one does that, not even Monsieur."

"Hell! How was he to know you're such a humourless bastard? He thought you'd take it as a jest."

"A jest? Dammit, George, he *kissed* me!"

"The problem, I suspect, is not that he kissed you but rather that you enjoyed it when you thought he was a woman!"

Philip had no intention of admitting that, not even to Buckingham, but it was the truth and the mere thought of it made him hot with shame. "He is a stupid man," he muttered.

"And you're a stubborn one. I warned you not to get involved with him but you took no more notice of me than you ever do. Now you must humble your great pride and win back his friendship or you're finished here, and so am I."

"If he desires my friendship then he must apologise to me and not the other way about," Philip said obstinately.

"In the name of heaven, is that what I'm to tell Louis?" Buckingham demanded.

"Tell him what you please."

If they had been at home one or the other of them would probably have stormed out of the room, but here they were trapped in the same tiny space with nowhere to go, so they both had to be content with remaining resolutely silent and Philip was determined that he was not going to be the one who spoke first.

"Monsieur was most distressed that you were offended with him," Buckingham said after a few minutes.

"I doubt that."

"No, really. He was led away in tears from the dance floor and apparently refuses to see anyone but you."

Philip considered the situation. He truly did feel a little sorry for Buckingham in his predicament, for those of his enemies who had criticised his appointment for such an important diplomatic mission would delight in his failure. Philip also had not forgotten that he had his own mission to fulfil. Perhaps if he was clever he could still turn matters to his own advantage.

"Very well," he said, with sudden decision. "To please you I will go to see Monsieur, but I am damned if I'll apologise, in public or in private."

Monsieur's valet de chambre admitted him right away, looking relieved to see him. He ushered Philip into Monsieur's bedroom and withdrew rapidly.

Monsieur's costume was strewn over the floor, thrown there in a fit of pique, Philip guessed as he stepped over the fabulous, pearl-encrusted bodice he had so admired.

Monsieur himself was spread across his bed, still wearing his stays. He was sobbing loudly, though Philip suspected that the sobs grew louder when he realised who was there.

Philip stood still for a moment, not knowing quite what he should do. He decided that, since Monsieur liked to play the woman, perhaps he would enjoy being treated as one.

He recalled how he had used to act when Barbara had thrown a tantrum and, heaving a sigh, he slapped Monsieur firmly on the rump.

"Come, enough of that. You'll make your face swell and your eyes red, and then the world will think you're ugly."

"What do I care what the world thinks?" Monsieur dabbed his eyes nonetheless and reached for a dainty little vinaigrette, from which he inhaled deeply. "Excuse me, but I fear that I might faint, so gravely has this affair upset me. You are not at all the charming man that I took you to be, my Lord. You abandoned me tonight in front of everyone."

"You made a laughing stock of me," Philip reminded him. "I find it dashed hard to be charming whilst I am being ridiculed by you in front of the Court."

Monsieur sniffed. "It was nothing but a harmless little prank."

"I don't like pranks. According to the Duke of Buckingham I am a humourless bastard!'"

"Well how was I to know that? I thought you liked me."

In fact, Philip did like him, although he was not sure why! "I do, Monsieur. Here, have this." He took out his handkerchief and passed it to Monsieur, whose own was damp with tears.

"And have you come to beg my forgiveness?"

"No," Philip said firmly, "but to console you if I can."

Monsieur reached to take a crystallized fruit from a silver tray, for food was his biggest consolation after any upset. He offered one to Philip, who declined. "Don't you think I make a handsome woman?" Monsieur asked him.

"I think you are handsomer as a man, without all this." Philip indicated the beribboned ringlets, which were not part of wig but made from Monsieur's own hair.

Monsieur attempted to tug the ribbons out but they only adhered to his fingers, which were sticky from the fruit.

"I'll do it," Philip said heavily, thinking that he had never been in such a ludicrous situation in all his life.

Monsieur licked the sugar from his fingers. "Ouch! There is no need to be so rough with me!"

"Your pardon, Monsieur, but I am not trained as a manservant," Philip pointed out sarcastically. "Perhaps if I were to call your valet?"

"No, no," Monsieur said hastily. "You're doing very well. I could grow quite used to having you around."

"But I don't laugh at your jokes, Monsieur," Philip said, a little absently, for he was studying the many crystal jars and silver pots on Monsieur's dressing table. "What do you keep in those?"

"I'll show you." Monsieur obligingly opened up the dainty containers to reveal his rouge, his carmine, his perfume and all the other substances he evidently deemed essential to his looks. "Try some if you like."

Philip disdained the paint and powder for, although he was fair, he had good pigment in his skin and he felt his looks could not be bettered by such aids, but he was tempted by a jar of perfumed oil.

"If you had worn that at the ball I would have recognised you," he said, for the oil had that distinctive odour he had already come to associate with Monsieur.

"Quite." Monsieur cast a sidelong glance in his direction. "I put that in my hair," he explained. "It makes it shine and keeps my curls in place. Sometimes, if I look a little fat, I have my servant massage me with it as well. You don't think I am too fat, do you?" he said anxiously, but Philip did not answer. He was totally absorbed in applying the sweetly-scented oil to his own blonde curls.

Monsieur pinched him on the arm. "I said am I too fat."

Philip looked away from the mirror and regarded him. "I can't really tell. You're wearing stays."

Suddenly the absurdness of the situation struck him and, in spite of himself, he began to laugh.

Monsieur looked relieved. "You are no longer angry with me," he guessed. "That's good, for you must know that I never meant to upset you."

"But why did you do all this tonight?" Philip asked, helping him out of his stays and passing him his dressing gown. "I can't believe it was totally for my benefit."

"It wasn't," Monsieur confessed. "I like to dress up as a woman. I often do so, here in my apartments. There's nothing wrong with that, is there?" he asked anxiously as Philip raised an eyebrow.

"I suppose not, if it gives you pleasure."

"My mother used to make me do it all the time. She bought me lots of pretty dresses. I had a friend, Francis de Choisy, and when we played together our mothers said we must pretend that we were girls. I grew to like it."

Philip recalled what Buckingham had told him about Monsieur's mother but, whatever her motives, it seemed incredible to him that any woman, even a queen, would go to such lengths to emasculate her son.

Any disgust he might have felt for Monsieur drained away, replaced by pity for a man who had never truly had the chance to be a man. Now that he realised the incident had not been planned as a spiteful act against himself, Philip could find it in his heart to feel remorse for the way he had treated Monsieur in front of everyone. Under those circumstances he decided that an apology might not be so hard to make.

"Monsieur, I am sincerely sorry for what I did. I trust it will not lose me your most gracious favour."

"Not at all." Monsieur kissed him on both cheeks but not, this time, nor ever again, upon the lips. "In fact, I think we two could become good friends. I am tired of all I have."

"You may grow tired of me too," Philip warned, "for whilst I would be most honoured to be counted as your friend you may as well know now that I will not be anything more."

Monsieur shrugged. "Oh well, it's better than nothing. But you must still apologise to me before the Court."

Philip shook his head. "I shall not do that, but I will make amends to you in some other way, if I can."

"What way?"

"Any way you like," Philip promised rashly.

"You must pay a forfeit, that's what you must do." Monsieur danced around the room, happy at the prospect. "This is it - for every minute that you made me wait for your apology you must spend one day with me. Do you agree?"

Actually, nothing could have suited Philip's purposes better. "Since you are the one imposing the forfeit it is not for me to agree or disagree," he said, "but I am supposed to be returning to England in a few days with the Duke of Buckingham."

"He can go without you." Monsieur turned to an ornate little clock adorned with four golden monkeys, one perched upon each of its four corners. "By this clock I waited one hour and forty minutes before you came to me, therefore you must stay one hundred days - let us say four months, one for each of these little monkeys."

Philip smiled. He could scarcely believe his luck. "Whatever you say, Monsieur."

Monsieur clapped his hands in glee. "That's settled then. You will travel to Paris with me in the morning." He treated Philip to an impulsive little hug. "Oh, I'm so happy I could cry!"

Buckingham was less happy when Philip told him of the arrangement.

"You can't stay here with him. You know what he's like."

"I ought to humour him. After all the outcome of your mission is at stake," Philip reminded him wickedly.

Buckingham snorted. "As if that mattered to you at all."

"But you distinctly said that I must win back his friendship."

"Win back his friendship, yes. Not become his companion."

Philip laughed. "Why, George, I do believe you're jealous!"

"Not at all," Buckingham, said crossly, but Philip suspected that he was, a little, for he knew that the Duke was proud of him and delighted in showing him off as his protégé. "I simply wonder why you choose this moment, of all those in your life, to be compliant."

"Because it suits me," Philip confessed. "I don't know why you're making such a fuss. It's only for four months. You can surely spare me for that long."

"You might as well say four years," Buckingham said sadly. "I fear when you return you will be so changed by Monsieur that I shall scarcely recognise you."

THIRTEEN

Philip made an elaborate bow and struck a pose, one hand upon his hip, the other resting upon a silver-headed cane.

"I am delighted to find you in such happy circumstances, my Lord Shaftesbury, as I now must call you."

Ashley had been created Earl of Shaftesbury whilst Philip had been away and he had finally been appointed to the position he had coveted, that of Lord Chancellor. He owed much of his good fortune to Philip.

"And I am delighted to find you in such fine spirits, Lord Devalle. As I recall you were a little disillusioned when last we met."

It had been some time ago, for Philip had stayed a good deal longer than the four months originally agreed with Monsieur, a year longer in fact. He had absorbed a great many influences from the French Court, and particularly from Monsieur. He had even begun to darken his long eyelashes and to heighten his colour with a touch of rouge. His blonde curls were perfumed and from his ears dangled diamond earrings, a parting present from Monsieur.

Philip clothes, too, were unmistakeably French. He wore an embroidered scarlet waistcoat and a white brocade coat, which was edged with a dazzling amount of silver lace and had a scarlet bow upon the right shoulder.

"You are a most impressive sight," Shaftesbury said.

"I thought I always was! I gather you were able to make good use of the letters I obtained for you."

"Most certainly, although I don't know how you managed to get them."

"It was fairly easy actually. Monsieur is quite besotted with me."

Shaftesbury nodded. "Yes, I know of Monsieur's weakness for good-looking men. Did you have to bed him for them?"

"Indeed not! I do have some principles."

"Precious few, from what I've heard. Tales of your exploits with the ladies of Paris have reached us across the channel! What does surprise me is that Monsieur would allow anyone, even a favourite, access to the private correspondence between his late wife and his brother-in-law."

Philip laughed. "It was case of mere necessity, my Lord. Monsieur wished to know what secrets Minette was keeping from him and, since he understands no English, he required a translator who he thought would be discreet. He read the letters out to me and I explained them to him, or at least as much of them as I thought he should know. Unbeknown to him, I retained the two which I dispatched to you, which were those I deemed of most significance."

"You did me a great service. Those letters proved what I had suspected, that the treaty Buckingham negotiated with King Louis was entirely worthless."

"Yet you signed it," Philip pointed out.

"Most certainly I signed it. There were great rewards to be had from pretending first to be duped and then aggrieved. I did not, of course, disclose the source of my information but Charles' conscience was so heavy that he did not trouble me for my proof. He well knew how dishonourably he had been in acting without consulting all of his ministers. He also knew that if he wanted my cooperation after I had discovered him then he would need to offer me both an earldom and the chancellorship."

"It is evident to me that to advance oneself in politics the prime requisite is a mind more devious than that of one's opponents," Philip said.

"Quite right, but the matter is far from over. When William of Orange paid a visit here last Winter he was well received by his Uncle Charles and by the people, yet the King mortgages the country to the hilt in order to raise money to fight with the French against the Dutch. Your guess is as good as mine as to which way this wind will blow, but the bellows may rest in the muddling hands of York."

The Duke of York had lost his wife the previous year and Philip had heard that he was looking for a successor. "If he should choose a Catholic for a wife, that would serve your purpose very well," he guessed.

"It would indeed, and it would make him almost as unpopular as the Brêton bitch that Buckingham brought back from France. Just as you feared she is now firmly established as Charles' mistress. What do you propose to do now, my Lord?" Shaftesbury asked him.

"I have decided to follow a suggestion you yourself once made. I'm going to join the French Army and fight the Dutch."

"Do you go with Monmouth to join Turenne?"

"No. I would like the chance to win some glory for myself, and I shall not do that whilst I am in the Duke of Monmouth's shadow," Philip said. "Through Monsieur's influence I have been offered a commission as a captain under Condé. I am home only to settle my affairs and see my father, for I need a considerable amount of money to equip myself for war. I bade him visit me today, since I refuse to go to Heatherton, and directly I have obtained the sum I require I shall depart again for France."

"Will he give you what you need, do you think?"

"I should hope so, since it is the first time I have troubled him for anything save my allowance in eight years," Philip retorted. "Besides, after all the years he let me suffer my brother's spite, he owes me this, and well he knows it."

"You may not always be able to rely upon a father's guilt to pay your way," Shaftesbury said. "Neither will you ever make your fortune fighting wars, as I'm sure you know. There may come a time when you need to consider other ways to make your living."

"And what do you suggest, my Lord?"

"Work for me," Shaftesbury said. "If you became my agent I would pay you handsomely. We made a bad beginning, you and I, but you have well redeemed yourself in my eyes and I would welcome the opportunity to redeem myself in yours. Until I can do that I shall consider myself to be in your debt."

Philip was surprised. He had not expected Shaftesbury to allude to the incident in Drury Lane so long ago. He had practically erased it from his memory, for he had found himself gradually falling deeper and deeper under the Earl's spell. Shaftesbury had great charm and a confidence about him which commanded respect. Philip certainly did not attribute only virtuous motives to his actions, but he could see some good in him now where previously he had seen none.

He took the hand which Shaftesbury offered him. "I count myself honoured to have as my debtor a person of your rank and standing in the world, Lord Shaftesbury," he said. "I hope that we shall meet again before too many years have passed."

"I hope so to. In the meantime, I shall follow your career with interest, Philip Devalle. A very great amount of interest."

Philip was staying at Buckingham's house and when he arrived back he found that the Duke had company, a tall and rather handsome man whom Buckingham introduced as Colonel John Scott.

"The Colonel owns extensive property in the Americas," Buckingham explained. "He has come to show me a map of it, for I have a mind to invest some money in the Colonies."

Philip went over to the fireplace and leaned upon the mantelshelf, a favourite attitude of his, taking in every detail of the stranger who spoke so earnestly to Buckingham. He had an easy and confiding manner, like one who made his living by his wits. His clothes were of good quality, but by no means new. The lace around his cuffs was frayed and his velvet coat had been carefully mended. Philip deduced from this that Scott periodically came into large sums of money, which he probably spent upon his pleasures and his person, and then suffered long periods of poverty. All in all, he could believe their visitor was an adventurer but not that he was a military man, especially not one with such an elevated rank as that of a colonel.

"In what regiment do you serve, Colonel Scott?" he asked him, during a lull in the conversation.

Scott coughed. "I am not, at present, serving his Majesty in a military capacity, my Lord. The Duke of York relieved me of my command in New York."

"And why would he do that?"

"Why, for no better reason than that he dislikes me, just as your dear friend the Duke here has suffered on account of York's spite."

"That I have, as Philip well knows," Buckingham said. "Not only did he make it impossible for me to be a part of the glorious fleet that did battle at Southwold Bay against the Dutch last year but he also refused me the command of land forces. This was after I had been honoured by the King of France to such a degree that he pronounced me the only true English gentleman he had ever met and presented me with a sword set with so many pearls and diamonds that it has been valued at no less than forty thousand pistoles!"

"It is plain that York is jealous of your Grace," Scott said sympathetically. "He could not bear to think you might eclipse him with your courage as well as with the magnificence of your person."

Philip remained very quiet, although he knew that Buckingham actually had been offered a command of land forces at Blackheath the previous year but had quit them after he found the military life more tedious than he remembered!

"I will be plain, Colonel Scott, there are those who seek to do me harm," Buckingham said, "who even take away the simple pleasures that bring a man his peace of mind. Prince Rupert is permitted to wed Mrs. Hughes yet I am forced to send Lady Shrewsbury from this house, and by a sovereign who, in one year, has given a child each to Louise de Quéroualle, Moll Davis and Nell Gwynne. Two actresses and a French whore! A sovereign, moreover, who let go free a thief who tried to steal the Crown jewels, because he said he could admire the courage of the villain! I ask you, is there any wonder that one loses faith in England and turns one's eyes towards the Colonies?"

"None at all," Scott agreed. "Are you interested in the Colonies, my Lord?" he asked Philip.

"Not in the least."

"There are fortunes to be made there," Scott assured him.

Philip thought he would have a little fun, He drew out a scented handkerchief and waved it before his face in a glorious imitation of Monsieur. "For the clever one's perhaps. Myself, I am an empty-headed thing. I confess that if I have the latest fashion to wear and the latest step to dance then I am well-contented with the world!"

Buckingham smiled to see him play the part of a giddy fop. It was an act that would have fooled no-one who knew him, but Scott did not know him.

"Still, my Lord, perhaps you would like to see a sample of my work?" Scott suggested cunningly, showing him the finely drawn map, fringed in blue silk.

Philip gave it a cursory glance. "Very pretty. Where is it supposed to be?"

"Why, the Americas, my Lord."

"Really?" Philip made a fluttery gesture with his hand, another of Monsieur's affectations. "I know very little of geography. I was expelled from school, you know."

"You were?" Scott looked at him disbelievingly, then glanced at Buckingham, who was having difficulty keeping a straight face.

"He's telling you the truth," he assured Scott.

Philip shrugged. "Would the ladies swoon for me in greater numbers if I were a scholar, Colonel? Could it make me handsomer or more modish?" He studied himself in a mirror, winking at Buckingham as he did so. "I believe that I have all the talents any man needs."

"Indeed you have, my Lord." Scott packed up his maps and made ready to depart. "I shall look forward to making your better acquaintance at some future time."

"You are a devil, Philip," Buckingham chided him when they were alone. "Why did you assume those airs with him?"

"He is a trickster, you can surely see that. I think I may have intrigued him sufficiently for him to try to gull me and I would like to see how he attempts it, that's all."

"He's no trickster," Buckingham argued. "He is a rich man, who travels for pleasure. He was introduced to me by Lord Sandwich."

Lord Sandwich, who was a cousin of Samuel Pepys, was an expert seaman but not the most astute man Philip had ever met.

"Very well, have it your own way, George. I still say he is trying to swindle you and has probably swindled Sandwich already."

"It is time you set your mind to such things as investments for the future," Buckingham said seriously. "You are monstrously extravagant with your money. Why, that French outfit must have cost you the equivalent of twenty pounds."

"A little more, in fact, but it becomes me, does it not?"

"You know well it does, but what has that to do with it? You are a wastrel, Philip. Every penny that you do not lose in gambling you spend on your appearance."

Philip laughed. "Don't you lecture me. My father will be calling here within the hour and I'm certain he will lecture me enough. You spend your money in the Colonies and I will put mine upon my back. At least when it is there I know exactly where it is, and that it is being displayed to best advantage!"

꒰Ꙭ꒱

If Philip's friends had seen a difference in him in just over a year then his father would have seen a far greater one in all the years since they had last seen each other.

He looked at Philip with a shocked expression. "So this is what life at Court has done to you," he said, shaking his head sadly. "You have changed beyond measure."

"I am likely to have changed. I was a child when you last saw me." Philip had entertained precious little respect for his father in the past but he had even less now that he himself was a man.

"I would have liked to see you, but it is difficult for me to leave your brother and I have no desire to come to Court. Since coming here today I have heard stories which only confirm my opinion that Whitehall has become a place of wickedness, where men's weaknesses are upheld as virtues and their crimes condoned. I was even told that your patron lived in this very house with Lady Shrewsbury, and that he actually buried their illegitimate child in Westminster Abbey with full honours, just as though it was his proper heir."

"I will hear nothing spoken against Buckingham, by you or anyone," Philip warned.

"Then what about your friend, the Duke of Monmouth? Is it true that he attacked Sir John Coventry and slit his nose to the bone?"

"Coventry made a disparaging remark about the King," Philip said, for he was not about to be disloyal to Monmouth either.

"From what I hear he did no more than allude to his Majesty's disgraceful fondness for the women of the stage, which brings me to a point concerning yourself. Is it true that one of the actresses is a friend of yours and that you helped her to become the King's mistress?"

"That's true enough," Philip admitted. "Who's been telling you all this anyway?"

"Lord Arlington. He's deeply shocked by what goes on around him."

Philip laughed. "Arlington? Did he also tell you that it was in his house Charles first bedded Louise de Quéroualle? The man's a hypocrite! Besides, he's recently argued with Buckingham so you will hear no good of the Duke from him."

"I hear no good of anyone, particularly those you count amongst your friends," his father said. "Buckingham, Monmouth, that despicable conniver Shaftesbury - not a worthy man amongst them."

"Always disapproving," Philip said irritably.

"What can you expect when you associate with such people?"

"Buckingham, the first lord in the land? Monmouth, the King's son? Shaftesbury, the Lord Chancellor? Certainly, these people are quite unworthy of the friendship of an earl's son," Philip returned sarcastically.

"Our family is one of which you should be proud, for the Devalles have earned the respect of those and better men."

"So well are the Devalles respected that, although I spent a year or more in France, my mother's family never once invited me to visit with them."

"The Pasquiers never did approve of our marriage," Philip's father admitted.

"Nor can I truly blame them. It is unlikely I would approve of any of my children marrying into a line of madmen."

"You have children?"

"I am told so, but you need not worry for they are by different mothers and so well-placed they have no need of my support."

The Earl shuddered. "This grows worse. You are as bad as all the rest, worse, probably, for I heard today that you were living with Monsieur whilst you were in France. Is there no limit to your immorality?"

"I did not invite you here discuss my morals, or my relationship with Monsieur, Philip said firmly.

"You did not invite me here at all. You summoned me."

"I felt that such a step was necessary since you had never once taken the trouble to visit me."

"You were always welcome to come home to Heatherton," his father pointed out.

Philip laughed harshly. "Home? You call that place my home? Where a maniac stalks me with a lash? Do you need to see my scars to be reminded of how happy I was at High Heatherton?"

"Perhaps things might be better between you now."

"They will never be better. Henry is incurable. There are inmates in Bedlam who are saner than my brother. Are you still not prepared to commit him into care?"

"I can't do it, Philip, not even for you, but your brother has much improved. He's even helping to manage the estate."

"It's only right that he should since, as he constantly reminded me, it will be his one day not mine," Philip said pointedly.

"Is it my fault you are not my elder son?" the Earl cried. "Do you not think I have wished many times it could be so. But he is my heir and I'll not take from him what is lawfully his. Besides, he needs High Heatherton far more than you. You can make your own way in this world whilst he cannot, for you have looks, intelligence and grace."

"Unfortunately, what I lack is education."

"Is that to be blamed upon me too? Did I not enrol you at a good school?"

"Yes, you did, but too late, oh, far too late. I should have had a proper tutor when I was a child, and well you know it. I would have had one too, but for your precious Henry, who threatened them all with violence," Philip said passionately. "It is through his insanity and your neglect that I went to school a total ignoramus, bettered by the sons of clerks and merchants. Is that fitting for the youngest of the noble Devalle line of which you speak?"

"Have you no compassion for your brother or for me?"

Philip's father reached out and touched his arm but Philip shook him off. He had never loved his father and saw no point in pretending. "I asked you here because I need some money to equip myself for war," Philip told him. "I have to purchase my commission and a good horse, and then there will be my uniform and sundry other articles. I think a thousand pounds should cover it."

"A thousand?" The Earl looked taken aback. "That is a considerable sum of money."

"Is it? Buckingham loses that much on the turn of a card and wins it back threefold the next day. Of course, I could always ask him for the money instead but I hardly like to, not when he has been so good to me already."

"That won't be necessary. We must not trouble the Duke any further on your account, for I expect you have been trouble enough to him already. I have the money available here in town and you can have it in a few days, if that is what you want."

Philip made him a formal bow. "I thank you for your generosity, my Lord. I shall attempt to be a credit to you on the battlefield and to uphold my family's name with honour."

It seemed pointless to prolong the meeting. Neither of them had ever enjoyed each other's company and they had never been able to hold a proper conversation.

"Take care, Philip," the Earl said awkwardly as he prepared to take his leave. "I would not wish to hear that anything had befallen you. No matter what you may believe, I love you and I always have."

"I will endeavour to remember that," Philip said stiffly, and showed him to the door.

Nell looked shocked when Philip related the meeting to her later. "How could you be so unfeeling towards him, your own father?" she said. "I never knew mine but I am certain if I had I could have been more affectionate, particularly if he had just agreed to give me a thousand pounds!"

"Perhaps you could but I could not. Don't try to understand, Nell, for you can't unless you have lived my life."

"But I do understand, far better than you think. It's not just for the scars upon your back that you hate your father, terrible though they are. It is because to him you will always be the second son, and you can never tolerate being second best," Nell guessed, sagely as it happened. "Well? Can you? You must always be the favourite, is that not so?"

Philip did not often hear such a shrewd assessment of himself, though that was not to say he would admit it to be true!

"What nonsense! With you I am second best to the King, and I don't mind a bit."

"Different. Altogether different," she said, "for you had the chance of me first. Why, it was you who pushed me into Charles' arms."

He smiled. "Aren't you glad I did?"

"I certainly am. I have this beautiful house in Pall Mall and two magnificent royal bastard sons! Not a bad achievement for a low-born slut!"

"And do you love the King?"

"I do. He is kind and tender to me. How could I do other than love him, and I will for all my days. You should fall in love," she said. "It would be good for you."

"I haven't time. I'm off to fight a war, remember?"

"I hope," her voice faltered for a moment, "that you'll be coming back."

"I won't be killed in battle, if that is what you mean," he reassured her. "Athénais de Montespan insisted that I went with her to see a fortune-teller whilst I was in France."

Nell's eyes opened wide. "What was he like?

"It was a woman, Mademoiselle Monvoisin. She wore a crimson velvet robe, embroidered with gold, two-headed eagles, and she chanted words I did not understand at all, though her predictions were clear enough."

"What did she tell you? Was it exciting?"

Philip smiled wryly. "Not a bit. When she looked into her device, which she claimed enables her to see into the future, she predicted I would suffer many misfortunes and that I will be constantly searching throughout my life but will never find what I seek."

"How curious!"

"The rest is worse. Whilst I am, apparently, going to rise to great heights I shall end my days in prison."

Nell clutched his hand. "In prison? But that's dreadful. It can't be true!"

"I trust it will be a few years before you discover whether it is or not, but Athénais thinks very highly of La Voisin, that is what they call the woman, and it is said half of Paris comes to her for love potions and the like, as well as for predictions. They are a superstitious bunch, the French, for all their outward show of religion."

"You are superstitious too, I fancy. You pretend, for my sake, not to heed this woman but I can see it troubles you. Oh, Philip I can't bear to think about your death, especially not in gaol."

"Probably a debtor's prison! Buckingham has often predicted that my gambling and extravagance will land me there. Come now," he added gently, seeing that she had turned her face away. "Don't worry about me, you silly girl."

"You are my very dearest friend."

"A fine friend to upset you so!" He held her close to him. "I am a thoughtless bastard, aren't I?" She felt warm and comfortable in his arms. Philip's feelings for Nell had not changed since the day he had helped her flee the Plague, and they never would. "Are you completely happy with your life, Nell?"

"Completely."

"How I envy you, my pet."

No matter how Philip's own feelings had changed towards Charles, he would never say a word against him in front of Nell. Charles had been good to her and she was happy, and Philip would not have spoiled that for all the world.

⁓

The landlord of the Horseshoe Tavern turned his back on Colonel Scott.

"Credit? Man, you must think me a fool. You've owed me twenty pounds these last three weeks and now you have the gall to come to me for credit?"

"Call it an investment," Scott said. "I have a gentleman that I must entertain this afternoon."

"A victim, don't you mean?" The landlord knew Scott's line of work.

"That's right, and what a victim. A mincing fop, son of an earl and pampered by the Duke of Buckingham; a fashionable young blade, just returned from France, who can think of nothing save his clothes and his handsome face. He's ready to be plucked, I tell you, and with your help I can be the one to pluck him. All I ask is credit for a bottle of wine whilst I work upon him."

"I know your skill at taking money from the unsuspecting, but I'm still loath to throw good money after bad."

"Just think, a week from now my debt to you might be repaid in full," Scott reminded him.

"And it might not. I've heard Big Jack Tate is chasing you."

Scott shuddered, for he was not a brave man. "That's the truth. I'd leave the country if I had the money. This coxcomb would be the end to all my worries."

"You are very sure of him, but what if he suspects you and is handy with a sword. Fat chance I'd have then of getting my money."

Scott laughed. "Him? He looks as though he has not the strength to lift a weapon, much less the energy to use it. Quickly, I've just seen a carriage stop outside and I must have your answer. Shall you give me credit, for he has to think me a substantial man."

The landlord sighed. "I'll probably regret it, but you have your credit, Colonel, for one hour only. Use it well."

"Don't worry, I will." Scott said, watching Philip step down from the vehicle. "If I could persuade the Governor of Barbados to part with a fortune I am certain I can fleece this pretty, golden lamb!"

Philip guessed that Scott would be watching out for him so he deliberately paused to admire his own reflection in the carriage window. "Ah Colonel," he said, as he entered the tavern. "I received your message, as you see, although I am curious as to why you sent it."

"Why, my Lord, to do you a great service." Scott escorted him to an empty table in a corner.

"And why should you wish to do me any service, sir? I scarcely know you."

"But upon our previous meeting, brief as it was, I recognised you as a shrewd man." Scott said knowingly. "A man with whom I could do business, but first allow me to offer you some refreshment." Scott snapped his fingers and a wench appeared swiftly. "A bottle of the landlord's finest claret, Mary, that which he keeps in reserve for me. Well go on, girl, what are you gawping at?"

Mary was staring at Philip, who winked at her. "That's Lord Devalle!"

"Well? What of it?"

"You never told me he was friend of yours," she whispered.

"I have many influential friends," Scott told her airily. "Go and see to our needs."

Mary nodded and backed away but kept her eyes on Philip as long as she could.

"I do apologise, my Lord. She is a simple and ill-mannered girl," Scott said.

"Don't let it trouble you. I'm used to it. Now, what is this service that you are so anxious to perform for me?"

"Ask rather what wondrous opportunity do I place in your grasp." Scott took from his pocket a piece of paper, carefully rolled, and spread it on the table. "And here it is."

"Well?" Philip asked. "What is it?"

"An investment in the Colonies, my Lord, and your chance to make a fortune." He paused as the landlord brought the claret and set the bottle down between them, looking curiously at Philip as he did so. Scott frowned. "Does everyone know you?" he said suspiciously.

Philip only smiled and begged him to continue. Scott produced another piece of paper. This one he claimed to be conclusive proof that he owned the land.

Philip passed it back to him. "I take your word that it confirms what you have said."

"You do?" Scott looked pleased. "And are you interested in the investment which I offer you?"

"I am more interested in the four men who have just entered this establishment and are watching you with most determined expressions," Philip said quietly, inclining his head in the direction of the door.

"God in heaven, I am done for!" Scott had turned quite white. "Your pardon, Lord Devalle. I must leave you now."

"You'll never make it through the door, so you might as well stay where you are and keep your dignity," Philip said.

"Right now my dignity is less important than my life." Scott looked around him frantically.

"Is it as serious as that? What have you done to them?" Philip asked him.

"I cheated them," Scott admitted.

"Well of course you did," Philip said heavily. "Not with Long Island land, surely?"

Scott swallowed. He obviously realised that the game was up for certain now, and the four men were purposefully approaching him. "No, my Lord. With another trick."

"What trick?"

Scott had risen to his feet, although he had no escape. "Does it matter?"

"It matters if I am to help you save your worthless skin. Sit down, man, and I want the truth, if you still know how to tell it."

Scott looked at him and then back to his advancing enemies. "I sold them a secret scientific process that I claimed turned copper into silver, but it was a fake. I thought to be gone from London before they had discovered it. Now will you help me out of this? I shall be ever in your debt."

"Much good that will do me, I should think," Philip muttered. "Sit tight, and do not make a move until I tell you."

"Well, if it ain't Colonel Scott," snarled the biggest of the four men who now surrounded them. "He who cheated us out of seventy pounds."

Philip raised an eyebrow. "Seventy? My, but you're a greedy man, Scott."

Big Jack sneered. "Who's this perfumed popinjay? Your bodyguard?"

"Something like that." Philip seized the bottle from the table and, in one movement, smacked it down upon the nearest fellow's head. He dropped, unconscious, to the ground. Philip nodded toward the table and together he and Scott heaved the heavy piece of oak at their assailants, trapping two of them beneath it.

"Keep them there." Philip took a swing at Big Jack, who had been caught completely off guard. It seemed he had not expected the cowardly Scott and the 'popinjay' to make a fight of it.

It was a good blow and well placed, but Big Jack did not even stagger. Philip pulled a face and, after a quick glance behind him, retreated slowly towards the wall.

Scott had added his own weight to that of the table so that those pinned beneath it were powerless to assist, but he winced as he saw Big Jack aim a blow at Philip's head.

Philip dodged the huge fist easily and reached the wall. Just above him was fixed an iron sconce. Because it was a dark day the candles were already lit. He pulled them out and hurled them straight into Big Jack's face.

Big Jack cursed and hurtled towards him in a rage but the candles had given Philip the vital seconds that he needed. Leaping up he grasped the sconce and brought his feet up sharply, aiming them at Jack's advancing chin.

There was a sickening crack as Philip's boots collided with the bone, then Big Jack staggered back, dazed, clutching at his broken jaw. Philip and Scott watched in fascination as he wheeled about, as though to aim another punch, before falling headlong, knocked off balance by his own action, to land at Philip's feet.

"Now for these two." Philip helped Scott lift the table, but the pair wedged underneath it had evidently seen enough. They scrambled up and ran out into the street as fast as they were able.

"Shall we go after them?" Scott said.

"For God's sake!" Philip cried. "Five minutes ago you were near paralysed with fright. Now, suddenly, you've found the courage of a lion!"

"Five minutes ago I had no notion of how formidable you were," Scott said admiringly.

"Now you know the reason I was expelled from school! Would you mind if we left this establishment before these other two recover consciousness? My carriage waits outside."

Scott followed him, although Philip knew that he must have had no hope now of selling him Long Island land or anything else.

"You are a scoundrel, John Scott," he said to him, before getting into the coach.

Scott looked at him sheepishly. "I don't know what to say, my Lord."

Philip carefully flicked the dust from his velvet coat. "I'll warrant that is not a situation with which you are familiar! You've a glib tongue and an easy manner, and good looks as well. You would be better off using your talents on rich widows!"

"Oh, I do," Scott told him brightly. "I do best of all with them and with…rich, young gentleman of fashion."

Philip smiled at that. "You should choose your victims with more care. I'm not even rich."

"That is not the only mistake I made concerning you," Scott admitted. "With all your airs I took you to be no more than a peacock."

"Just a trick or two I picked up from Monsieur in France! You really didn't find out half enough about me, did you?"

"No, but I would like to find out more," Scott said. "Would you allow me to take you to some other inn? It is the very least that I can do."

"It is indeed," Philip agreed, "but you will understand, I'm sure, if I decline to remain in a public place with a person whose acquaintances are likely to appear at any time to finish him off!"

Scott nodded dejectedly. Philip guessed it was only a matter of time before Big Jack caught up with him again and he was no nearer to improving his finances now than he had been before. In fact, if anything, he was probably further away, for he now owed the landlord of the Horseshoe for a bottle of claret!

He watched Scott with amusement, for he thought he had rarely seen the mettle drain so quickly from a man. "You're in a lot of trouble, aren't you?"

"I confess it. I had hoped to take you for enough to pay off my most pressing debts and get me out of England for a while. Would you have suspected me if Big Jack had not arrived at so unfortunate a time?"

"I suspected you at Buckingham's. You claim to be rich, yet you have torn lace upon your coat. That is how I knew you were a liar from the very first, but you are an audacious liar. I have a suggestion for you, Scott - go to Holland. It may be that you can compose some preposterous maps of the English coastline and persuade De Witt to base an invasion on them! That should help the English war effort and keep the Dutch busy whilst I am away fighting them for the French!"

"Do you know, that might not be a bad idea," Scott said, brightening. "He'd pay well, don't you think? Especially if I claimed to be a geographer to King Charles!"

Philip groaned. "What have I done?" He had little thought Scott would take him seriously.

But Scott had warmed to the theme. "Major-General Scott of Scott's Hall, one of the greatest engineers and chart makers in the world! That is," he finished lamely, "if I could only raise the money to sail to Holland."

Philip studied 'Major-General' Scott's handsome features. There were no strong lines of character there. He saw an opportunist, an unscrupulous rogue, a heartless villain, with neither principles nor honour. He saw a liar and a cheat, but he did not see a fool. Philip's brief association with Lord Shaftesbury had already taught him to appreciate a devious and scheming mind and Shaftesbury's parting words, that he may not always be able to rely upon a father's guilt to pay his way, had made a deep impression on him

He made a decision.

"Would fifty guineas clear what you call your pressing debts and get you overseas?" he asked Scott.

Scott looked at him suspiciously. "What would I have to do to earn that?"

"Nothing now, save promise you will not trick Buckingham the way you have Lord Sandwich, for I will allow no-one to hurt the Duke," Philip warned him. "I am a gambler, Scott, and I am wagering that you will be useful to me some day."

Scott grinned. "You are a gentleman, my Lord, and no mistake."

"I am of gentle birth, it's true, but not of gentle nature," Philip reminded him, "and I am certainly no simpleton. I see a hundred ways in which your talents might be harnessed for my own advantage, but I have neither the time nor the need to employ them now, for I leave for France in a day or two. If I let you fall victim to your enemies then I shall forever lose the opportunity to make use of you, therefore I shall help you to escape them." Philip held open the carriage door. "Come back to Buckingham's with me, for I do not carry such sums upon my person, not with the streets so full of thieves and blackguards!"

Scott leapt in eagerly beside him. "But what if I am unable to return to England? Supposing I am hung by the authorities in Holland or knifed by enemies in some Dutch tavern before I ever have the chance to serve you?"

"Then I will have lost fifty guineas," Philip said simply, "but I was taught a long, long while ago that I should never gamble any amount which I was not prepared to lose!"

FOURTEEN

Philip reported to Condé at Sedan in the beginning of May. He regarded the famous General with considerable interest. Buckingham had told him that Monsieur le Prince, as Condé was known, had fought with the people of Paris against the Court in the Fronde, although he was Louis' cousin. He had even fought against France in the Spanish Wars and it was a mark of his return to favour that Louis had entrusted him with a command in such an important campaign.

Condé was to take forty thousand men, called the Army of the Ardennes, and march upon Maestricht, there to meet up with the Army of France, commanded by Louis and Marèchal Turenne, who were to start from Charleroi. Ironically Condé had fought against Turenne in the Spanish Wars.

"You are my English captain?" Condé asked Philip.

"I am, Monsieur le Prince."

Condé nodded approvingly. "I like the look of you."

Philip knew that he did look rather splendid in his uniform, which was black with a gold sash.

"What service have you seen?" Condé said.

"Only the defence of the English coast against the Dutch navy. We did not fare very well against them," Philip admitted, recalling how the Dutch had managed to tow away the 'Royal Charles'.

"This will be different," Condé said. "The Dutch may still be able to hold their own upon the sea but the policy of peace which De Witt has carried out these last few years has meant the neglect of their land forces."

"Does Monsieur le Prince infer that this will not be an

enemy worth fighting?" Philip said in dismay, for he wanted the chance to seek a glorious revenge for the humiliation the English had suffered in the Medway.

Condé chuckled. "The Dutch are always worth fighting, my young lion, but our army has been preparing for three years and I do not believe it has ever been nearer to perfection. You will ride with my son, the Duc d'Enghien, and my nephew, the Duc de Longueville. You will be directly answerable to the Comte de Guiche."

Philip was pleased, for he knew that the Comte de Guiche was an experienced leader who had fought in the Polish Wars. Longueville was as yet untried in combat, but he was a reckless kind of person and Philip took to him right away. For Enghien, however, known by his title of Monsieur le Duc, he conceived an immediate dislike.

Ever since the death of his beloved daughter, Condé had doted on Enghien, his only remaining child, and Philip thought him spoilt and petulant. All Condé's love could not make the boy the son his father wished him to be. Enghien was cold-natured and much given to ridiculing others, which was not a trait that endeared him to Philip and, although he was almost thirty, Philip found him oddly immature.

They marched in the second week of May, to join up with the Army of France at Visé nine days later. Since Louis and Turenne were following the left bank of the River Meuse, which was a shorter, straighter, route, they had already occupied Tongre, Bilsen and Maaseik before they joined them.

Condé knew the strategic importance of the nearby town of Maestricht and thought it wiser to delay further advance until the siege of that town was completed but, rather than cause a delay which would give the Dutch time to reinforce their defences, Louis abandoned the idea of a siege for the time being. Leaving ten thousand men to mask the town, the main forces marched northwards up the Rhine.

Condé crossed to the right bank of the river at Kaiserwerth and by this time Philip and Longueville were hungry for action for, so far, they had met with no resistance. On the first day of June they reached Wesel and Condé summoned the Governor of the town, Van Santen, to open the gates and surrender.

To Philip's delight, Van Santen declined, although from the sign of alarm in the town it was obvious that the garrison was in no state to resist them.

"Do we attack?" he asked the Comte de Guiche, who had been attending a meeting with Condé.

"We wait," came back the disappointing reply. "Monsieur le Prince says we are to let them be defeated by their own panic."

It was a strategy which ill-suited Philip and Longueville. Even Enghien seemed discontented, although he was always dutiful towards his father.

A petition reached them on the morning of the following day. It was from thirty ladies of high rank and requested their safe passage from the town. Philip himself took the letter from the messenger and presented it to Condé. He was surprised when the General threw back his head and laughed.

"We have them now, Captain. Tell the messenger that no passports will be issued on any pretext, and if he asks you why say that on no account will I deprive my conquest of its fairest adornment!"

Puzzled, Philip obeyed, but the wisdom of Condé's plan soon became clear.

As he had anticipated, the ladies of Wesel were not about to let themselves become the innocent victims of a battle between the desperate forces of the town and the might of the French army. These formidable females scaled the ramparts and seized poor Van Santen and forced him to surrender! Condé's experience had won the day without a shot being fired or a soldier put at risk. His troops went in and made the entire garrison prisoners of war before marching on to take Emmerich.

Turenne, meanwhile, advancing on the left bank of the Rhine, had occupied the fortresses of Büderich and Orson. To avoid the Waal, a wide tributary taking water to the sea, he crossed the river to join with the Army of the Ardennes at Emmerich, where Louis established his headquarters.

The campaign had so far been ridiculously easy. In less than a fortnight the two French armies had, between them, taken all the defences along the Rhine.

Resistance did await them, however, in the person of William of Orange himself. He was waiting for them at Westervoort, where the Yssel River joined the Rhine.

Condé called the Comte de Guiche and some of his other officers, including Philip, to his tent. "The Prince of Orange will expect us to attack when we get to the Yssel but the King suggests that we outwit him and cross the Rhine before we reach that point. Our task, therefore, is to select a place where we can safely cross and occupy the territory."

The Rhine was wide and the troops would be at the mercy of the enemy during the crossing. De Guiche had forded the rivers of Eastern Europe during the Polish Wars and was the man with the most experience in these matters so, whilst he and Philip went on a reconnaissance, Condé advanced to the higher ground to view the Orangeman's troops.

They found a local who was willing to act as a guide and he took them to a place, near the village of Tolhuys, where the river could be forded in the Summer drought. There was an old toll tower by the crossing but it had been abandoned, against William's orders, the man told them.

Materials were quickly gathered for a floating bridge to be constructed at the spot and, before the following day was out, de Guiche announced that the river was ready to be crossed. Louis was so excited at the prospect that he determined to view the operation, which greatly pleased Philip, who had been chosen as one of the officers to cross with the Comte de Guiche.

At Condé's signal the first squadron entered the river, following the course of the ford which had been marked. The water came no higher than their horses' shoulders.

De Guiche crossed next, with Philip by his side. They had barely stepped into the water when Enghien, furious that he had been forbidden by Condé to ride with them, broke free of his father's restraining hand upon his horse's bridle and hastened after them.

There was no cover at the spot where they were crossing and many looked nervously at Tolhuys in case it had been reoccupied. There were now seven lines advancing in the water.

Suddenly the guns of the fort blazed into life.

Twelve French guns answered them from the other side. The horses, trapped in the sudden crossfire, panicked.

Condé watched helplessly as his precious son was caught up in the confusion.

Those horses that had swerved from the ford were swept into the current and many of their riders were drowning. Philip managed to keep control of his mount and would have reached the Dutch side of the bank without difficulty but, when he had only a few yards to go, he looked back and saw Enghien fall from his horse.

"Damnation! Why does it have to be you?" Philip muttered, but he knew what he must do. He leapt from his horse and swam to Enghien, who was powerless to save himself, for he was not a strong swimmer.

It had been many years since Philip had pitted his own strength against water but he had cause now to be glad of his early contests with John Bone. Despite being hampered by his boots and sword, he managed to reach the panic-stricken Enghien. With a supreme effort he succeeded in steering him through the water, now filled with the floating corpses of both men and beasts, back to the French side of the bank, where Condé and the King were waiting.

Condé rushed forward and took his exhausted son in his arms, but it was Louis himself who reached out a hand to help Philip from the river.

No words were spoken between them, nor were any necessary. Philip knew, at that moment, that he could have done himself no greater favour that day than to have saved Enghien.

However, the day was not yet done.

Condé, accompanied by the Prince de Marcillac and Longueville, made the crossing in a small boat. Enghien, somewhat recovered, went with them and Philip, too, for his horse was now upon the other side of the river. By the time they arrived the Comte de Guiche had beaten back the Dutch and several young officers were pressing the pursuit.

Philip, Marcillac and Longueville were determined not to miss the last part of the action, even if they had been forced to miss the rest, and each grabbed a mount and set off after them.

Before long, on the road to Huissen, they came upon a company of infantry.

"We have some Dutch to fight at last," Longueville said. "They're going to make a stand!"

The soldiers certainly had their muskets raised, but an officer stepped forward as the Frenchmen approached.

"He asks for quarter," called one who understood the language. "He says that now their cavalry has taken flight there is no point in the infantry resisting."

"No," Longueville cried, enraged. "I say death and no quarter for these cowardly dogs."

He raised his pistol, but Philip tried to stay his arm.

"I am as eager for a fight as you, God knows, but these men plainly have us at a disadvantage, for their muskets are already primed and pointing at us at close range. Allow them to surrender. We will get another chance, and at men more worthy of our trouble."

"I am sick of waiting for a chance." Longueville shook him off and without more ado discharged his pistol across the barricade.

The Dutch fired back immediately. Longueville toppled from his horse.

He was dead.

Philip was unharmed but, as he looked about, he saw three others lay upon the ground and many more were wounded, including Marcillac.

For the second time that day he cursed the impetuosity of the relatives of Condé, but there was no time to reflect or even spare a thought for poor Longueville, for the Dutch still fired upon them. He dragged Marcillac to cover behind some rocks and then, drawing his pistol, fired carefully and accurately, with a steadiness of hand that surprised himself.

"You're a cool bastard and no mistake," Marcillac panted. "I can hardly believe this is your first campaign."

"If help does not arrive soon it will surely be my last," Philip said grimly, as he reloaded yet again. He had counted at least four men dead by his own hand but they were hopelessly outnumbered.

He was relieved to hear the sound of approaching horses' hooves.

It was Condé himself, come to investigate the musket shots, but he had only a handful of men with him. He was immediately recognised by the Dutch.

Philip watched in horror as a Dutch officer rode straight at Condé and fired at his head. He raised his left arm to shield himself but cried out in pain as the bullet struck his wrist.

The Dutchman turned to flee but Philip fired and the officer never made it back to his troops.

"The Comte de Guiche is coming," Marcillac cried. "Thank God!"

It was indeed the Comte, accompanied by a company of cuirassiers. The Dutch surrendered but it did not seem too much like a victory as Condé knelt by the lifeless body of his nephew.

Condé spent that night in a fisherman's hut, overcome with

grief. The Comte de Guiche visited him for a few moments and then sent for Philip.

"Monsieur le Prince desires to see you, Captain, but he is weak from sorrow."

Philip entered quietly, to find Condé sitting in semi-darkness, with his head resting upon one hand. The other hand and arm were bandaged.

"Does your wrist cause you much pain, Monsieur le Prince?" Philip asked him.

"The pain in my heart is far greater," Condé said sadly. "Do not come too close, my young lion, for it is not seemly for a junior officer to see tears upon the face of his commander, yet I do shed tears, and not only on my own behalf. Longueville was my sister's favourite son. This will destroy her."

"The Duc de Longueville's death is a mighty loss to us all and to his country." Philip said. "I only wish I had been able to prevent it."

"But you tried, I am aware of that, for I have spoken with the Prince de Marcillac, He told me how you hazarded yourself to get him to safety and also that it was you who killed my attacker. You have earned my gratitude upon another count, too, for you undoubtedly saved the life of my impulsive son today. You may have little experience in the field but you have proved that you are both brave and level-headed, and you have shown that you have qualities of leadership. Accordingly, King Louis and myself have decided to award you the rank of major."

Philip was astonished. The rank of major could not be purchased but must be earned, and he had expected no such reward for his actions, particularly from one who was reputed to be a hard, fierce master.

"I trust Monsieur le Prince will never have cause to regret the confidence he places in me," he said, very conscious of the honour Condé did him.

"I'm sure I won't. Now leave me, if you please. I am too full of grief to be good company tonight."

The Comte de Guiche was waiting for Philip outside. "Well? What did he want?" he asked.

Philip liked the Comte and was pleased that he would be the first to hear his news. "Believe it or not, Monsieur le Prince has made me a major!"

Not everyone was as happy for Philip as the Comte de Guiche. Enghien, forgetting all too easily that Philip had saved his life, complained bitterly that a foreigner should rise above French officers but his father, who had always prided himself that he could judge men, adhered to his decision.

In fact, Philip was not to serve under Condé again for a while. The injury to which he had paid so little heed was to cause him a great deal of pain, for his wrist was shattered and the gout, from which he frequently suffered, entered the wound.

He was forced to retire from the battle for several weeks and Philip was transferred to the Army of France and the leadership of Turenne. If he had ever desired action his wish was now granted. Turenne's first move was to be against Arnheim, where the Prince of Orange waited with his troops.

Philip also had the chance to meet up with Monmouth, who was overjoyed to see him again and to learn of his promotion. With him was Thomas Armstrong and his friend, Richard Lindsey, both of whom Philip had met in London, and another man, who Philip did not know. Monmouth introduced him as John Churchill.

Philip found little to like about him, for his manner was so stiff as to be almost impolite.

"Have you heard the news from England?" Monmouth asked Philip.

"Not a word."

"It's bad, I fear. My uncle was supposed to join with Admiral d'Estrées to fire upon the Dutch fleet but the 'Royal James' was fired instead and blown out of the water, and the Earl of Sandwich with it. It is reckoned more than two thousand Englishmen were killed, and all on account of the French admiral's refusal to obey my uncle's orders."

"It is well we are here and not upon the North Sea then," reckoned Philip. "Here we at least stand to gain a little glory."

"I'll be frank with you, my friend, glory or not I don't care too much for this army life," Monmouth admitted. "How I miss London."

"I confess this suits me very well," Philip said truthfully.

"Doubtless one of Lord Devalle's temperament feels this more barbarous environment is better suited to his nature," put in Churchill, who had been listening.

Philip raised an eyebrow but said nothing, although Monmouth worriedly took Churchill away, as though fearing a dispute would start between the pair.

"Who is this John Churchill?" Philip asked Armstrong.

"He arrived at Court whilst you were in France. His sister, Arabella, is York's new mistress and Churchill joined his household as a page."

"He seems a dull sort of fellow to me," Philip said, recalling Churchill's somewhat vacant features.

"Oh he is, but Barbara's made a pet of him. She bought his uniform and horse and sent him off for all the world as though he were her champion. I tell you, frankly, he detests you."

"But he has never met me before today."

"He says you treated her disgracefully, even that you brutally assaulted her and caused her to miscarry. Is it the truth?"

"It's half the truth," Philip said, "the half that Barbara wishes to be known. If he feels so strongly he can always challenge me to a duel."

Armstrong grinned. "He's got more sense, or else he has been better advised. You are gaining quite a formidable reputation. Besides, he is only a captain and you are a major now. It would be unwise for him to give offence to a superior officer!"

⚛

The battle for Arnheim was fierce. Prince William was beaten back from the frontier and the whole district of Betuwe, between the Waal tributary and the Yssel River, was taken. Utrecht, the only sizeable town between Arnheim and Amsterdam, refused to defend itself and the Army of France, with Louis at its head, took no less than thirty fortresses in the next ten days. William, who had only ten thousand men, retreated behind Holland's last defence – the Water Line.

The Water Line was a ring of sluices that held back the sea. As Louis' forces pressed on to Naarden, but a day's march from Amsterdam, William reached Muyden and opened up the great sluice gates. For the first time in the campaign the French were driven back. The countryside was flooded and impassible.

Nevertheless, the return to Paris was triumphant, with Louis hailed as the conqueror of the Rhine. Leaving the Maréchal de Luxembourg in charge of the occupation, Louis announced confidently that he would take the remainder of Holland in the Spring.

Monmouth took the opportunity to return to England, using Anna's pregnancy as an excuse, but Philip knew that, in reality, his friend craved a soft bed, an indulgent father and the attention of the ladies. For himself he was content to remain with Turenne, and it was not long before the Army of France was once more on the march.

The Hollanders had turned again against the unpopular De Witt and the Prince William was now in sole charge of the state. The rest of Europe had begun to pay attention to the invasion too. Spain, Austria and Brandenburg, fearing France's increasing power, joined with William. At the head of their armies was Count Montecuccoli, a brilliant soldier of fortune.

There was to be, therefore, no easy Winter in Paris preparing for a Spring campaign. Turenne's task was to prevent

Monteccucoli from joining his troops with those of the Orangeman and they advanced with sixteen thousand men to guard the frontier between Wesel and Mayence. Condé, who was still far from well, was given a less important stretch of the river to guard, between Mayence and Strasbourg, with only six thousand men. The Occupation had drained the resources of the French army.

After some hard fighting, Turenne finally drove Monteccucoli back into the heart of Germany and Philip was once more transferred to Condé's force, bringing with him a thousand of his own men, the first he had been given to command.

Condé seemed well satisfied with what he saw, for the troop was disciplined and a credit to Philip, who had grown strong and fit during the campaign. He had never in his life felt or looked so well, and he knew it.

"I have read good reports of you throughout the Winter campaign, Major," Condé told him. "It would seem my faith in you was fully justified. You've seen some action, I hear."

"Indeed! We were a match for Monteccucoli," Philip said proudly.

Condé sighed. "Would that I could have played a more active part. To be set to guard such an insignificant frontier, and with such an insignificant number of men, is an insult to my experience and reputation. It is plain the King considered that the enemy would never attack at such a place."

"No doubt his Majesty wished to allow you time recover fully from your injury," Philip said, though he suspected that the real reason for Louis' shabby treatment of his cousin was to remind him that he was still not fully forgiven for his part in the Fronde.

"Our task now is to inspect the fortresses at Alsace," Condé continued. "After that I am to return home to Chantilly to await further orders. You are to take your troop to help Luxembourg keep order in the provinces."

Philip pulled a face. It was not a duty which appealed to him, not after spending so many exciting months in the thick of battle.

"Have you not had your fill of fighting yet, my young lion?" Condé asked, smiling. "Well don't despair. If the weather is cold enough the country which the Dutch have flooded will freeze over and you may be taking Amsterdam before the Winter ends."

But in the early part of Autumn there was nothing but rain.

FIFTEEN

✑

Philip's troop was billeted in Woerden. To alleviate the boredom of the endless damp days he was forced to spend in that flat, bleak, sodden landscape he purchased a string of horses and set about training them himself.

He did not doubt that the disreputable band of gypsies who sold the animals had stolen most of them from the Dutch army or from neighbouring farms, but he didn't much care. There was one horse of special interest to him, an Andalusian cross of fully seventeen hands high, which was tall for the breed. He was a magnificent black stallion, with a curling mane and a proud tilt to his head. Philip named him Ferrion. He was so wild that none of the soldiers would go near him but with Philip, who had an uncanny knack with horses, he was little more than skittish. Philip saw to all Ferrion's needs himself, treating him gently but firmly so that within a few weeks the stallion was as responsive as his own bay, that he had ridden since the start of the campaigns.

Louvois, the Minister of War, had sent word from Paris that the pillaging of the captured towns must cease, for otherwise King Louis' new Dutch subjects would be hard pressed to pay their taxes, but there was no ruling from the government upon the usage of the local girls. Philip allowed his men to associate with them as they pleased, for he knew that a normal, lusty man needed an occasional woman as much as he needed his daily ration of food and drink. At times his own sexual cravings grew almost too much to bear, but he reckoned it beneath his dignity to sport with the peasant girls.

Philip's second in command was a captain called Leventier who, Philip suspected, shared Enghien's opinion that a foreigner had no business commanding French troops. Leventier made it clear that he disapproved of Philip's ruling in the matter of the women and he was not alone in his disapproval. The fathers from the town visited the French headquarters frequently with complaints that their daughters had been badly used by the soldiers. In the majority of the cases it appeared that the girls were as eager to be seduced as the army was to seduce them, so Philip generally dismissed their claims with a few terse words to the effect that his men were there in order to protect the inhabitants from Monteccucoli, whose soldiers would likely do far worse to them than the French!

Philip had chosen the Governor's house for his lodgings, as befitted his station. Leventier interrupted him one afternoon during the second month of their occupation and, from his expression, Philip anticipated the arrival of yet another irate father who held him personally responsible for the loss of his daughter's virtue. He was wrong.

"There is a disturbance in the town, Major," Leventier said. "The Sergeant is having difficulty in restraining a man who demands to see you. He claims to be one of your countrymen."

"You say the Sergeant is restraining him? Does he desire to do me harm?" Philip asked.

"We are not too certain what he wants. He seems to be a violent sort of person and of rough birth, by the look of him."

"Is he armed?"

"He had a knife, which we took from him."

"Then I dare say I can cope with him. Bid the Sergeant bring him here."

"If you will be advised by me…" Leventier began, but Philip cut him short with an impatient gesture of his hand.

"You heard my order. See to it."

When the cause of the disturbance was brought in to him, however, Philip saw that the man struggling in the Sergeant's grip did, indeed, look to be a violent sort of person. What was more, the words in which he was cursing the Sergeant were not in any language that Philip had ever heard before.

"Let him be," he told the Sergeant, more curious than alarmed, "and get out of here."

"You want me to leave you alone with him, Major?"

"That's what I said. My God, must every order I give be questioned?"

"As you please, Major, but I shall wait outside the door in case you need me."

The Sergeant turned to go but, with a quick movement, the man stood in his way.

"I want my knife, you great French ape."

Those words were in plain enough English and Philip could not hide a smile.

"What did he say, sir?" the Sergeant asked him.

"He says he wants his knife. I suggest you give it to him, since you have no valid reason for withholding it."

The Sergeant reluctantly obeyed and Philip observed that his visitor kissed the handle of the weapon as though it were his child returned to him before he thrust it into his leather belt.

He was not a tall man, but stocky and swarthy-skinned, with tangled black hair. Philip noticed, too, that the fellow wore a seaman's garb and gold earrings, though he could not imagine what a sailor might be doing so far inland in enemy territory.

"You're not English, are you?" he said when they were finally left alone.

"No, my Lord. I'm Welsh,"

"What the devil is a Welshman doing out here?"

"What is an Englishman doing in the French army?" came back the swift reply.

Philip was slightly taken aback. "I am half-French," he explained, without knowing quite why he should feel the need to justify himself to this person. "Now, what do you want of me?"

"I heard that this troop was commanded by an English officer. When I learned that it was you, who I know by reputation, I reckoned I could do no better than to offer you my services."

"You wish to join my troop? Why did you not say so at the start? The Sergeant could have easily arranged that," Philip said.

"I do not wish to join your troop," the man contradicted him. "I've heard good things about you and I have decided that you are the man who I would like to make my master."

Philip stared at him, astounded at this effrontery. "You wish to become my servant?"

"That is my wish. Your servant and bodyguard."

"The deuce!" Philip poured himself a glass of brandy whilst he thought of a reply. As he drank it he noticed that his visitor watched him enviously. He filled up the glass again and held it out to him. "What's your name?"

"Morgan, my Lord." The Welshman took the measure gratefully and downed it in one. "Edwin Morgan."

"Well, Morgan, let me put this in as kindly a way as I can. Whilst I am flattered that you should have chosen me to be your master, I fear that, at present, I have no need of a servant. When I return to France I may well consider engaging one, but I imagine you require a position right away. As for a bodyguard, I have no need of one, now or at any other time. In fact, I have no employment to offer you save as an ordinary soldier in my troop. If you accept that honourable post then you will be fed and quartered straight away, that I promise, and your opportunity to serve me will come daily, as you fight for France's glory. I pay five sous a day, although the government will relieve you of one sou and six deniers of that for your bread. Meat and wine are supplied free whilst you are on the march."

"Very well," Morgan said resignedly. "I am in sore need of some vittles and a bed."

"Some clothes as well, it would appear." Philip had noticed the fellow's worn-out shoes and the holes torn in his stockings. "Have you walked far?"

"That I have, my Lord. I left my ship in Flanders."

"On what ship did you serve?"

"I was on 'The Dragon', under Captain Tyrwhitt."

"Isn't that one of the frigates that patrol the channel to protect the East India Company's flotillas from the Dutch?" Philip said. "I am surprised they would set ashore so close to Zeeland."

Now that he thought about it Philip decided that, despite his garb, Morgan did not have the look of seafaring man, but he looked fit enough and the opportunity to recruit even one man in that isolated spot was too good to miss, especially one who spoke his own language.

After the Welshman had gone Philip poured himself another brandy and went to his room. Kicking off his boots he lay down upon his bed. The conversation with the stranger had reminded him of a different way of life, one he seemed to have left far behind him.

Not that he missed such trivialities as the masked balls or the supper parties, or even the gaming tables. What he truly missed was female companionship.

He closed his eyes and for delicious moment allowed his thoughts to wander. It seemed as if he could almost feel Barbara's trembling fingertips as they caressed the inside of his thigh and hear her quickening breaths in his ear. His fantasy was rudely shattered by the sound of a woman's laughter outside his open window. He guessed it was one of the local whores visiting his men.

"Dammit! This is more than I can stand." Leaping from the bed he hailed the guard posted in the street beneath. "Bring that bitch to me. I don't care what she looks like."

"But Major, that one's nowhere near good enough for you," protested the young musketeer.

"Few women here are but I must have one now and she appears to be the closest."

Even as the guard sped off to do his bidding a young lieutenant rushed up the stairs.

"Major, we have news. Our northern patrols report the movement of a Dutch troop toward Naarden."

By the time the guard returned Philip was pouring over a map with his officers.

The soldier coughed discreetly.

"Yes? What is it?" Philip said, without turning around.

"I have brought the woman, Major."

"Woman? What woman?"

"The one you wanted right away."

"Good God, man, do I look as though I want a woman now? Take the pox-ridden whore away! I reckon, gentlemen, from the position of those troops they are those of Prince William, and he appears to be intending to engage with Luxembourg."

"Should we send aid to Naarden?" Leventier asked.

"I think not. The Maréchal has enough men to retain it," Philip reckoned. "It is my guess the Orangemen will fail and, having failed, he will move swiftly south and attempt to take us here, at Woerden."

"Can we hold them off alone?"

"We may have to. Zuylestein has his forces here." Philip drew a circle on the map to indicate the position of the other Dutch commander. "He may attempt to stop Luxembourg reaching us with aid. If he does then we will face at least ten thousand men, commanded by the Prince of Orange himself."

"What should we do?"

"Why, what else but make ready? The Orangeman may outnumber us but his troops are neither so experienced nor so disciplined as mine. We must hold this place until the Maréchal de Luxembourg arrives."

"And if he does not arrive?" Leventier said.

"Then we must make as brave a show as our men and weapons will allow," Philip said determinedly. "Speaking for myself, I would die before I surrendered even so insignificant a town as this to an enemy I have come to detest."

Philip received no word of Luxembourg's position and guessed that his predictions had been accurate. His scouts reported that the Prince of Orange was marching southwards and he stood by his decision to attempt to hold the little garrison alone.

Since he knew that they could not hold out against a siege from such a large force Philip resolved to advance to meet them. To do this he had to split his own force. Leaving a third of them to man the walls he took the remainder, protected by the rampart guns, to face the enemy. In the blessed event of aid arriving, Philip's troops would retreat and join the rest on the ramparts, leaving the field clear for Luxembourg. It was a gamble and a desperate one, but all that he could do.

Philip proposed to lead the attack whilst Leventier took charge of the guns on the ramparts, but the Frenchman seemed unhappy with the plan. Even as Philip sat ready to advance, the relentless rain dripping from his plumed hat and soaking his shoulders, Leventier rode out to speak to him.

"Major, I do feel that you would be better advised to remain at a safe distance behind the cavalry charge and not expose yourself to danger."

Philip knew very well that it was not concern for his welfare which had prompted Leventier's words but only that the Captain could not endure the thought of him gaining more acclaim.

"We had a great English general, the Duke of Albemarle, perhaps you've heard of him? When advised to keep himself clear of danger in a battle he replied that if he had been afraid of bullets he would never have become a soldier!"

"But what if anything should happen to you?"

"You will assume command and attempt to hold this miserable town until the Maréchal de Luxembourg arrives to relieve you."

Leventier said no more because, like Philip, he could see the first line of the enemy's cavalry in the distance and he hastened back to his position.

Philip signalled the Sergeant, who was waiting by the infantry, to be prepared. They did not have long to wait. As Philip caught his first glimpse of the famed Prince of Orange the Dutch began their charge.

Philip let the first three lines through to within firing range of Leventier's guns, then raised his hand. The Sergeant barked an order and his twelve cannons fired simultaneously with those upon the walls. Immediately the musketeers opened fire from the trenches.

With the first three lines decimated by the musket volley and cannon fire, the Dutch cavalry fell into chaos. Their mounts were out of control as they stumbled over the bodies of men and horses strewn over the ground.

They pulled back apace, ready to make another attempt, but before they could properly reassemble Philip gave the signal for his own cavalry to charge. Four hundred horsemen, with Philip at their head, thundered towards the Dutch lines, their swords ready. Some of the musketeers followed whilst the piquers leapt from the trenches to finish the dismounted Dutchmen.

The guns resounded from the town at regular intervals, wreaking havoc, but it became evident that the French were not dealing with cowards. Despite their disarray, the Dutch started forward to meet them.

The two cavalries engaged and Philip fought more fiercely than he had ever done, cutting his way through the human wall before him with a viciousness he never knew that he possessed.

Outnumbered though they were, his men gave of their best until, above the clashing of steel and the crash of guns, Philip heard the sound he had hardly dared hope to hear. He glanced at the skyline and gave a yell of joy. It was Luxembourg. They had been relieved!

Leventier had seen Luxembourg too and ordered the bugler to give the signal to retreat. The Dutch now saw that they were trapped between the two forces and those who had been unhorsed battled desperately for a mount. Even as Philip fended off blows with his sword a Dutchman tugged at his leg, attempting to unseat him. Philip brought out his pistol and fired it directly into the man's face.

Most of his troop had already pulled back to the town but, as Philip and the remaining French cavalry rode to join them, the Dutch infantry opened fire to stop them escaping.

Philip was untouched but, as the ground came up to meet him he realised that his horse had been shot. The next moment he hit the rocky earth with a force that he thought had cracked his spine. Before he had recovered from that shock the heavy body of his lifeless bay crashed down on top of him.

Horses' hooves pounded all around him, sometimes missing his head by only inches. Amidst the mud and deafening noise, he struggled furiously to free himself, cursing the Dutch and then La Voisin, who had never predicted he would die like this.

His every instinct told him to fight for survival but, even as he sensed the futility of his efforts, he became aware of a figure crouching beside him. Strong arms locked around his chest.

He cried out in pain as he was tugged, but he felt his body move and, although it was only a few inches, it gave him hope.

"Get me clear and you shall be rewarded with more money then you ever had in your life," he shouted above the turmoil, as the soldier heaved again.

Once more Philip felt a fierce pain and then it seemed as if his head exploded as the cannons again spurted flame from the ramparts of Woerden. Blackness enveloped him and he no longer heard the battle's din or smelt the smoke of the guns.

The next time he opened his eyes he was lying on his bed, with the surgeon bending over him examining his legs. Philip tried to sit up, but fell back groaning. His back ached and so did his legs, which he saw now were black with bruising, although not broken.

The surgeon smiled. "Major! You are with us once again. Heaven be praised! I'll tell the Maréchal de Luxembourg, he has been most concerned for you."

Philip struggled to recall what had happened.

"Luxembourg arrived with a full troop shortly before you went down," the surgeon reminded him. "We routed the Dutch and retained the town. You are a hero, Major!"

"I am?" Philip said weakly. "That's good to know. I certainly owe the Maréchal a debt of gratitude, but I think I owe an even greater one to the bloody fool who stopped to rescue me. Who was it?"

"Just a common piquer, sir."

"With an uncommon amount of courage, I would say. Send him to me as soon as you can, please."

When the piquer entered Philip stared at him. "You!"

It was the Welshman.

"Yes, Major."

"Then you have my grateful thanks, but what induced you to risk your life to save that of a man you hardly know?"

"I know enough to realise that you are a man worth saving, Major."

"Thank you. Since you have troubled to find out so much about me you must be aware that my father is the Earl of Southwick, and a rich man. You will be well rewarded for your bravery this day, Edwin Morgan."

"I have no wish for your father's money," Morgan said. "You can offer me no greater reward than that of remaining by your side."

"That again? I've already told you I don't need a servant."

"You also said you didn't need a bodyguard," Morgan pointed out.

"I can't always be right! Why do you want to stay with me anyway?"

"You have the qualities which I look for in a master."

"Have I indeed!" Philip could not help but smile at the audacity of this shaggy-headed Welshman who had determined on him for an employer. "That's all very well, but what makes you think you have any of the qualities which I might seek in a servant?"

"I believe you would grow accustomed to me in time," Morgan said.

Oddly, Philip felt that too. He had never bothered to engage a personal servant of his own, for he had always been able to make use of Buckingham's or Monsieur's staff, but he wondered whether now was not the time to consider it, especially since fate had brought Morgan to him at such an opportune moment. "As you please. If this is the reward you want for saving me, then so be it. We'll see how well we suit each other, and I hope you don't find that you've made a damned poor bargain!"

Less than three weeks later the Prince of Orange was on the move again, this time from Rotterdam with thirteen thousand men. He marched through Roosendaal toward Maestricht but, before he reached it, he swung southward to Charleroi. Luxembourg hastened to intercept him once again, for the garrison at Charleroi was weak. Philip went with him this time, mounted on Ferrion, who was now properly trained for war, leaving Leventier with a small force to keep control of Woerden.

As luck would have it a sudden frost prevented William from digging trenches around Charleroi and gave the French the long-awaited opportunity to invade the once-flooded fields of the part of the country known as Holland.

Each soldier was supplied with a pair of skates. Two days after Christmas, the most austere and miserable Christmas that Philip had ever known, the army of the Maréchal de Luxembourg prepared to skate and march across the ice of what had previously been the impenetrable Water Line. They were finally to make for Amsterdam.

Philip stood with the other officers listening in the bitter wind to the words of the Maréchal, words which chilled him more than the icy weather.

"Go, my children," Luxembourg commanded his men, whose dislike of the Dutch had turned into plainest hatred during the long, harsh months they had spent in that desolate country. "Plunder, murder and destroy! Let me see that I am not deceived in my choice of the flower of the King's troops."

The sack of Holland had begun.

Philip was forced to look on whilst his men raped women in the streets and set fire to their houses with their men and children trapped inside. It sickened him, but there was nothing he could do to stop it. Luxembourg maintained it was a show of force that would cause the whole Dutch nation to fear France and accede to her demands. Philip had his orders and he had no choice but to obey.

On they pressed to Amsterdam but the weather changed again. The ice had helped them to victory but the thaw was their enemy.

They trudged back the weary miles, often waist deep in cold water. Some men drowned in the deep, dark bogs, their horses and equipment lost. Philip was unwilling to risk any harm coming to Ferrion and led him the entire way, so that he was as sodden and filthy as any of his men. Morgan plodded on stoically beside him and Philip was glad to have him there.

Luxembourg himself fell from his horse and was ill for several days, but at last they reached Nieuwerburg. To their amazement it was undefended. The Dutch commander had deserted his post and, encouraged by this easy acquisition, the exhausted French army rallied sufficient strength and spirit to retake Utrecht.

Condé joined them in the early Spring to take charge of the 'Army of Holland' as Luxembourg's forces had been named. Philip was pleased to see him, though not so pleased to receive his latest orders, which were to return to Woerden.

"The duty of the Army of Holland is to keep the Dutch forces at bay whilst Turenne besieges Maestricht," Condé told him. "I advised them to take that town a year ago, though none would listen to me. By the way, your friend, the Duke of Monmouth, is to lead a troop."

"Monmouth is back in France?"

"He's back, and recently appointed Lieutenant-Général." Condé's expression showed that he understood how galling that news must be to Philip, who had not spent his Winter enjoying the comforts of the English Court!

"That scarcely surprises me," Philip said heavily. "Are we to play no part, then, in this siege?"

Condé snorted. "None at all. What need have they for tried and tested soldiers such as you and me? This is a spectacle, to be witnessed by the King, the Queen and Madame de Montespan, can you believe it? Maestricht, mark my words, will go down in the annals of our country whilst our achievements will be all forgotten six months from now. All we are to do is hold back Prince William's entire army so that the actors upon the stage of Maestricht may prettily play their parts!"

Philip thought Condé's words a little unjust, although he understood the reason for his resentment. For himself, although he would dearly have loved to be present at the siege, he was certain that his record throughout the campaign would earn him recognition.

Maestricht fell in July, after holding out for a month against Louis' force of over thirty thousand men. Monmouth was fêted as a hero and Philip, along with many of the Army of Holland, was ordered to return in triumph to Paris, first meeting up with the King and Turenne at Charleroi. Condé returned too, for his health had failed him yet again, and it was Luxembourg, now once more in charge of the depleted Army of Holland, who bade Philip farewell.

"We leave you with scarcely any men, Maréchal," Philip said, watching his own troop leaving Woerden.

"I have enough, Major. Your English navy is soon to invade Holland at Schevingen. We'll best these bastard brandy-guzzling cheese worms then," Luxembourg predicted. "Besides, the Orangeman has lost his spirit for fighting."

Philip was not so sure. William, though no more than Philip's own age, had shown himself to be enterprising, brave and, above all, determined.

Charleroi was in a glorious confusion as the armies met after their long separation to congratulate each other upon their successes.

Louis received Philip graciously and told him of the excellent reports he had received of him from Condé, Turenne and Luxembourg.

Monmouth greeted him like a brother and told everyone how proud he was of him. He had some surprising news from England too. King Charles, at Shaftesbury's insistence, had finally brought in the Test Act, prohibiting any Roman Catholic to hold a public office. This had forced the Duke of York to yield up to Prince Rupert his position as Lord High Admiral.

"Then your uncle is ruined?" Philip could hardly believe it.

"And so is Shaftesbury. I fear that he has overreached himself. My father could foresee the further trouble he would have with him and Shaftesbury is dismissed from office. He is now in league with the Opposition."

"I'll warrant this is not the last we hear of him." Philip could imagine no more formidable leader of the Opposition Party than the clever, scheming 'little limping peer'."

"Come back to London with me," Monmouth pleaded as he left Charleroi a few days later. "You have done more than your duty for France and you must be tired of army life by now."

"I do welcome the thought of returning to the comforts of civilisation for a while," Philip admitted, "but, having no commitments in England, nor any family that cares for me, I really think I would prefer to stay in France."

"I beg you not to do so." Monmouth sounded dismayed. "*I* care about you greatly."

"I am most flattered that you want me with you, James, but surely you have other friends."

"None as dear as you."

"Not even John Churchill?" Philip nodded over to the haughty, blonde captain who had been with Monmouth at Maestricht. "He seems attentive towards you."

"Him?" Monmouth pulled a face. "He's bold enough, I'll grant you that, but he's ill-natured. He does say the most dreadful things about you, too, and I will not have it."

Philip smiled. Monmouth had not changed one jot from the time when they had been boys together. He was still as earnest and still as loyal to Philip as he had been then, but Philip had changed a great deal. Always the cynic of the pair, he had already learned more of the harsh realities of life than the pampered Monmouth.

"Let him tell his lies about me, James. He can't hurt me, or disillusion those who know me best. I promise I'll return to England one day, but I can't say when."

"You pledged once that you would give your life for me," Monmouth reminded him. "You do recall that?"

"I recall it well and, what is more, I meant it truly. If you ever need me I will come to you without delay," Philip promised. "Go home to your father and your wife and your little son, whose ill-health, I know, causes you such distress. A glorious return awaits you, James, but there are few who will welcome me back to

England. I am happy in France and I have Monsieur, who will be pleased to see me. I pray you give me leave to discover for myself what course my life should take."

The march back to Paris was slow and Philip was not sorry when they made camp for the last time, only ten miles outside the city. The following morning Philip felt jubilant as Morgan helped him prepare for his ride into the capital.

He had become agreeable to the Welshman's presence in a remarkably short time. Although Morgan rarely spoke of his own accord, there was something quite companionable in his silence, whilst Philip found himself talking to him as naturally as though they had been together years instead of mere weeks.

One thing was perfectly plain - Morgan had never in his mysterious life been a servant, but he obeyed orders willingly enough, though with little of the deference usually accorded to Philip's rank. Philip was not offended by his manner, for there could be no doubt of Morgan's desire to adequately fill his new post.

Philip resolved to ask no questions of him at all, not wishing to disturb the easy intimacy which had grown between them. He concentrated, instead, on teaching him the duties of a personal servant, for if Morgan was to remain with him when Philip returned to Court there were a great many things he would need to learn in order to be satisfactory.

One such thing was the combing of his master's hair, a province not only new but totally alien to him, Philip guessed, from the usual state of the Welshman's own unkempt black locks! Morgan was engaged in this task when Captain Leventier interrupted them with the news that there was an English officer of the law waiting to see him.

"For what reason?" Philip asked.

"He is searching for a fugitive from English justice and suspects he might have joined one of the divisions. He is questioning all of the commanders."

"Then I had better see him, I suppose," Philip said irritably. "Dammit, Morgan, need you pull my hair so much?"

Morgan mumbled an apology but, when the visitor appeared, he tugged so fiercely that Philip took the comb from his hand.

"Your pardon, Major, for taking up your time on such a day. I need to ask you some questions before you reach Paris and your troop is disbanded, for this concerns your soldiers. Are they all Frenchmen?"

"I believe so, though there may be some Swiss amongst them," Philip said.

"I meant are there any of your countrymen?"

"There are no English here, save for myself," Philip answered carefully, handing the comb back to Morgan, who swiftly turned to pack it away.

"It is a Welshman that I seek, Major. An outlaw wanted by Lord Harleston."

"Fancy!" Philip raised an eyebrow. "Why do you suppose he may be here?"

"We've traced the captain of the ship on which he made his escape from England, Major. Apparently, he attacked another member of the crew and cut off some of his fingers, then jumped ship in Flanders. I thought maybe he might have joined up with you or one of the other troops."

"Was he, then, a soldier or a sailor?"

"He was neither. Morgan Davis is his name and he was once a tenant, farming on Lord Harleston's land."

"He must have grievously offended this Lord Harleston for you to have pursued him all this way," Philip said, observing Morgan closely.

"He did more than offend his Lordship, Major. He killed Lord Harleston's son in cold blood."

"A rogue indeed!" There had never been any doubt in Philip's mind as to what action he was going to take. "If I should come across him I will let you know. Now, if you will excuse me, sir, I must attend a meeting with my fellow officers and leave this place within the hour."

When he had gone Morgan viewed him silently.

"Well?" Philip said at length. "Well, Morgan Davis, have you nothing to say to me? No protestations of your innocence?"

Morgan hung his head. "No, my Lord. I'll lie to you no longer."

"Then he was right? You are a murderer?"

"I had good cause."

"I'm sure you did."

Morgan looked surprised. "You don't care?"

"Not too much. I killed two men in a single day during the plague and I have slain many more upon the battlefield. I do confess to being curious, however, so tell me why you did it."

"I was inflamed with passion."

"Now you have intrigued me!"

"I was to have been married to a girl on Harleston's estate," Morgan explained. "As you now know I was once a farmer and my betrothed was a farmer's daughter, a simple little country maid, but pretty and she caught the eye of the Honourable Edward Harleston. He took her by force." Morgan ground his teeth at the memory. "She was with child before we could even be wed."

"You know that it was his?"

"Aye, for he flaunted it in front of me. Boasting he was, the bastard, but he picked a sorry moment. I was standing with a pitchfork in my hand and before I knew what I was doing I had thrust it into his breast. I knew straightaway that he was dead and I ran before they could string me up. I swore from that day I would choose my own master, and would choose carefully."

"Why, thank you, Morgan. I will take that as a compliment! Am I to assume it is also true that you mutilated a member of the 'Dragon's' crew?"

"It's true," Morgan admitted." He drew the long knife from his belt and held the hilt out to Philip. "I did it with this. You may take it if that would cause you to feel easier about me."

Philip shook his head. "You keep it. Every man in this wild age has need of a weapon to protect himself. All the same, I shall ensure that you never have access to a pitchfork! Now help me dress, for I am eager to get to Paris."

"Shall you still take me with you?" Morgan asked uncertainly.

"But naturally. The last place anyone will ever think of searching for you is at Court in the employ of one as conspicuous as me."

He was right, of course. The search for Edward Harleston's killer was abandoned in due time and, although Morgan was to become a familiar figure at his master's side, it was to be some years before anyone discovered the dark secrets of his past.

He spoke occasionally of the homeland that he loved, but with regret rather than bitterness. Philip never again raised the subject, for he was learning to evaluate men for what they really were, not for what circumstances made them appear. Nothing he had learned that day concerning his new servant was to detract from the regard he had for him, nor weaken the bond which was to grow between them in the many years that they would spend together.

SIXTEEN

∽

Paris was a very fine place to be that Summer and Philip, fêted and fussed upon all sides, enjoyed himself immensely. He was invited everywhere; no ball, no party, no reception was complete, it seemed, without it was graced by his presence. His slight English accent and the little affectations he had cultivated became so modish that half the Frenchmen at Court attempted to copy them. Monsieur was more devoted to him than ever.

To Philip's amusement, Morgan appeared quite unimpressed with any of the fashionable people who surrounded them and for the majority he managed only the most basic civility. Even Monsieur could not overawe him!

"Monsieur thinks I ought to take a wife," Philip told him one sunny afternoon as they strolled the short distance from the Palais Royale to the Tuileries.

Morgan's expression did not change. "If that is what you want, my Lord."

"I'm not altogether sure that it is," Philip admitted, "and Monsieur only suggests it because he wishes me to stay in Paris. Shall we take a promenade about the gardens?"

"As you wish." Morgan always seemed content merely to be at his side and, indeed, Philip went barely anywhere without him. "Who do you hope to see, my Lord?"

"Whoever's to be seen. If I'm to take a wife I ought to view all that is available! Now who do you suppose is over there?"

Morgan followed his gaze to a small group about fifty yards away, noticeable by their loud laughter, which travelled across the park on the light Summer breeze. "A popular person by the sound of the merriment they are causing," he guessed.

Philip frowned. "Do you think so? I don't. That is mocking laughter we are hearing. They are taunting some poor soul, as like as not."

"Shall you stop them?"

"No. Is it my concern? Let them have their sport. The courtiers here are just like children and King Louis does nothing to discourage them, in fact he's just as bad. He puts hairs in Athénais' butter to make her scream! I really don't know why the world considers them sophisticated."

They would have walked on had not one of the group turned and seen them.

"My Lord Devalle, will you not join us?" It was the Marquis de Villeroy, who had grown more and more jealous of Monsieur's attentions to him.

"Blast! Now we're caught. Best go along and laugh like all the other apes, I suppose," Philip muttered sourly, though he managed to force a smile before he drew near.

"There is someone here that you really should meet," Villeroy said.

"I feared that. What poor wretch is suffering at your hands now, Villeroy? A hunchback? A blind beggar? Or is it some old lady so senile that she smiles even when you poke a stick at her or let a frog loose inside her petticoats?"

"You don't enjoy our games?" Villeroy winked at his companions. "Let his Lordship through, so that he may reassure himself that the person we wish him to meet is none of those things."

The crowd parted and Philip saw what he first took to be an old man, seated upon a bench with his head bowed. His hair, which hung in wispy waves about his shoulders, was as white as snow and he clutched a rug across his knees.

"This is our little poet," Villeroy said. "Monsieur Gaspard, won't you speak to our fair English visitor?"

The man slowly raised his head and Philip gasped in surprise. Gaspard was not old, as he had thought, but looked only in his early twenties and his face was more perfect than the face of any man or woman that Philip had ever seen, but there was something else. His skin was as white as his hair and his eyes had no pigment in them.

"An albino?" he asked, when he had drawn himself away from the oddly compelling sight. "I have heard of such people."

"That's right," Villeroy laughed. "An albino, a freak."

"Perhaps," Philip allowed, "but a beautiful one. He looks just like an angel."

"You think so? Then I had better show you the rest of your 'angel' before you decide to worship him! Rise, Gaspard. Have you no respect for Lord Devalle, the hero of the Rhine?" He prodded Gaspard with his cane.

Gaspard looked at Philip pleadingly and shook his head.

Philip had a sudden inkling of what he might be hiding under the blanket. "Leave him be," he said quickly. "I have no wish to torment the man. I've seen enough."

"Seen enough? You have not seen the half."

Villeroy poked Gaspard quite savagely, so that the poet had no choice but to rise. As he did so the blanket fell to the ground, exposing the sight he had clearly wished to hide.

"My God!" Philip turned away, sickened. Gaspard's legs were so twisted and malformed that they would not have supported him without the crutch he leaned upon.

"Come away," Morgan urged him. "There is nothing you can do here. Paris has a hundred cripples in every quarter."

But Villeroy stepped in front of him, obviously not intending to let his quarry escape so easily. "Well, my Lord, what do you think of our handsome poet now?"

"Get out of my way," Philip snapped, annoyed that he had fallen victim to Villeroy's jest. "He is grotesque, and well you know it."

Philip became aware of Morgan watching him anxiously as they walked home in silence. He was more deeply affected by the incident than he cared to admit and he knew that his parting words, spoken in his anger towards Villeroy, must have been extremely hurtful to Gaspard.

The following day a letter was delivered to Philip at the Palais Royale, where he was once again residing. He was seated in Monsieur's apartments idly watching whilst his host was massaged with his perfumed oil.

"Who is sending you letters?" Monsieur said jealously.

"I've no idea." Philip fanned himself languidly with the paper, for the day was warm, even for August. "I'll read it later." Although he spoke the language fluently, he still found reading French quite difficult.

Monsieur screamed as the servant entrusted with his massage pinched a fold of skin too hard. "You clumsy imbecile! I'll have you whipped. You see the discomforts that I must suffer in order to be beautiful?" he asked Philip.

Philip was unimpressed. "You should take more exercise if you want to lose some fat."

"I can't. You know how bad the fresh air is for my complexion."

"Then don't eat so many sweets."

"Oh, I do try." Even as he spoke Monsieur stretched out his hand and took another piece of marzipan from the dish beside his bed. He wiped his fingers on the sheet, much to Philip's disgust, and held out his hand. "Give me your letter. I will read it to you. Why, it's from that poet fellow, Jules Gaspard!"

"Why would he write to me?" Philip said, taken aback.

"How should I know? Villeroy told me that you met him in the Tuileries."

"Villeroy made sure I met him, and I tell you now that if he ever plays such a trick on me again I swear I will draw my sword upon him," Philip warned.

"Very well, my beauty," Monsieur soothed him, looking surprised at the vehemence of his tone. "He meant no harm, you know. We all use Jules Gaspard for our amusement from time to time."

"Why?"

"Why do you think? He's hideous," Monsieur said, laughing, "although he does have a way with words. If you were to ask for truth you would discover that a great many suitors have given their lovers Gaspard's tender poems and claimed the sentiments came from their own heart, including me!" Monsieur still fell regularly in and out of love with handsome young men, although Philip, who he would never manage to seduce, would always be his overriding passion. "That's how he's made his living since he came to Paris whilst you were away, and it's why he must tolerate us."

"I think that I would rather die than live my life deformed and the object of other's mockery," Philip said quietly.

"Well you don't have to, so why think upon it?" Monsieur unfolded the piece of paper. "Let's see what he wrote to you. 'My Lord, I pray you will forgive my great effrontery in sending this to you but, since the occasion of our meeting yesterday, I have been troubled at the displeasure which my appearance gave you. I would never wish to offend one as brave and honourable as yourself and I, therefore, beg your forgiveness. You may be aware that I am considered to be a poet and I have taken the liberty of preparing a short poem for you in the hopes that it will, in some small way, compensate for any affront I may have given you.'"

Philip was astounded. "Well, what do you make of that? He talks of giving me offence when, by rights, I should beg his forgiveness for the distress which my thoughtless words evidently gave him."

"I trust you will not do so," Monsieur said sternly. "It does not do to apologise to those of lower rank."

"Whatever you say." Philip generally found it easier to agree with Monsieur. "But I'd have you read his poem all the same, if you would be so kind."

Monsieur did read it and Philip could not be other than delighted by the work, for it was full of praise for his looks, his accomplishments and his valour.

"I told you he had a way with words. I wish I'd bought this from him and given it to you myself." Monsieur laid the poem down and seized Philip's hand possessively. "Damned impertinence I call it. I will rid you of him if you like."

Philip shook his head. "He has done nothing wrong."

"He is deformed. He belongs with others of his kind, who once begged in the Cours de Miracles."

"No, for those monsters used to feign their disabilities and strap up their limbs or pretend to be deformed. This poor devil has been truly blighted by nature, yet it seems he has a brain and feelings for which those less sensitive, including me, I'm afraid, do not give him credit."

Monsieur shrugged. "Oh, have it your own way. Perhaps you ought to purchase one of his poems to impress Mademoiselle de Bellecourt. I have decided she would make an admirable wife for you, for she is of a good Huguenot family, like yourself, and I believe she has more sense than to forbid you the company of your dearest friends."

"Which means she would accept my spending almost every minute with you," Philip smiled, glad that the subject of the conversation had been changed. "Even if they were the only qualities which I sought in a wife, I'm not too sure that I am ready yet to be a husband."

"Why, my dear, there's nothing to it." Monsieur had just taken a second wife, a large, outspoken German woman called Liselotte. "Just keep them satisfied once a month and the rest of the time's your own! At least Bellecourt is good-looking, whilst Madame is ugly, fat and quite inelegant."

"That's true! It should be she who is the husband and yourself the wife," Philip teased him, for Monsieur grew more and more effeminate as time went on. "I'll think on it, I promise, Monsieur."

"Where are you going now?" Monsieur wailed as Philip put on his hat.

"For a walk."

"In the Tuileries?"

"Not necessarily."

"You're lying! Wait, I'm coming with you," Monsieur decided. "Help me dress."

Philip sighed. Dressing Monsieur could take a long while and the stifling heat of the room was beginning to oppress him. "At times you are a tyrant to me," he complained, throwing down his hat again. "Now why do you want to come? You hate to walk."

"Well today I like to walk," Monsieur said perversely, "and, besides, in the gardens of the Tuileries we may meet with Gaspard. If we do then I shall employ him on your behalf to write a love poem to Mademoiselle de Bellecourt."

"You'll what?"

"You heard," the artful Monsieur giggled. "That will bring you one step nearer to becoming a husband."

Fortunately, Jules was not in the gardens that day, but Philip did manage to escape from Monsieur the following morning to exercise Ferrion in the Tuileries. As he had hoped, he found him in the same place, and alone this time.

Jules was writing but he looked up at the sound of the horse's hooves and Philip noticed the violet hue of his eyelids where the blood vessels showed through the almost transparent skin.

"Lord Devalle!" He looked startled

"Monsieur Gaspard, I would have a word with you," Philip began, a little awkwardly. He was not much in the habit of making apologies, but he knew that he must make this one, no matter what Monsieur said.

"I hope you are not upset at my sending you the poem, my Lord."

"Not in the least," Philip assured him. "I was very flattered by it, indeed I don't see how I could be otherwise, so greatly does it extol my virtues! No, it was rather your letter which has upset me."

"That was never my intent. I do sincerely beg your pardon, my Lord."

Philip dismounted and sat down beside him on the bench. "In fact, Jules Gaspard, I have come to beg yours. It was a hurtful thing I said in front of you and I am sorry."

"You have come to apologise to me?" Jules said disbelievingly. "You should know, my Lord, that no-one ever does that, though they say much worse than you did."

Their eyes met Philip experienced the most curious sensation of calm. "Well I'm an Englishman. Let us say that we have better manners, though not necessarily more tact," Philip said ruefully.

"You are very gracious, Lord Devalle."

Philip smiled. "Should I not be gracious to an angel?"

Jules smiled too. "I hardly think God would have so blighted one of his own creatures, do you?"

Philip's eyes were drawn involuntarily to the blanket which covered the poet's legs. "How can you endure it?" he asked, filled with overwhelming pity for him.

"I have no option but to endure it," Jules said quietly. "Please don't trouble yourself on my account. I am most grateful to you for your kind words. They will help me to bear the cruel tongues of those from whom I must earn my living."

"Will you let me pay you for the poem that you wrote for me?" Philip said, feeling he would like to help him, yet not knowing how.

"No, it was a gift," Gaspard insisted. "I consider it an honour that you should accept my humble offering."

There was no more to be said on that, for Philip did not want to hurt his feelings, yet he wished there was something he could do for Gaspard all the same. "Perhaps I'll see you here another day," he said as he mounted Ferrion again.

"I shall eagerly await that pleasure, Lord Devalle".

Philip spoke about the meeting to Morgan later, though he could not explain the feeling that had come over him when he had looked into Gaspard's strange, colourless eyes. "It really was uncanny," Philip told him. "I have never felt anything quite like it, and there is something else that's strange; I've seen men injured on the battlefield, men with broken bones or bullet wounds, but none have ever affected me in the way he has."

After that Philip often went to the Tuileries to talk to Jules Gaspard, though he never told Monsieur.

He learned that Jules was of bourgeois birth, and he had been treated as an outcast by his parents on account of his strange pigmentation. As a child he had existed upon the scraps left after the rest of the household had eaten and, on account of this poor diet, he had developed rickets. The disease had left him so horribly deformed that his family had decided to rid themselves altogether of such an unwholesome freak and had taken him to a monastery so that they need no longer look upon him.

Jules had remained there, shut away from the sight of men until he was himself a man, but he had no love of the monastic life. The monks were strict but they taught him a great deal and by the time he left them Jules had received a thorough education. At first he sought employment as a tutor for the sons of noblemen but there were none, it seemed, who wanted such an unsightly creature in their home.

Though nature had been cruel, she had bestowed upon him two gifts; beauty and the ability to write words that could fire the imagination and excite the senses. Jules had decided to become a poet and, armed only with his courage and his talent for verse, he had set out to survive amongst people who mocked his deformity but bought his work.

Despite all he had suffered he was filled with neither self-pity nor bitterness, but only resignation for his misfortunes and great patience. All in all, Jules Gaspard was like no person Philip had ever met.

The Summer passed and Philip was not recalled to action but in September he was summoned to the Louvre, and he was certain he would soon be reunited with his troop.

"Just in time for another Winter campaign," Morgan complained as Philip left him in the courtyard of the palace.

"Well for myself I shall be pleased to set off on campaigns again," Philip said. "I am beginning to tire of being idle."

But Louis' first words dispelled all his hopes for an early recall to action.

"I have some sorry news that I wished to convey to you myself," Louis told him. "Naarden has fallen to the Orangeman and the Maréchal de Luxembourg was powerless to prevent it, for he had insufficient men. I have sent orders for him and his forces to return home."

"Your Majesty is abandoning the United Provinces?" Philip could scarcely believe what he was hearing. "We fought so hard for it."

"I know, but I have no choice. It is too far away," Louis said. "I have enemies for neighbours now that the Prince of Orange has acquired some allies, so I must attend to my own frontiers. The Dutch are even now moving with the Emperor of Austria toward Bonn."

"And what of Woerden?" Philip asked, remembering the long, tedious months that he and his troop had spent there.

"I'm afraid I have had to give orders to pull down your fortifications. Louvois has persuaded me it is for the best."

Philip smiled wryly at that. Louvois was a minister, not a soldier. The decision was a cold and practical one, and could never have been made by any who had fought with the Army of Holland.

"I understand how you must be feeling," Louis said sympathetically, "and I dare say it seems harsh to you, who nearly lost your life holding it for me, but you will see, in time, that he is right. I shall certainly have need of you again but not, I think, for several months. I'm sure you can amuse yourself in Paris, unless, of course, you would prefer to return to England. Your own King may need you now that Prince Rupert has been defeated by De Ruyter at Kikjduin."

Philip had heard that the English navy had failed in their attempt to invade Holland but he had no wish to go home. As for serving King Charles, Philip had not forgiven him for his deceit and never would.

"I would rather fight for you, your Majesty," he said.

Louis looked pleased with that. "And I would rather keep you here, for you have served France well, but that is not the only reason I would have you stay. I will be frank with you, Philip, you have proved yourself to be an excellent companion for my brother. He thinks the world of you."

"And I like him," Philip said truthfully. Irritating though Monsieur could be at times, Philip would have done almost anything for him.

"I know you do. I can tell those who only want him for their own advantage, even if he can't. That is why I banished the Chevalier de Lorraine, although I have allowed him home now and, no doubt, he has already found his way back into Monsieur's heart."

Philip shared Louis' opinion of Lorraine who, he felt, exerted nothing but evil influence over the besotted Monsieur.

"As you say, your Majesty, but there is little I can do to save him from himself," he pointed out.

"But he takes great note of you," Louis said, "and he talks about you all the time. He wants you to choose a wife and take up residence in France, so I understand."

"That is correct, your Majesty, but I am not yet in a position to do so," Philip said, a little embarrassed, for he had no wish to discuss his finances with Louis.

Louis, it seemed, had already made it his business to discover them. "If you were to find a property in Paris which you liked, and which was close to my brother's palace, then I do not believe you would find me ungenerous to a Hero of France," he said, smiling.

Philip knew that he was being bought, for Monsieur's sake, but the offer was attractive all the same, and certainly not one that he could turn down without causing offence. "Your Majesty is generous. I will begin my search immediately."

"Well?" Morgan asked, when Philip met him in the courtyard afterwards. "Do we ride to rejoin Luxembourg?"

"We do not ride," Philip said flatly. "The Maréchal de Luxembourg is even now engaged upon a tactical withdrawal from the United Provinces whilst I, it seems, am to be married and remain in Paris. What do you think of that?"

"I think you will not be contented with that arrangement for very long."

"And you are right, even though the King offers to help me buy a house to sweeten my enslavement to him! Hell's teeth! Why did we fight, Morgan? To meekly give back all we gained? A pox on Louvois, who wages his war on paper and not up to his belly in a bog!"

Philip purchased a property near the Place Royale in the Marais district, which was rapidly becoming the fashionable quarter, inhabited by the nobility and the richer bourgeois.

It was an elegant building of pink and white stone with tall iron gates in front, leading to a courtyard with stables and a large, walled garden. He employed a young married couple, Monsieur and Madame Bisset, as gardener and housekeeper, and also, at Monsieur's absolute insistence, two coal-black Negroes, for blackamoors were all the rage in Paris. Their job was to drive the carriage he had bought and to care for the horses. Morgan was put in charge of everyone and everything, and took on his new responsibilities with his customary impassiveness.

For the next few weeks Philip was absorbed in selecting the furnishings and decorations, aided, naturally, by Monsieur. He still found time occasionally to walk or ride in the Tuileries but Jules, it seemed, had disappeared. No-one had seen him or knew what had happened to him.

Philip's house was soon transformed into a very smart dwelling. King Louis was more than generous to him and so were his many friends. Monsieur presented him with a magnificent Boulle cabinet, inlaid with tortoiseshell and decorated with gilt cupids, whilst Monmouth had a mosaic table imported for him from Florence.

Yet Philip was not completely happy. This fact did not escape Monsieur, who came almost daily to cast a critical eye over the progress and make suggestions.

"Did you ever employ that poet fellow to write a verse for Mademoiselle de Bellecourt?" he asked Philip one day, as he walked from room to room regarding the finished decorations.

"No, I never did." Philip had often pondered on what might have happened to him. "Why do you ask?"

"Do you know I think the tapestries would be better hung in here and not the salon." Monsieur went back into the salon and considered the four tapestries, which showed Flora, Ceres, Vulcan and Neptune as the four seasons of the year.

"I like them where they are," Philip said firmly. Although many of Monsieur's suggestions were agreeable to him he resolutely ignored those that were not.

Monsieur sniffed. "Oh, suit yourself dear. Now, what was I saying?"

"The poet," Philip prompted.

"Oh, yes. If you still want Gaspard to write for you I understand that he is once more plying his trade in the Tuileries. Strange. I thought he might have died of some disease, didn't you? He is a sickly-looking creature."

Philip and Morgan rode to the gardens directly Monsieur had left. They found Jules there, alone and working upon a composition, but even the undemonstrative Morgan looked shocked to see how thin and drawn he was.

Philip noticed, too, that he shivered in the raw November wind and that, beneath his patched cloak, he wore the same thin coat he had worn throughout the Summer.

"He'll not survive this winter out of doors," Morgan said as they reined their horses a little way away.

Philip feared he was right. "I have to help him. Morgan."

"Why?"

Philip shook his head. "I don't know. All I know is that if I do nothing then his death will be forever on my conscience."

"He may not take help from you," Morgan pointed out. "From what you say he has some pride, despite his circumstances."

"A great deal of it," Philip agreed. "Oh well, I'll see what I can do." He dismounted and handed his bridle to Morgan. "I had best do this alone. It might be easier for him."

Jules looked up from his work and smiled with pleasure to see who was approaching him. "Lord Devalle! I have missed the sight of you."

"It is good to see you again, too," Philip said, "but you should not be sitting out here on such a cold day."

"You are probably right, my Lord, but I have little choice, for it is here I meet my clients and without them I would starve."

"But you have not met them here for several weeks."

"Alas, I had a fever, which left me too weak to walk," Jules explained.

"I trust you are recovered now?"

"I have to be, my Lord." Jules pulled a wry face. "I owe my landlord several weeks rent and if I do not pay him soon then I may find myself spending my nights as well as my days in these gardens!"

"I would like to help you," Philip said hesitantly. He had never offered to help anyone before and he was not quite sure how to go about it.

"If you would be so kind as to encourage your friends to buy my work it would help me a great deal."

Philip looked at him pityingly, for he knew the abuse the poet had to suffer at the hands of his paying customers if he wanted to exist upon their money. "How much do you owe?"

"A great deal, I'm afraid, my Lord, nearly seventy francs, but I can earn it if the gentlemen of Paris are feeling generous."

"And in the meantime you are at the mercy of their spite."

"I don't mind that so much as I mind being hungry."

"You shall not be hungry, nor shall you be homeless," Philip said. "I will meet you here tomorrow at midday and I will have with me one hundred francs, to pay your debts and for you to buy yourself a warmer Winter coat."

Jules looked astonished. "I cannot take your money, my Lord."

"Nonsense! Don't protest, Jules. This is something that I wish to do for you." Before Jules could argue any further Philip returned to his horse and he and Morgan rode away.

Philip told him what he had said. "You don't approve," he guessed when Morgan made no reply.

"It is not my place to approve or disapprove your actions, my Lord."

Philip gave him a sidelong glance. "Since when have you known your place? You venture your opinions, unasked, upon everything else, including Monsieur and my taste in decorations, so why not upon this?"

"Very well, if you must have it from me, no, I do not approve," Morgan said, "though perhaps not for the reasons you suppose.

It is a kind thing you are doing but I fear if you become too involved with him you may get hurt, that is all."

"I don't see how," Philip said stubbornly.

"Don't you?" Morgan said, in the tone of someone who saw only too well. "You cannot take responsibility for him."

Philip knew, if he admitted it, that Morgan was right but it was the first time in his life that he had been prompted to a totally unselfish act and he was not prepared to give thought to the consequences.

"It's not as though I can't afford it," he said defensively. "The paltry sum he needs is only a quarter of what I spent on those blasted Gobelin tapestries that Monsieur persuaded me to buy! In any case my mind is quite made up. I shall meet him, as agreed, tomorrow morning and that will be the end of it."

They returned to the Tuileries the following morning, in Philip's coach this time, for they were to drive straight on to Fontainebleau. The King and Monsieur always visited the palace in the Autumn and Philip had been invited to join them.

They left the vehicle at the entrance to the gardens and walked over to the bench where Jules usually sat but, although it was past midday, there was no sign of him.

Philip tutted irritably, for he was not due to return to Paris for a week.

"Perhaps it was too wet for him today," Morgan said, for it had rained heavily overnight and the air was still damp and chill.

Philip recalled how cold Jules had looked the day before and thought Morgan was probably right. "Well, for whatever reason, he is not here, more's the pity, and we cannot wait. I'm in sufficient trouble with Monsieur already for not travelling to Fontainebleau with him."

Philip was about to turn and go when he heard laughter and, looking about, saw a circle of people he recognised, apparently being well entertained by something.

He was in no mood to join them and would have left had he not heard his own name clearly mentioned. He silently approached the group and saw Captain Leventier amongst the revellers.

"Leventier! Since you appear to be sharing a joke at my expense, shall you not be gracious enough to share it with me?"

Leventier looked a little uneasy. "Major! It is not at you we laugh, I assure you, but at the temerity of one who dared to employ your name in his defence."

"And who is this bold gentleman?"

"The poet. He claimed to be here today at your invitation. We thought to make him pay for his presumption, that's all."

Philip stiffened. "What have you done to him?"

Leventier's smile faded and he stood aside. Jules lay on the wet ground. His crutch was broken in two and his hat trampled in the mud beside him. His clothes and face were stained with dirt and a sheet of paper with his writing upon it was torn to pieces and scattered over him.

"Dear God! You're animals, the lot of you." Philip swung round on them furiously. "How could you do this to a helpless cripple?"

"Major, you must understand that we little thought he was really here to meet you," Leventier protested. "We assumed you were on your way to Fontainebleau."

"Well I am not, as you can plainly see. He told the truth. He's here at my request and let it be known now that if any of you filthy cowards are again tempted to vent your spite on Monsieur Gaspard they will find themselves facing my sword."

It was a rash threat for, by order of the King, duelling was now illegal, but none seemed about to question his intent as they all made haste to leave.

Morgan was already helping Jules up from the muddy ground. He was considerably shaken and Philip looked at him with concern.

"You have suffered this on my account, I fear," he said regretfully. "Are you much hurt?"

"Only my pride," Jules said. "You must not mind the things they do to me, my Lord. I am well used to it and I would not have you make enemies on my account."

"I do not fear to have such men as enemies," Philip assured him.

Morgan retrieved Jules' hat, which was battered beyond repair. "It's ruined, I'm afraid."

"It does not matter," Jules told him. "I shall miss my crutch a good deal more, for I cannot walk a step without it."

"We will take you home in my coach," Philip said, offering his arm for Jules to lean upon.

Morgan went on ahead, and Philip knew the reason for the Welshman's stony expression.

"Why did they turn on you today?" he asked Jules.

Jules' pale eyes met his. "I was on my way to meet you with a poem I had composed to express my gratitude at your generosity, but they tore the paper from my hand and ordered me to be gone since I was spoiling the beauty of the gardens for them. When I explained that I could not leave because I was to meet with you they set upon me. I am most grateful for your intervention, my Lord, although," he added sadly, "I could wish they had not shamed me so in front of you."

"They have done you more favours than you know," Philip said, an idea forming in his mind whilst he helped Jules into the coach.

They crossed the Pont Neuf to the other side of the River Seine and soon were in the narrow streets of the quarter known as Saint Michel. Philip looked about him distastefully, for the dingy hovels crowded together bore little resemblance to the fine dwellings of the Marais. The women washing their clothes by the banks of the river stared curiously at the rich conveyance and the two blackamoors.

"You live here?" Philip said, as they stopped before a dilapidated lodging house.

"For the moment, but I hope one day to finish writing my play and then I may be able to move up in the world," Jules said with a little smile. "They are only humble rooms but I would be most pleased if you would accept my hospitality, although, of course, I would quite understand if you declined," he assured Philip hastily. "I gather you were upon your way to Fontainebleau and I have already delayed you far too long."

"Never mind Fontainebleau. I can go there later." Philip helped him down.

"But what about Monsieur?" Jules said. "Will he not be angry with you?"

"Monsieur can forgive me absolutely anything if I make sufficient fuss of him!"

A savage barking began as soon as they set foot upon the stairs. "Is that animal yours?" Philip asked him,

"He is my protector," Jules explained. "This is a rough district and I am, as you know, a weak and helpless person."

As he unlocked the door the largest, most ferocious-looking dog that Philip had ever seen bounded toward them. Jules spoke to him and the beast quietened.

"No-one would ever attack me in the streets of Paris, even at night, if Brutus is with me," Jules said, patting the dog's massive brown head with obvious affection. "It is a pity I did not take him with me to the Tuileries today, but I fear the mere sight of him would frighten away those from whom I try to earn a living!"

As Philip looked around the shabby little dwelling his mind was quite made up. "I have thought of a way to ensure that you will no longer suffer at the hands of the courtiers and the so-called 'gentlemen' of Paris."

"My Lord?"

"I recently purchased a house in the Marais, one that is far too large for me. Monsieur has become so dependent on me that I must accompany him everywhere he goes and, consequently,

I am scarcely ever even at home. It would please me greatly if you would reside there as my guest when I return from Fontainebleau."

Jules stared at him. "You mean to become my patron?"

"Why not? If you have talent, as I think you have, then it should be put to better use than helping the Parisians woo their mistresses," Philip said. "Write your poems, Jules Gaspard, write your play, or whatever else you wish. I am offering to support you until you can earn a decent living."

"My Lord, your kindness overwhelms me," Jules stammered. "What can I say?"

"I beg you to say yes, for it will save us both a most uncomfortable Winter, since I shall not then have to ride out to the Tuileries if I wish to talk to you!"

Jules laughed, which was a thing Philip suspected he had not done for a very long time. "When did you think of this, my Lord?"

"Just now," Philip confessed.

"You may regret it," Jules warned him. "There will be many who will condemn you for your generosity to someone they despise."

"On the contrary, I believe that when you are successful there will be many who will compliment me on my foresight in befriending you but, whether they do or not, you are most welcome to my hospitality for as long as you need it," Philip said sincerely. "You can live as separately from me as you please and you will not be imposing on me one bit."

"In that case," Jules decided, "I would be delighted to accept your offer."

Now all Philip had to do was to tell Morgan!

SEVENTEEN

❦

Philip's decision was the talk of Paris, but he did not care. Monsieur sulked for a full two weeks but he could not manage without Philip for longer than that and became even more possessive of him than he had before, so that he had very little time to call his own.

What time he did have he enjoyed spending with Jules, taking him riding in his carriage or to the theatre, and a real friendship gradually struck up between them. It was a friendship more binding than Philip had enjoyed with John Bone and far deeper than his relationship with Monmouth had ever been. In some ways it was as if Jules was the brother that Henry had never been to him, a companion with whom he could share his innermost thoughts and confide his hopes and dreams.

Jules brought little with him save for his dog, from which he would not be parted, but Philip saw to it that he wanted for nothing. There was one thing, however, which Philip was unable to give his friend, and that was acceptance in society, although he was determined to set even that matter straight as soon as the opportunity presented itself.

It did after about three months. Monsieur came to call one day and told him of the funeral to be held for the playwright Molière, who had died that week.

"There will be many literary people at his commemoration service," Philip guessed. "I think I shall attend it."

"You?" Monsieur scoffed. "But you are an utter Philistine, my sweet!"

"May I not still mourn Molière, whose plays have entertained me, especially if by doing so I might meet, say, Racine or La Fontaine."

"You always said you hated intellectuals," Monsieur reminded him.

"I've changed my mind," Philip said, "or rather I have my reasons now for cultivating them."

"To sell Gaspard's poetry, I suppose," Monsieur said jealously, moving closer to him.

"Jules does not only write poetry but plays as well and, as his patron, I intend to use what influence I have to advance his interests."

"Why not hold a salon?" Monsieur said sarcastically. "Madame de Scudery has Sarazin as her star, Madame de Lafayette has Segrais and Madame de Suze has Pellisson. You have Jules Gaspard."

Philip seized his hand and kissed it. "What a very excellent idea!"

"I was joking," Monsieur protested, though he did not withdraw his hand.

"I rarely joke, you know that. If I held a salon could I count upon you to attend?"

Monsieur pouted. "I might, but you would have to coax me."

Philip told Jules of his idea. "If Monsieur comes, as I know he will, then the rest of Paris society will follow him."

"But is this what you really want?" Jules said. "To fill your lovely home with the very people who sneer at you for your goodness to me?"

"It is exactly what I want," Philip said. "I want to see the bastards forced to pay you homage. That will be sweet justice in an unjust world."

"But what if they do not care to pay the crippled poet homage?" Jules said. "Then you will be a laughing stock, my friend, all on account of me."

"They'll come," Philip predicted confidently. "They will all come once, if only out of curiosity. It is up to us to make sure they wish to come again."

Even Philip was amazed at the number who accepted his invitation and he threw himself into the preparations with an enthusiasm he had never previously felt for entertaining.

First, he contacted his tailor, Monsieur Bonhomme, who had already learned that dressing him was a profitable occupation!

"I am most honoured that your Lordship should see fit to call upon my unworthy talents yet again," he greeted Philip, bowing very low. "I shall endeavour to create a garment fit enough for one whose looks are so esteemed, but then, my Lord, the poorest rag would be as a king's richest raiment when it was fortunate enough to adorn such a magnificent figure as yours."

"You are wasting your time in flattering me today," Philip told him, "for I am not your customer."

"Then who?"

"Monsieur Gaspard."

Bonhomme looked horrified. "But, my Lord, he is... misshapen."

"Monsieur Bonhomme," Philip said heavily, "do you only ever accept the easy tasks in life? Whilst I'm sure it enhances your reputation greatly to be famed as my tailor, I, as you rightly say, would probably manage to look delightful in whatever I wore! In short, Bonhomme, the meanest tailor in the Rue Saint Jacques could dress me, whilst to dress Monsieur Gaspard requires a man of quite considerable talent. I consider you to be that man, and I am prepared to pay you handsomely for the trouble that you take. Shall you prove me wrong?"

Bonhomme was also susceptible to flattery, as Philip suspected!

"That is a different matter, my Lord. Indeed, when you put it that way there is not a tailor in Paris or the whole of France who could dress Monsieur Gaspard better but, I beg you, do not expect him to look as magnificent as yourself."

"But I do expect it, in fact I expect him to look better," Philip emphasised. "If you feel yourself to be unequal to the task then I pray you to say so now, for I'll not have his feelings hurt by your failure."

Bonhomme looked nervous. "What if, despite my best endeavours, I should fail?" he asked, a little apprehensively.

"Then I shall not pay you, nor shall I grace you with any future business, but I have every confidence in you, Monsieur Bonhomme. Shall you accept the challenge?"

Bonhomme sighed resignedly. "I accept it. Take me to him, my Lord. I will do my best."

"Of course you will and, what is more, you will compliment him, exactly as you do me."

Jules was writing at his desk in one of the rooms Philip had given over to him. It was a fine room in which to work, light and airy with large double doors that led into the garden, and it was furnished to Jules' own taste, which was simple and much more modest than Philip's own!

He looked up from his work as they entered and smiled a little wistfully. "Is this your tailor, Philip? I regret that you have summoned him against my wishes, for I know that you are wasting his time and your money."

"Monsieur Gaspard," Bonhomme cried, as though shocked, "did Bernini think his time was wasted when he was commissioned to fashion a likeness of the King from a block of marble? Should I, then, deem my own time wasted when I am commanded to create a masterpiece from silks and satins, the tools of my own art?"

Jules turned to Philip despairingly. "See how he runs on, my friend? Dispatch him upon his way now, before he tricks you into parting with good livres to deck me out in his expensive baubles."

But Philip was not listening to his protests. The tailor had already taken out his pattern book and was holding samples up against Jules' pale skin. By the time he turned back to Philip his face was alive with inspiration.

"My Lord, I have it! Monsieur Gaspard shall be a God of Snow! Since every colour is harsh against his complexion he should wear only white. White satin, embroidered with gold thread," he produced a sample with a flourish, "white velvet encrusted with pearls, white brocade with silver lace."

"Bonhomme, you are a genius!" Philip said, warming to his theme. "Silver buttons on his coat, silver buckles for his shoes."

Jules looked from one to the other in disbelief. "Philip, I beg you to stop before he thinks you are in earnest."

"But I am in deadly earnest," Philip assured him. "I can't wait to see the faces of our guests when they are confronted with a God of Snow!"

Philip's evening was well attended, both by the Court and by some of the most famous literary names in Paris.

Monsieur came, even though he had threatened right up to the last that he would not, for he dearly loved to tease, and also Athénais de Montespan. Philip was pleased to see them both for, where those two went, the rest of fashionable society soon followed.

Lest any should forget the rank and fame of their host, guests were confronted in the main salon by a larger than life-size portrait of Philip, clad in full military uniform and mounted on Ferrion. He was very proud of the magnificent study, and rightly so. The artist had caught his handsome looks to perfection, whilst the haughtiness of his expression reminded those who looked up at the canvas that they were the guests of Condé's proud 'young lion'.

Philip was an impeccable host, but the real wonder of the evening was Jules himself.

Monsieur Bonhomme had truly excelled in his art. Dressed so splendidly, and with a silver tasselled rug across his knees, it was easy to forget Jules' deformity. If any had come to mock, none did. In this setting Jules Gaspard had acquired dignity and, when he spoke, folk discovered that the beautiful, crippled poet from Saint Michel was capable of more than a verse with which a man might woo his sweetheart or a lady send a secret message to her lover!

Philip contributed very little to the conversations, indeed he had little in common with most of his guests, but he was content. The Beaux Esprits, as the select group of Paris intellectuals were known, discoursed lengthily upon subjects about which he knew nothing, and cared even less, but Jules was the centre of every discussion and those who talked also seemed prepared to listen to him, even Racine and La Bruyère, both of whom Philip had prevailed upon to attend when he had met with them at Molière's funeral.

"This will become a fashionable gathering place," Athénais predicted. "You have done well."

"Philip always does well," Monsieur interrupted, giving them both a kiss upon the cheek. "I must rush, for I left an admirer at home positively panting for my return."

"Don't tell me you are being unfaithful to your precious Chevalier de Lorraine already? You are a dreadful man!" Philip scolded him. "I'm so pleased I am not in love with you."

"But I would be faithful to you," Monsieur protested. "I would, I would," he insisted, his voice rising as they both broke into loud peals of laughter. "Oh well." He joined in with them good naturedly. "Perhaps I wouldn't!"

When Monsieur had gone upon his noisy way Philip looked toward a plainly-dressed woman who had been watching them most disapprovingly. "Who is that dowdy creature over there?" he asked Athénais. "She came with you, I think."

"That's Françoise Scarron, the widow of Scarron the poet. I brought her because she claims to be an intellectual.

"Is she a friend of yours?"

"Of sorts. I obtained employment for her with the King."

Philip was surprised, for Louis generally liked those around him to be colourfully dressed and livelier.

"She is the governess to my children," Athénais explained. She already had two sons by Louis and he had acknowledged both of them. "She's trustworthy and very intelligent so I thought her a fitting companion for them."

"And yet you don't like her," Philip guessed, for he had noticed Athénais' expression.

"To be honest no, I don't, not anymore," Athénais confessed. "We used to get along quite famously but now she worms her way into Louis' favour behind my back. He is always talking about her."

"But surely such an insignificant female could never replace you in his affections," Philip said, with a conviction that might not have been so strong had he been able to see ten years into the future!

"Well I intend to take no chances," Athénais said. "I am trying to find another husband for her."

"What about the Duc de Villars?" Philip suggested. "He is looking for a wife and, since he is so old, she would not need to put up with him for very long, just long enough, perhaps to turn the King's attention from her."

"That's a very good idea," Athénais said, "and speaking of husbands, weren't you meant to become one?"

"Don't you start," Philip begged. "I have enough of that from the King and Monsieur! To tell the truth I don't believe I'm ready yet to take on such responsibilities."

"What nonsense! You are twenty-four years old and should be settled," Athénais said. "There must be someone here in Paris who takes your fancy."

"There is," Philip told her, looking directly into her eyes, "but not only is she already married but she has as her lover the King of France."

"Philip Devalle, you are as preposterous as Monsieur," Athénais scolded, striking him with her fan, but not too hard. "Do you think I don't see through your pretty words?"

In fact, Athénais de Montespan was exactly Philip's type of woman, with her rounded figure and her infectious humour. He thought she looked exceptionally lovely that night, for she had dyed her dark hair blonde, the same shade as her old rival, Louise de La Vallière, for Louis preferred blondes. "When I find a woman just like you I'll marry her," he pledged.

"You are a charmer, Philip," Athénais said, smiling, "but I tell you this, I pity the woman who does manage to snare you, for she'll never have you to herself!"

Philip asked Morgan to bring her cloak, for Athénais was about to leave, but he fastened it around her shoulders himself. The royal mistress had very fine shoulders and, since none were looking, he could not resist the temptation to lightly kiss each one.

"Thank you for coming, sweetheart. You have done me a great favour."

"You deserve support for what you're doing for Jules," Athénais said seriously. "It is a fine and noble thing, and quite unlike you."

"Are you surprised to find that I have a better side to my nature?" Philip asked, feigning hurt.

She laughed. "Frankly yes! I'd better see if Françoise wants to ride with me, I suppose. It seems she is leaving too."

Françoise Scarron was indeed approaching them. She accepted Athénais' offer then nodded stiffly to Philip. "Goodnight, Lord Devalle."

She would have passed straight on but Philip felt incensed at her offhand manner.

"Have I offended you, Madame Scarron?"

"Only a person such as you would need to ask that question, my Lord," she said stonily.

Athénais gasped in horror at this rudeness. Françoise went to walk on, but Philip was not about to that remark pass.

"What the hell does that mean?" he demanded. "Explain yourself, Madame."

Scarron looked imploringly at her friend. "Do you hear the way he speaks to me? Must I endure this?"

"Don't look to me for help," Athénais snapped.

Françoise turned back to him. "Lord Devalle, I know you as a soldier of some repute, one who has served France well, and for that reason I was prepared to overlook the unfortunate fact that you are a Protestant."

"Damned decent of you, I'm sure!"

"What I cannot overlook, however, are your morals. You are one of Monsieur's set but, even so, I little thought that you would bring your depravity into your own home."

"My depravity?" Philip looked at her in disbelief as he caught her meaning.

"What else do you call it when you take a creature from the streets, a creature which God in His wisdom has seen fit to blight with weakness, and possess him so that he has not the will to see your evil for what it is? The rest of Paris may uphold your generosity if they please. For myself I shall go to my confessor tomorrow and beg forgiveness for entering such a house of wickedness."

Philip controlled his temper for the sake of Athénais, who looked mortified. "Madame Scarron, for all your pretended piety you must have the mind of a gutter slut if you can think of my taking indecent advantage of the twisted body of a cripple."

"Why else would you have him live with you? In my opinion he has but a mediocre talent for verse."

That did it.

"You will not dare to insult Jules in my house, you odious woman." Philip pointed to the door which Morgan, who had heard everything, swiftly opened. "Get out of here with your foul insinuations, and be thankful for your friendship with Madame de Montespan. She is a lady and, in deference to her feelings, I will say no more to you than that you would do well to emulate her manners even though you can never match her beauty."

Philip paused only to kiss Athénais' hand before he strode away.

He had made himself an enemy for the future, and a more powerful one than he could possibly have envisaged, but the scene had fortunately passed unnoticed by the remaining company. What was more, it seemed that if any were of similar opinion to Scarron they had the good breeding, or good sense, to keep it to themselves.

Most, on the contrary seemed enchanted by Jules, and the courtly Racine took a particular interest in him. It was to be a most advantageous friendship for, through his influence, Jules' play, 'Le Touche-à-Tout', was performed by the King's Troupe at Molière's theatre in the Rue de Valois.

It was a huge success. Soon Philip's house was crowded with visitors, for it suddenly became not only acceptable but positively fashionable to associate with Jules Gaspard.

Still only half-believing what was happening to him, Jules collected together all the poems he had written and published them in three volumes, copies of which he charmingly presented to the ladies of their rapidly increasing circle at a special party Philip gave in his honour, to mark his most recent venture into the literary world.

There was one guest at the celebration whose presence even Philip had not dared to hope for - Louis himself.

Never slow to patronise talent, Louis had evidently decided that, since Gaspard appeared, after all, to be an author of some promise, he should be seen to be encouraging him.

He entered unannounced. A hush immediately fell over the room and the musicians Philip had hired for the evening ceased their playing. Philip turned from a conversation with Marie de Bellecourt to ascertain the reason for the lull.

He could not have been more delighted. He was relieved too. Philip had feared that Françoise Scarron might have managed to poison the King's mind against him with her insinuations but it appeared that, if she had spoken against him, Louis had taken no notice.

"Well done," Marie whispered, as he left her to welcome his illustrious guest. "Your triumph is now complete!"

"I am most honoured by your Majesty's presence," Philip said.

"It is more honour than you deserve, you know," Louis told him with mock severity, "for you have disobeyed me. You were supposed to be spending the Winter becoming a husband, not a patron of the arts!"

"But did your Majesty not observe me, as you entered, intent upon carrying out your orders?" Philip protested, although he had decided long ago that if he had to take a wife to please the King then it would not be Marie de Bellecourt, for she was listless and bored him very quickly.

Louis did not look convinced. "It seems to me that one with your reputation with the ladies could have moved a little faster in the matter if you desired, particularly since you can be sure your efforts will be crowned with certain success," he said dryly, "but what I really want to know is how you were able to judge Gaspard's talent, since you claim to be illiterate! I suspect that this whole enterprise was designed solely to spite those you threatened in the Tuileries." Very little escaped Louis' intelligence network! "No matter. You gambled on him and you won. Now you had better introduce him to me."

Those surrounding Jules stood aside to let the King approach and, as he did so, Jules struggled to stand, but Louis motioned him to remain where he was.

"You suffer great disabilities, Monsieur Gaspard. On account of that I will always permit you to remain seated in my presence."

Philip was stunned by that, for such a favour was rarely granted, even to those of aristocratic blood.

"Thank you, your Majesty, you are very gracious," Jules said.

"I come to offer you my felicitations and encouragement," Louis told him. "I hope you will continue to enrich France's store of literary works, for it is my most earnest desire that this nation should be regarded as the cultural centre of all Europe."

"I am most grateful for the honour of being permitted to participate in that great aim, your Majesty," Jules replied softly.

At Louis' signal the musicians once more commenced to play and he took Philip's arm.

"How much is all this costing you, I wonder? Probably more than Gaspard earns from the performing of one play and the publication of three books of verse," Louis said, as they walked together through to the little salon, where Philip's caterers had laid out a tempting feast of delicacies. Louis was a prodigious eater, just like Monsieur.

"My army pay is all gone," Philip admitted, "but my father sends me money when I ask him."

"And does he know exactly how you spend it?" Louis said. "What if he decides that the patronage of a Paris poet is a cause undeserving of his money? I think, perhaps, it is time you took up arms for France again."

Philip was pleased. He had been a man of action too long to really enjoy a life of idleness. "I can't believe your Majesty came here tonight just to tell me that," he said with a smile.

"Does it matter why I am here, only that I am?" Louis said. "I have done you a great favour by attending your reception, and well you know it, and by doing so I have properly established Jules Gaspard in the eyes of Paris. He will not need you to advance him now and I would like to take you back into my service, if you are willing to serve me again, that is."

"I am at your Majesty's command," Philip assured him.

"Good, for I do need you, but before I press you to rejoin my army you should first know that your country has now declared itself neutral."

Philip was surprised by that but undeterred. "Since I am of mixed blood I do not believe that England's decision needs to affect me for I am loyal, above all, to the interests of France."

"You should also know that we have only Sweden now remaining as our ally. Two powerful armies stand poised to attack us as we speak, from the north and from the east, so that I must, regrettably, relinquish the towns we took along the Rhine, but Turenne and I march soon to retake Franche-Comté."

Condé had taken the province of Franche-Comté seven years before, only to see it returned to Spain in the Peace of Aix-la-Chapelle.

"Am I to ride with your Majesty?" Philip asked eagerly.

Louis smiled at his enthusiasm. "Alas no, for Condé has particularly requested that you be assigned to his division. He is to resume command of the northern frontier."

That was even better.

✑

Turenne regained Franche-Comté in only six weeks and moved on to Alsace.

Condé was preparing to leave in May and Philip was glad to see the great man looking so much better.

"I am well enough for what we have to do," Condé assured him. "The gout still troubles me but I dare say active service will do me more good than all the remedies of Bourdelet, my physician. I have told him that if I cannot get my boots on I shall ride into battle in my slippers!"

Philip laughed, for he could picture that. "Is the Maréchal de Luxembourg going with us?"

"Yes, and Enghien, but not the King, thank God! It is one thing to play games at Franche-Comté but quite another to fight upon the Northern Frontier. It will be no place for King Louis but you, my young lion, are another matter."

When Philip arrived home after his meeting with Condé at the Louvre he found Morgan on his knees packing the wooden travelling case that Philip took upon campaigns. It was a fine object, covered with Savonnerie tapestry, and it had spaces especially made in its lid and base to hold all the articles he needed whilst away from home, from cups, plates and a spoon to his hair brush and, of course, a mirror, for Philip never travelled far without one of those!

"It will be good to be away from Paris," he confessed to Morgan. "I have had enough of the erudite set for a while, although I would not wish Jules to hear me say it. It is his world, but it is not truly mine. Where is he, by the way? I ought to try to spend some time with him before we leave tomorrow."

"Monsieur Gaspard is in the garden," Morgan said. "I thought he ought to take advantage of the pleasant weather, for he gets so little fresh air these days, and scarcely any exercise."

Philip smiled at him fondly. "Morgan you have turned into a fussy mother hen! Seriously, I should thank you for the consideration you have shown Jules since he came here. I know you thought that I was wrong to involve myself with him but, as you see, everything has turned out splendidly and your fears for me were all in vain."

The campaign, which culminated in the battle of Seneff, was to be one that neither side could truly claim as a victory, although both did. Condé drove his troops to the very limits of their endurance. Condé's son, Enghien, was wounded and the number of French dead was estimated to be more than seven thousand. There were a good many officers amongst them, and Condé raised Philip to the rank of Lieutenant-Colonel, since the position had become available.

Philip and Morgan arrived home at the end of October, unharmed but battle worn and weary. Philip was ordered almost immediately to Saint Germain, where Louis confirmed his promotion, following Condé's recommendations.

Jules had not been idle during Philip's absence. He had completed a second play and Philip had arrived back in Paris in time to see the first performance and to hear his friend hailed as the new comic genius of the French stage.

He was quite a different person from the long-suffering and pathetic waif that Philip has rescued from the Tuileries. Jules had blossomed in the environment that Philip had provided for him. He was confident and had even become a trifle vain, which was scarcely surprising since his face was constantly being praised by the ladies who now jealously surrounded him. Jules found that amusing, in fact Jules found a great deal amusing these days and, through his eyes and his perceptive wit, Philip had learned to see life in quite a different way.

He returned to the Netherlands with Condé a few months later. This time Louis would not be left behind, although he did allow Condé to remain as Commander-in-Chief.

Philip found that campaigning with the King was a very different business, for Louis could not dispense with ceremony, even under such circumstances! Despite being impeded by the royal train, the 'Army of Flanders' managed to achieve an impressive series of victories and a satisfied Louis returned home in July. Philip accompanied him, planning to spend a few months in Paris, but, in August, came the devastating news that Turenne had been killed in action at Hainault.

Condé was summoned from the Netherlands to take Turenne's place and restore order amongst the demoralised troops and Philip was preparing to rejoin him there when another, far more personal, misfortune struck.

EIGHTEEN

❦

Jules caught a chill in the Autumn and took to his bed, where he remained for two weeks. Even after Philip allowed him to come downstairs again he spent nearly the whole of each day upon his couch, for the mild illness seemed to have sapped most of his strength.

He was lying there one day, propped up on a pile of pillows, looking out onto the damp, windswept garden when Philip came home with a little box in his hand.

"What's this, a gift?" Jules said as the box was tossed onto his lap.

"Only a trifle," Philip said as Jules opened the box and took out a bracelet made of silver and set with sapphires. "Do you like it?"

"Of course I do, it's beautiful," Jules said, slipping it onto his delicate wrist," but you should not spend your money on me."

"I thought it would cheer you up and it will go well with the blue-edged satin coat I ordered for you from Monsieur Bonhomme. I hope he will have it finished in time."

Jules fingered the bracelet. "In time for what?"

"I just heard that I am to leave in a week to join Condé at Utrecht. I assumed you would want to be at Court to see me on my way?"

"I would not miss it for the world," Jules assured him.

"I trust you will be well enough by then."

"I'm sure I will."

Philip studied him. He was more than a little concerned that his friend was still unable to walk more than a few steps without tiring.

"Well I am not so sure, in fact I'm not even certain I ought to leave you whilst you are so weak. Perhaps I should not be going."

"That won't be necessary," Jules insisted. "I feel stronger every day."

Philip didn't know whether to believe him or not. He turned away, appearing to glance at himself in a mirror but, in reality, he was looking at Jules' reflection, not his own.

Jules, unaware that he was being watched, had reached for his crutch and was attempting to get to his feet, but he collapsed back on the couch, wincing.

Philip turned back to him. "Why are you lying to me, Jules?" he said gently. "You're getting worse, not better, aren't you?"

"My legs are aching, that is all."

Philip frowned. "You've never complained of that before, in all the time I've known you."

"It's just a twinge, not worth mentioning," Jules reassured him quickly. "All this cold, damp weather has occasioned it, no doubt. Why, in a week I shall be walking as well as I did before. The ache has gone already, see?"

To prove his words Jules once more raised himself and this time managed to take a step, then bit upon his lip as though a red-hot pain had shot through his twisted limbs.

"Stop it, do you hear me? Stop it!" Philip sat him down again. "In heaven's name, why are you doing this?"

Jules did not reply, but he had no need to, for Philip knew the reason right enough.

"This is my fault, isn't it? You are trying to please me in my selfishness." He lifted Jules legs and laid him back upon the cushions. "I will stay in Paris until you are fully recovered," he decided.

"No, Philip," Jules said. "I'll not have you sacrifice your career on my account, not when you've done so much for me. Besides, you cannot disobey the King."

"King Louis cannot order me, for I am not his subject but his guest," Philip reminded him.

"Then what of Condé?"

"I will report to him when I can. First, though, we must get you well, completely well," Philip stressed. "I shall take care of you myself."

"You are such a stubborn man," Jules cried despairingly. "A brilliant future lies ahead of you. You can't discard it all on account of me."

"I don't intend to, but it's no use asking me to go away when you are like this, for I won't," Philip said firmly. "There will be other wars and other chances for me to win my laurels. Your friendship means a great deal to me and I tell you now that I will see you fully restored to health before I rejoin my regiment."

Jules sighed. "You are resolved on this, I see."

"Completely. I pray that whatever ails you passes quickly but, until it does, you will just have to endure my company, for I shall not leave your side!"

Philip was as good as his word. For the next few weeks he attended to Jules' every want, but there was little he could do to ease his friend's pain.

The Court went to Fontainebleau and returned to Paris for the Winter. Philip then found himself inundated with callers concerned for Jules' state of health. Philip welcomed them all but, directly he saw any signs of fatigue in Jules' face, the visitors, regardless of their rank, would be politely asked to leave.

This did not, of course, apply to Monsieur, who became a surprising source of strength to Philip. He visited daily, bringing with him a fund of entertaining stories and usually some outrageous cure sent by his German wife, Liselotte, who prided herself upon having a better knowledge than the physicians, in whom Philip had no faith at all. He was sceptical of Madame's cures as well, but he was growing desperate, so Jules patiently swallowed all the concoctions she sent him, had a spider tied to each of his ankles and allowed his legs to be rubbed with a substance called Pomade Divine, prepared especially for Madame by her chemist.

Whether on account of these methods or because nature had temporarily affected her own cure, by the end of January Jules was well enough to be taken out into the garden in his special chair on wheels that Philip had purchased for him, but he had lost what little use he had once had in his legs and he was never to walk again.

With this last vestige of independence wrested from him Jules became, of necessity, more and more dependent on Philip. He still wrote, though not so prolifically, and during February his third play, a romantic comedy, was staged. It was played at the Palace of Saint-Germain before Louis and the Queen, and Philip took him there to see it and to hear the King acclaim it as a masterpiece.

Before the month was out, however, Jules took sick again, this time with a fever which raged for a week. He was delirious and burning to the touch, and sick if anything but water passed his lips. Philip, watching anxiously for signs of the ever-prevalent smallpox, nursed him once again but, though no pustules formed and the heat passed at last from his body, the fever seemed to have sapped the remaining strength from him.

Visitors still called, including Condé. His task in Alsace was now completed and he had retired from the army, for his own health had deteriorated yet again.

"That was to be the last campaign not only for myself and poor Turenne but for Monteccucoli too," he said. "His health is as poor as mine. I think we were both as anxious as each other to be done with fighting before the Winter set in!"

"The world will never see the likes of such commanders as you again," Philip reckoned.

"Especially Turenne. I tell you I did wish that I could talk with his ghost that I might learn of his designs and the methods of that devil, Monteccucoli."

Condé had often been accused of jealousy toward Turenne so Philip was pleased to hear him speak so generously of him. "What will you do now, Monsieur le Prince?"

"What will I do? Enjoy Chantilly, my friend, and you must visit me there one day, for there is good hunting all about. I did hope to see my son succeed me but, alas, Louis sets no great store by him and I fear he has no future in command. You now, my young lion, you could rise to great heights if you put your mind to it."

When Philip returned from escorting Condé to his carriage he found Jules, who had been privy to the conversation, looking up at the portrait of him in his military regalia.

Philip followed the direction of his gaze and understood the thoughts which were passing through Jules' mind.

"If that troubles you I will take it down."

"Don't do that," Jules pleaded. "I enjoy seeing how grand you look in your uniform."

"Well I do not. I'm tired of it, and of visitors who talk about the past," Philip said crossly. "If you're so fond of the wretched thing then I will have it hung in your room."

He did so and replaced it with an oval portrait he had commissioned of Jules himself.

Monsieur raised an eyebrow in surprise when he saw it the following day.

His Lordship will be with you in a moment," Morgan told him. "He is helping Monsieur Gaspard dress."

"What? Does he attend to him himself?" Monsieur looked shocked. "It is not fitting for a man of his rank to do that."

Morgan only grunted. For once he was in complete agreement with Monsieur!

Philip entered then and looked from one to the other. He sensed the unaccustomed bond between the pair and guessed its cause.

"I do believe you are discussing me and, from the looks on both your faces, neither holds me in very high regard!"

"Nonsense! It is because I do regard you so highly that I disapprove of your behaviour. It is one thing to house and patronise Gaspard but quite another to act the part of his valet," Monsieur said. "Your reputation would suffer if it were known," he warned.

"I don't much care, so long as I can count on your friendship," Philip told him frankly.

"You will always have that, although I feel that you are taking me a lot for granted lately." Monsieur tossed his head.

"No," Philip protested. "I am always glad to see you. If I lost your company I should be distraught."

Monsieur beamed. "Would you really? I came to tell you that another friend of yours is here in Paris, the Duke of Buckingham."

Philip's face lit. "That is splendid news." he could think of no-one he would rather see.

It was an emotional reunion. Philip could confide in Buckingham as he could in no other, and for the first time he talked of his despair.

"My poor fellow," the Duke said sympathetically when he had heard all. "Monsieur spoke of your trouble but he never said how badly it was affecting you."

"I must make light of it in front of him or else he may not come to see me," Philip said, "and I confess to you, George, that without Monsieur this would be, at times, too hard to bear. Forgive me for burdening you with my problems when I have not seen you for so long."

"I only wish that I could help." Buckingham regarded him with real concern. "I have never seen you so upset over anything."

"Shall you meet Jules?" Philip asked. "It would mean a great deal to him, and to me, for I have spoken of you constantly."

"Indeed I will, dear boy, and I confess to being curious to meet the only person who has ever managed to touch your sympathies!"

The Duke's curiosity was satisfied a few minutes later, when Morgan wheeled Jules through in his chair.

"Good Lord!" Buckingham quickly recollected his manners. "Your pardon, Monsieur Gaspard, but I have never in my life met an albino."

Jules smiled at that. "We are very rare, I understand, your Grace. Some call us freaks!"

"Not I, monsieur," Buckingham said. "I am to have the privilege of watching one of your plays performed in my honour before I leave and it will be doubly pleasurable to me now that I have been fortunate enough to meet its esteemed author."

Philip was grateful to him. Blundering and misguided as Buckingham often was, he could always be relied upon in company to say exactly what was right.

The Duke conversed with Jules for a while about the theatre and told them of how the King's House in London, had burned down and had been replaced by a magnificent new building. Philip made them smile as he talked of how he had met with Nell on Strand Bridge and given her the money to go to the opening night of the old theatre. How long ago that May Day seemed now, when they were both little more than children.

Afterwards Philip took Buckingham out into the garden. "What did you think?" he asked him, for Jules was looking exceptionally fragile that day.

"I think you must get help for him without delay," Buckingham said frankly.

"I know. He fades before my eyes and yet I am reluctant to abandon him to the so-called medical profession. Whether they are barber-surgeons or graduates of Saint-Côme, the barbarous fiends know only how to take a pint of blood or administer an emetic."

"There must be some who can do more."

"There is Vallot, the King's physician. He has certain drugs, they say, which cure as if by magic, or there is Guy Patin. He is a Professor of Medicine, for what that is worth."

"What have you tried?"

"At the start some superstitious cures suggested by Madame and other friends, but I refuse to employ their methods now that Jules has grown so weak."

"There are always the waters at Vichy or Bourbon-L'Archamboult," Buckingham suggested.

There was a little pavilion in the garden. Jules had loved to sit there and write in the Summer. At the entrance Buckingham noticed a stone statue of Jules' dog, Brutus.

"A present that amused him," Philip explained. Jules was still very attached to the animal, which lived in his quarters and rarely left his side, much to the consternation of the servants, for the dog was only really docile with its master. "Now tell me all that's happened to you since we last met."

"Oh, I am in disgrace again at home," Buckingham told him cheerfully, "and your friend, Monmouth, has been the gainer by it. Charles has given him my Chancellorship of Cambridge University and my position as Master of the Horse. He has, as well, been made Commissioner of the Admiralty and Lord High Chamberlain of Scotland. He was invited to be Commissioner of Scotland to replace old Lauderdale, but he refused that and declared that he wished to be a general!"

"But Monmouth hates the army life," Philip said, laughing.

"Not in retrospect, it seems. He and York re-created the siege of Maestricht at Windsor Castle in a meadow at the foot of the Long Terrace, and huge crowds came to watch them. There were a great many guns fired and mines exploded, and prisoners taken too, exactly as it must have been. You weren't there though, were you?"

"No. I was fighting elsewhere," Philip said heavily, recalling Condé's prediction concerning the siege and thinking how right it had turned out to be. "Did Monmouth lose his baby son who was so ill?"

"He did, but Anna has since presented him with another. It seems all goes his way just now and he is popular with everyone.

Not so his uncle. York's marriage has set the country and the Parliament against him."

The Duke of York had wed a Catholic after all, Mary of Modena, and Philip could just imagine Shaftesbury's glee. It would be the final straw to those who abhorred the prospect of a Papist ruler in England and bring many over to the Opposition.

"What about the peace with Holland?" Philip wondered. "Is that popular in England?"

Buckingham pulled a face. "It might be if a man could trust the devils. Only last month they attacked some English ships in Chesapeake Bay. I can't pretend, though, to dislike the Orangeman, although I know you met him under slightly different circumstances! When Arlington and I were sent to smooth the way for peace I found William very reasonable, but Arlington, of course, must belittle my efforts, as he always does, and take all the credit for himself. He has been made Lord Chamberlain now and I'll have nothing to do with him."

Philip smiled. Fond though he was of Buckingham, he was not so biased that he could not acknowledge the level-headed Arlington to be the superior statesman.

"They all advance but you, it seems, George."

"That's so. Even your Nell is made a Lady of the Privy Chamber, in place of Barbara. What a king! Two years ago he arrests the buccaneer Henry Morgan and this year he makes him Governor of Jamaica!"

"What do you intend to do now?" Philip said.

"Why, dear boy, I'm going into business," Buckingham told him proudly. "I'm investing money shortly in a glass factory. What do you think of that?"

"I think you are as hare-brained as ever," Philip said affectionately, "but I wish you every bit of luck."

The afternoon sky was darkening into dusk when they went back to the house. As they reached the door Philip turned and glanced back at the pavilion.

There seemed to be a figure sitting in the shadows. He gasped, suddenly feeling icy cold, and gripped Buckingham's arm. "Look there! Do you see him?"

"See who?" Buckingham was watching him in alarm.

"Jules. It looked like his ghost." Philip's thoughts were racing, but whatever he had seen, or thought he had seen, had disappeared as the shadows lengthened. "Do you believe in premonitions, George?"

"No, I don't," Buckingham said firmly. "This is not like you. Take my advice and get some medical attention for him without delay, instead of driving yourself wild with flights of fancy."

Philip did take Buckingham's advice and they set off the following week for Vichy.

The gay atmosphere of the fashionable little resort caused Philip to recall the days that he had spent at Bath, so long ago. This time, however, he was not there for the social life but for a cure, if one was truly to be found.

Every morning at six o'clock Philip would take Jules to the Maison du Roi, where everyone assembled to drink the water. Jules complied without a murmur, pulling a wry face, like all the rest, at the taste of the saltpetre, but he rarely managed to keep it down. They would then go for a short promenade with Morgan pushing the chair and Jules well wrapped up against the cold. In the afternoon there would be showers. These were held in a subterranean room where a jet of hot water, directed at the naked patient, was supposed to ease rheumatic pains and other pains of the joints, but they caused not the slightest change in Jules' condition.

After three weeks Philip decided they might as well go home and, once back in Paris, he reluctantly abandoned Jules to the care of Guy Patin.

Patin was an ill-natured man who appeared to hate all of mankind, and particularly Vallot, the royal physician. "He is a charlatan," he told Philip, "as are any who reckon these new and mysterious drugs can do the work of phlebotomy and osteology. I am trained in both these fields. Do you have a copy of the patient's horoscope?"

"His horoscope?" Philip was certain he had not heard right. "I had it cast last year. Is it of interest to you?"

"I shall need to know his lucky numbers before I can begin to treat him and also the position of the sky at the time of his birth. It may be that there was a comet in the vicinity."

"Would that be bad?"

"It can often foretell a disease."

Philip sighed and fetched Jules' horoscope. Patin might call himself a Professor of Medicine yet Philip could not help but feel that the treatment the man would offer would be about as efficacious as that which the plague doctor had given to the wretched patients in the London pest house.

When Patin had gone Philip sat on Jules' bed and looked at him sadly. "I pray that I have made the right decision. I promised Buckingham before he left France that I would seek a cure for you."

"I don't believe that it will make much difference in the end," Jules said softly. "I am a mighty burden to you, aren't I?"

Philip denied it, but the past few months had taken their toll. He knew he looked careworn and he felt older.

"Poor Philip." Jules reached out and took his hand. "This is hard for you, I know, but, believe me, I am not afraid to die. But for you I would not even properly have lived."

"Don't talk of dying," Philip said, upset. "Patin claims he can cure you."

Jules nodded. They both had little faith in Patin's skill yet for each other's sake they both pretended to believe in miracles.

Alas, Patin was not able to work miracles. He called daily but, despite all his efforts, Jules grew weaker. Philip fed him with bread and milk or broth but he gained no weight and soon became too frail to even be lifted from the bed to his couch.

Monsieur still visited regularly but Philip saw no-one else, for he did not feel like socialising and rarely left the house any more. Occasionally, whilst Jules was asleep, he would take a little exercise and let the fresh March winds clear his lungs of the stale air of the closed and shuttered sickroom. Patin would allow no light or ventilation, and the heat from the fire, built up high, was stifling to one accustomed to being out of doors.

After one of these brief excursions he returned to find the house in uproar. He was surprised to see that Patin had arrived during his absence, for the doctor had already called that day, and even more surprised when Patin confronted him in a fury.

"Since when have your servants been trained physicians, my Lord? This man," he indicated Morgan, who stood glowering behind him, "stopped me in the midst of treating my patient."

"Is this true?" Philip asked the Welshman.

"Yes, my Lord," Morgan admitted. "I did stop him, but not before he had taken a full two pints of Monsieur Gaspard's blood."

"You have bled him again?"

"I have, and I have purged him too. It is customary in these cases," Patin said stiffly.

"But you have bled him once today already. It is plain to see that he has hardly any strength, yet you would sap what little he has."

"As to that, you need have no fear, my Lord. His humours are at the centre of his body, for it is the last quarter of the moon and at that time a man can spare a little blood."

"A dying man? A man too weak to lift his head?" Philip almost struck him, but he controlled himself in time. "You are a fool, Guy Patin, a superstitious fool, and I am a greater one to think that you could help us. Leave this house."

"But my fee…"

"Shall be accounted for in full," Philip assured him testily. "Fear not, Patin, I am a gentleman and rich enough in livres to pay you though I am, at this moment very poor in hope."

Philip went quickly to Jules' room and stood looking at the still figure, whiter even than the pillows on which he lay. By the side of him was a basin filled with his blood and Philip covered it with a cloth, sickened at the sight.

"Forgive me, Jules," he murmured. "I only did that which I thought was for the best."

He had spoken quietly but Jules heard him and opened his eyes.

"You have done all a man could do, my friend." The words were halting but coherent. "You have to let me go."

"I'm not sure that I can."

Philip stayed with him until he slept, and for a long while after that, lost in his own sad thoughts. He wished so much that he could give Jules some of his own strength, but there was no magical way that he could help his friend, in fact no way at all. Philip knew that now.

The next few weeks were ones which he was to remember only too vividly for the rest of his life. He hardly left Jules' side. Not concerned that the beauty of a Paris Spring was just other side of the shuttered window pane, Philip was ready, at any time of day or night, to offer him water or press a cooling towel to his brow.

For a lot of the time, however, Jules lay still, with his eyes closed, breathing so gently that he looked as though he were already in his shroud.

April passed and then, in the first week of May, came the final, cruellest blow. Jules lost consciousness altogether. There was no longer any way that Philip could fool himself. The violet-tinted eyelids did not flicker, nor did the cracked lips moan for water. Though he still breathed, Jules' soul, it seemed had fled its poor, twisted shell.

Morgan brought Philip up a tray of food, which he waved aside. He had no appetite, even though he had not eaten properly for several days. "Madame Bisset thinks that you should call a priest," the Welshman said soberly.

Philip drew himself from his reverie. "What did you say?"

"A priest should be summoned for Monsieur Gaspard. He is a Catholic, after all, and they set store by such things."

"I don't know a priest," Philip said helplessly.

"Madame Bisset will fetch one if you give permission."

"Tell her to do what she must."

Madame Bisset returned in half an hour, bringing with her a small man swathed in an enormous black cloak. Philip paid no attention to the ceremony, most of which he did not understand, but he managed to rouse himself sufficiently to show the priest to the bedroom door afterwards.

"My prayers are with you at this sad time, my son," the priest told him.

"You should know that I am a Protestant, Father, inasmuch as I believe in God at all at this moment."

"My Lord!" The priest looked shocked. "You must not say such things or God will punish you."

"He has already punished me." Philip looked at his dying friend. "Don't speak to me of God's goodness or His mercy, not when He would allow the world to lose such a sweet and gentle creature."

"But the earth's loss will be Heaven's gain, my Lord, for the angels will take him to live amongst them."

"Much use that is to me," Philip said bitterly. "I want him here, where I can talk to him."

"You will be reunited with him at the proper time, if you repent your sins and lead a worthy life," the priest said.

Philip turned away. "I don't believe you. You have done your duty, Father. Please leave me to my misery."

Now Morgan, too, kept a vigil in the darkened room. Although Philip had never asked him to stay he was, nonetheless, grateful for the Welshman's silent presence.

An hour before midnight he awoke from a fitful doze to find Morgan at Jules' bedside.

"What is it, Morgan. What does he need?"

"There is nothing more you can do for him, my Lord," Morgan said quietly.

"No!" Philip was nearly out of his mind from lack of sleep and sustenance. "The angels cannot have him yet. We have to help him."

Morgan looked at him pityingly. "He is beyond our help now."

Philip pushed him aside but one glance told him that Morgan was right. Jules was not breathing.

"It's too late," he said dully. "They have taken him."

Jules Gaspard was dead.

NINETEEN

❦

Shaftesbury offered his hand to John Locke, his physician, who he was dispatching to France on his behalf. Locke had given up his own work as a tutor to take the post of the Earl's personal physician, but he did more for Shaftesbury than merely look after his health.

"When you get to Paris seek out Philip Devalle," Shaftesbury said. "His father has been taken dangerously ill, so Buckingham says. If he dies then Philip will be left penniless and once more in need of an employer to provide the wherewithal for his extravagant style of living. This time I would rather that employer be myself than King Louis."

"Why is Lord Devalle so important to you?" Locke said.

"For one thing Monmouth adores him and, for another, he is well known and accepted by everyone at two Courts," Shaftesbury said. "Also, his career in the army has proved that he has the ability to lead and to gain the respect of the common man, and I need hardly remind you, Locke, that without the support of the common man my cause will be lost. I need him back in England."

"He may be disinclined to come. It runs through galleries that he has suffered a loss."

"That was a month ago," Shaftesbury said dismissively. "Time enough for one of his kind to be well over the death of a friend!"

❦

Philip was still devastated by Jules' death. During the short time he had known him Jules had made a tremendous impact on his life. It was also the only time he had ever really considered the well-being of anyone but himself. That consideration seemed to have opened up a part of him which had been closed before. When he had stood at Jules graveside in the Cimitière des Innocents he had vowed that from now on it would be closed again. Morgan had been right, he acknowledged that now, and he had been caused a great deal of pain yet, when he looked at the portrait of Jules, still hanging in the salon, he did not regret for a moment the friendship he had shared with the poet, the memories of which would remain with him all his days.

He had a great many visitors, for it seemed to have become almost a challenge to his friends to attempt to raise his spirits but, although Monsieur and Athénais were always welcome, in the main he wished that people would leave him alone for a while. He received Locke courteously enough, however, for he guessed he came from Shaftesbury.

He laughed hollowly when Locke expressed his regret at the news of his father's illness. That seemed very trivial after his recent loss. "Save your sympathy, sir. I have no feelings for my father whatsoever."

Locke looked shocked. "But shall you not go to England to see him?"

"For what purpose? His will must already be made out, leaving all, I don't doubt to my idiot brother, who will have played mightily upon his sympathies these last fourteen years."

"As you have played upon his conscience?" Locke guessed.

"Quite. We've played our own games, Henry and I, but I fear that mine is now played out. I have got all I shall ever get from my father. The estate, the earldom, everything will go to Henry and my only consolation is that he is not possessed of sufficient intelligence to properly enjoy it."

"And what will you do now, my Lord?" Locke said, after a short pause.

"I suppose I will go back into the French army, since that is the only way I ever earned a livre of my own."

"The Earl of Shaftesbury suggests that you return to London."

"And what does Shaftesbury want of me?" Philip asked.

"I believe he has a proposition which might be of interest to you."

"Very little is of interest to me these days," Philip said truthfully. "Besides, the Earl is no longer Lord Chancellor. Can he still wield any real power?"

"More than ever," Locke assured him. "You have lived in France too long if you cannot envisage the disrupting influence of a strong Opposition Party. King Charles is at the mercy of his Parliament, for they can refuse him the money he needs."

"Surely he can prorogue a troublesome Parliament."

"He already has, my Lord, but without it he gets nothing at all and if he decides to dissolve it then he knows full well that, after the elections, he might well find himself with a worse one than before! Much has happened since you were last in England," Locke reminded him. "The Declaration of Indulgence he devised was as great an insult as he could have flung in the faces of the Protestants and it lasted only a month before he was forced to abandon it. King Charles then swore before both Houses that he had never made a treaty with France save the one which had been made public knowledge. You yourself know well enough that is not the case."

Philip nodded. "I accept what you say, that the man is a liar, just as I accept that the Duke of York is unfit to follow him to the throne, but are there many who think that way?"

"More than you might imagine, and there are a large number who have been discontented ever since the Restoration. Your father was fortunate, for High Heatherton was confiscated by the state and so could be returned to your family after the Civil

War, but there are many Cavaliers who were forced to sell their lands for a pittance in order to pay the fines Cromwell imposed upon them. For them there has been no justice, thanks to an Act confirming the legality of all sales of property since the commencement of the War. Those estates will never be returned to their rightful owners. Truly it is said that King Charles has passed an Act of Indemnity for his enemies and an Act of Oblivion for his friends."

"And will they follow Shaftesbury on account of this?" Philip said dubiously. The old Cavaliers had been complaining for years but it was one thing to protest and quite another, he knew, to stand against the very king they had fought to put back on the throne.

"They and many more, my Lord," Locke said confidently, "but I am not at liberty to tell you more than that."

After Locke had gone Philip considered what he had said, but he could not work up any real enthusiasm for the prospect of returning to London, much less embroiling himself in English politics. He had to do something, though, that much he did know.

He seemed to be incapable of making any decisions at the moment. He had not even been able to make one concerning Jules' dog. Since the death of his master, Brutus had behaved in a most peculiar fashion, crouching in corners or under tables, growling with fangs bared, so that the servants were terrified of him. Torn between consideration for his household and loyalty to Jules' memory, Philip had done no more than relegate the animal to the garden, where he roamed, restricted by a chain, and howled so loudly at night that Madame Bisset told him the neighbours were recalling tales of the wolves which had once crept into to the city and taken children!

Philip retired to bed early that night, for Locke has been the last in a long stream of callers during the day and he was tired.

His servants were going about their usual last tasks of the day and the two blackamoor coachmen, Jonathon and Ned, were settling the horses for the night when Jonathon heard a low but distinct growl coming from the vicinity of the feed store.

"Listen!"

The sound came again and, this time, Ned heard it too. "The dog is loose!"

The Negroes stared into the darkness in terror, for they had feared Brutus from the start. Slowly they edged their way out of the stables and ran to the house to find Morgan.

Morgan cursed at the news. He had already incurred Philip's wrath by suggesting that the animal be shot but he could not risk the dog escaping now to wreak havoc in the city streets. He decided to take whatever action was necessary and suffer the consequences of his decision later.

Philip was nearly asleep when he heard voices in the servants' rooms below. Throwing on a shirt and some breeches he went downstairs and saw Morgan, armed with a pistol, heading for the stables.

Philip started after him but, before he could reach him, he heard a shout and a gasp of pain.

He broke into a run. When he got to the stables he could see that Morgan was pinned to the ground, with the dog attacking him like a thing possessed.

Philip was not armed, but there was no time to lose. He flung himself onto the animal's back and locked his fingers around its throat.

The slavering dog yelped in surprise, and then began to choke as Philip pulled its head back with all his strength until he heard its neck snap.

Jonathon and Ned arrived close behind him and they looked at the dead creature in disbelief, but Philip was already kneeling by Morgan's side.

The dog had bitten off most of his right ear.

Morgan was mercifully unconscious and remained so whilst he was carried inside, where Madame Bisset bathed and bandaged his wounds as best she could. The lobe and some of the upper part of his ear had been torn off and he was covered in bleeding bites and vicious scratches where the dog's claws had ripped through his clothes.

Philip passed an anxious night. He had grown much attached to the cussed Welshman who had saved his life at Woerden and followed him with such determination.

That had been three years ago and during that time he and Morgan had grown close. Philip realised, suddenly, how much he had come to take his servant's often silent presence for granted. He had dreaded the thought of being alone when Jules had gone and yet the most loyal friend he could have wished for was never more than a few feet from him, offering strength and comfort whenever he needed it.

Only now did it occur to Philip how thoughtlessly he had often treated him. He was contrite now, of course, but he feared it was too late. He knew that by keeping the dog alive he was to blame for Morgan's injuries, and he could not see how the Welshman could ever forgive him.

He went into Morgan's room early the next morning to find he was awake, but Philip was ravaged with guilt to see the extent of the bites and cuts upon his face and hands and the blood-soaked bandage over his ear.

"What can I say, Morgan, except that I am sorry," he said wretchedly.

"There is nothing to be said, my Lord," Morgan assured him.

"Nothing? Thanks to my pig-headedness you have been scarred and mutilated. In your place I would find plenty to say to a master who had caused me such affliction."

"The cuts will heal, my Lord. As for my ear, well I doubt if I shall miss that a lot. I was none too handsome a fellow to begin with," Morgan reminded him.

"You're being kind. I don't deserve that."

"Even though you saved my life?"

"If you consider that I did so then, surely, I have done no more than repay the debt I owed you for my own life."

"Which means you are no longer under any obligation to me, I suppose, my Lord," Morgan said slowly. "Since my looks will be even less of a credit to you now than they were before, perhaps it would be better if I left your service."

Philip sighed. It was what he had dreaded. He went over to the window, not wishing for Morgan to see that he was upset.

"If that is what you wish then I will let you go, though with reluctance, I confess. You see I have grown accustomed to you, just as you once said I would." He pressed his forehead to the cooling glass. "Oh Morgan, would that I had taken your advice about Jules. I could have spared myself so much grief. Now, on top of losing him, I am to lose you too. Not that I can honestly blame you for wanting to leave me, for I have scarcely lived up to all your expectations, have I?"

"On the contrary, I admire you more now than I ever did," Morgan reassured him. "I only thought you might want to be rid of me."

"Don't be ridiculous!" Philip returned quickly to his bedside, suddenly feeling more positive than he had for weeks. "I was thinking we might go to London and visit some old friends."

"You've never mentioned doing that before."

"Because I've only just decided on it. What happened to you has bought me to my senses," Philip said. "I don't feel quite ready to be a soldier again but neither can I stay here brooding on the past. Perhaps it is time I looked ahead to what the future may hold."

"When do you wish to leave?" Morgan said.

"Why, just as soon as you are fit, that is...," Philip paused, "... if you are coming with me."

Morgan managed a smile. "Most certainly I am, my Lord. The truth is I have grown accustomed to you too!"

...to be continued in

DESIGNS OF A GENTLEMAN: THE DARKER YEARS

ALSO BY THE AUTHOR